THE COMPLETE HOROWITZ HORROR

D0639531

Bath Night

Isabel lay there on her own in the hot water, trying to relax.
But there was a knot in her stomach and her whole body
was rigid, shying away from the cast-iron touch of the
bath. She heard her mother going back down the stairs.
The door of the laundry room opened. Isabel turned her
head slightly and for the first time caught sight of herself in
the mirror. And this time she did scream. And screamed.

In the bath, everything was ordinary, just as it was when
her mother had left her. Clear water. Her flesh a little pink
in the heat. Steam. But in the mirror, in the reflection…The
bathroom was a slaughterhouse. The liquid in the bath
was crimson and Isabel was up to her neck in it. As her
hand—her reflected hand—recoiled out of the water, the
red liquid clung to it, dripping down heavily, splattering
against the side of the bath and clinging there, too. Isabel
tried to lever herself out of the bath but slipped and fell,
the water rising over her chin. It touched her lips and she
screamed again, certain she would be sucked into it and
die. She tore her eyes away from the mirror. Now it was
just water. In the mirror…Blood.

She was covered in it, swimming in it. And there
was somebody else in the room. Not in the room. In the
reflection of the room. A man, tall, in his forties, dressed in
some sort of suit, gray face, mustache, small, beady eyes.

. . .

ALSO BY ANTHONY HOROWITZ

THE ALEX RIDER ADVENTURES

Stormbreaker

Point Blank

Skeleton Key

Eagle Strike

Scorpia

Ark Angel

Snakehead

Stormbreaker: The Graphic Novel

THE DIAMOND BROTHERS MYSTERIES

The Falcon's Malteser

Public Enemy Number Two

Three of Diamonds

South by Southeast

The Devil and His Boy

THE COMPLETE HOROWITZ HORROR

ANTHONY HOROWITZ

Previously published as
Horowitz Horror and *More Horowitz Horror*

PUFFIN BOOKS

PUFFIN BOOKS

Published by the Penguin Group

Penguin Young Readers Group, 345 Hudson Street, New York, New York 10014, U.S.A.

Penguin Group (Canada), 90 Eglinton Avenue East, Suite 700, Toronto, Ontario, Canada M4P 2Y3
(a division of Pearson Penguin Canada Inc.)

Penguin Books Ltd, 80 Strand, London WC2R 0RL, England

Penguin Ireland, 25 St Stephen's Green, Dublin 2, Ireland (a division of Penguin Books Ltd)

Penguin Group (Australia), 250 Camberwell Road, Camberwell, Victoria 3124, Australia
(a division of Pearson Australia Group Pty Ltd)

Penguin Books India Pvt Ltd, 11 Community Centre, Panchsheel Park,
New Delhi - 110 017, India

Penguin Group (NZ), 67 Apollo Drive, Rosedale, North Shore 0632, New Zealand
(a division of Pearson New Zealand Ltd.)

Penguin Books (South Africa) (Pty) Ltd, 24 Sturdee Avenue,
Rosebank, Johannesburg 2196, South Africa

Registered Offices: Penguin Books Ltd, 80 Strand, London WC2R 0RL, England

Horowitz Horror first published in Great Britain by Orchard Books Ltd, 1999
More Horowitz Horror first published in Great Britain by Orchard Books Ltd, 2000

Horowitz Horror first American edition published by Philomel Books,
a division of Penguin Young Readers Group, 2006
More Horowitz Horror first American edition published by Philomel Books,
a division of Penguin Young Readers Group, 2007
This edition published by Puffin Books, a division of Penguin Young Readers Group, 2008

5 7 9 10 8 6 4

THE LIBRARY OF CONGRESS CIP DATA IS AVAILABLE FOR *HOROWITZ HORROR* AND *MORE HOROWITZ HORROR*

Design by Gunta Alexander.

Puffin Books ISBN 0-978-0-14-241162-9

Printed in the United States of America

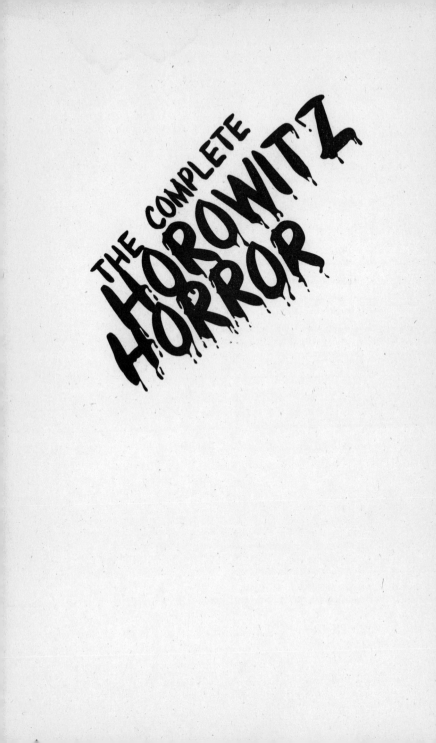

THE COMPLETE HOROWITZ HORROR

TABLE OF CONTENTS

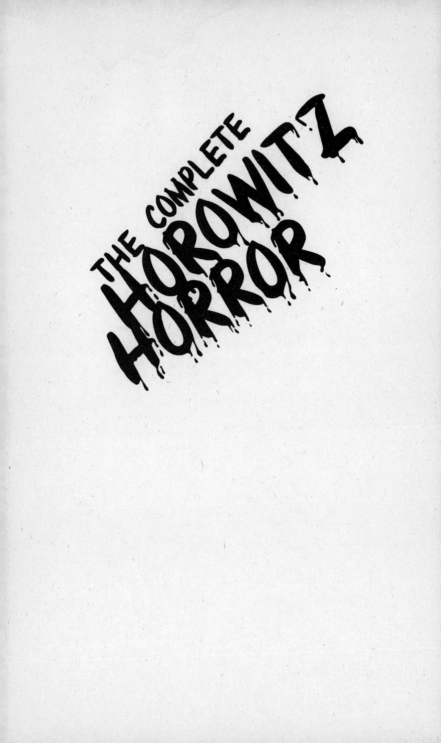

THE COMPLETE HOROWITZ HORROR

Bath
Night

She didn't like the bathtub from the start.

Isabel was at home the Saturday they delivered it and wondered how the fat, metal beast was ever going to make it up one flight of stairs, around the corner, and into the bathroom. The two scrawny workmen didn't seem to have much idea either. Thirty minutes, four gashed knuckles, and a hundred swearwords later, it seemed to be hopelessly wedged, and it was only when Isabel's father lent a hand that they were able to free it. But then one of the stubby legs caught the wallpaper and tore it and that led to another argument right in front of the workmen, her mother and father blaming each other like they always did.

"I told you to measure it."

"I did measure it."

"Yes. But you said the legs came off."

"No. That's what you said."

It was so typical of her parents to buy that tub, Isabel thought. Anyone else would have been off to the West End to one of the upscale department stores. Pick something out of the showroom. Out with the credit card. Delivery and free installation in six weeks and thank you very much.

But Jeremy and Susan Martin weren't like that. Ever since they had bought their small, turn-of-the-century house in Muswell Hill, North London, they had devoted their holidays to getting it just right. And since they were both teachers—he at a private school, she in a local elementary—their holidays were frequent and long.

And so, the dining-room table had come from an antiques shop in Hungerford, the chairs that surrounded it from a house sale in Hove. The kitchen cupboards had been rescued from a skip in Macclesfield. And their double bed had been a rusting, tangled heap when they had found it in the barn of a French farmhouse outside Boulogne. So many weekends. So many hours spent searching, measuring, imagining, haggling, and arguing.

That was the worst of it. As far as Isabel could see, her parents didn't seem to get any pleasure out of all these antiques. They argued constantly—in the shops, in the marketplaces, even at the auctions. Once her father had gotten so heated, he had actually broken the Victorian chamber pot they had been fighting about and of course he'd had to buy it anyway. It was in the hall now, glued back together again, the all-too-visible cracks an unpleasant image of their twelve-year-old marriage.

The bathtub was Victorian, too. Isabel had not been with her parents when they bought it—at an antiques shop in West London.

"End of the last century," the dealer had told them. "A real beauty. It's still got its own taps . . ."

It certainly didn't look beautiful as it squatted there on the stripped-pine floor, surrounded by stops and washers and twisting lengths of pipe. It reminded Isabel of a pregnant cow, its great white belly hanging only inches off the ground. Its metal feet curved outward, splayed, as if unable to bear the weight. And, of course, it had been decapitated. There was a single round hole where the taps would be and beneath it an ugly yellow stain in the white enamel where the water had trickled down for perhaps a hundred years, on its way to the plug hole below. Isabel glanced at the taps, lying next to the sink, a tangle of mottled brass that looked too big for the tub they were meant to sit on. There were two handles, marked *hot* and *cold* on faded ivory discs. Isabel imagined the water thundering in. It would need to. The bathtub was very deep.

But nobody used the bath that night. Jeremy had said he would be able to connect it up himself, but in the end he had found it was beyond him. Nothing fit. It would have to be soldered. Unfortunately he wouldn't be able to get a plumber until Monday, and of course it would add another forty dollars to the bill, and when he told Susan, that led to another argument. They ate their dinner in front of the television that night, letting the shallow laughter of a sitcom cover the chill silence in the room.

And then it was nine o'clock. "You'd better go to bed early, darling. School tomorrow," Susan said.

"Yes, Mom." Isabel was twelve, but her mother sometimes treated her as if she were much younger. Maybe it came from teaching in a elementary school. Although her father was a tutor at Highgate School, Isabel went to an ordinary public school and she was glad of it. They didn't allow girls at Highgate and she had always found the boys altogether too prim and proper. They were probably all gay, too.

Isabel undressed and washed quickly—hands, face, neck, teeth, in that order. The face that gazed out at her from the gilded mirror above the sink wasn't an unattractive one, she thought, except for the annoying pimple on her nose . . . a punishment for the Mars Bar ice cream she'd eaten the day before. Long brown hair and blue eyes (her mother's), a thin face with narrow cheekbones and chin (her father's). She had been fat until she was nine, but now she was getting herself in shape. She'd never be a supermodel. She was too fond of ice cream for that. But no fatty either, not like Belinda Price, her best friend at school, who was doomed to a life of hopeless diets and baggy clothes.

The shape of the tub, over her shoulder, caught her eye and she realized suddenly that from the moment she had come into the bathroom she had been trying to avoid looking at it. Why? She put her toothbrush down, turned around, and examined it. She didn't like it. Her first impression had been right. It was so big and ugly with its dull enamel and dribbling stain over the plug hole. And it seemed—it was a stupid thought, but now that it was there she couldn't make it go away—it seemed to be *waiting* for her. She half smiled at her own foolishness. And then she noticed something else.

There was a small puddle of water in the bottom of the bathtub. As she moved her head, it caught the light and she saw it clearly. Isabel's first thought was to look up at the ceiling. There had to be a leak, somewhere upstairs, in the attic. How else could water have gotten into a bath whose taps were lying on their side next to the sink? But there was no leak. Isabel leaned forward and ran her third finger along the bottom of the tub. The water was warm.

I must have splashed it in there myself, she thought. As I was washing my face . . .

She flicked the light off and left the room, crossing the landing to her bedroom on the other side of her parents'. Somewhere in her mind she knew that it wasn't true, that she could never have splashed water from the sink into the bathtub. But it wasn't an important question. In fact, it was ridiculous. She curled up in bed and closed her eyes.

But an hour later her thumb was still rubbing circles against her third finger and it was a long, long time before she slept.

• • •

"Bath night!" her father said when she got home from school the next day. He was in a good mood, smiling broadly as he shuffled together the ingredients for that night's dinner.

"So you got it plumbed in, then?"

"Yes." He looked up. "It cost fifty dollars—don't tell your mother. The plumber was here for two hours." He smiled and blinked several times and Isabel was reminded of something she had once been told by the brother of a friend who went to the school where he taught. At school, her father's nickname was Mouse. Why did boys have to be so cruel?

She reached out and squeezed his arm. "That's great, Dad," she said. "I'll have a bath after dinner. What are you making?"

"Lasagne. Your mom's gone out to get some wine."

It was a pleasant evening. Isabel had gotten a part in her school play—Lady Montague in *Romeo and Juliet*. Susan had found a ten-dollar bill in the pocket of a jacket she hadn't worn for years. Jeremy had been asked to take a group of boys to Paris at the end of the term. Good news oiled the machinery of the family and for once everything turned smoothly. After dinner,

Isabel did half an hour's homework, then kissed her parents good night and went upstairs.

To the bathroom.

The bath was ready now. Installed. Permanent. The taps with the black *hot* and *cold* protruded over the rim with the curve of a vulture's neck. A silver plug on a heavy chain slanted into the plug hole. Her father had polished the brasswork, giving it a new gleam. He had put the towels back on the rail and a green bath mat on the floor. Everything back to normal. And yet the room, the towels, the bath mat, seemed to have shrunk. The tub was too big. And it was waiting for her. She still couldn't get the thought out of her mind.

"Isabel. Stop being silly . . . !"

What's the first sign of madness? Talking to yourself. And the second sign? Answering back. Isabel let out a great sigh of breath and went over to the bathtub. She leaned in and pushed the plug into the hole. Downstairs, she could hear the television: *World in Action*, one of her father's favorite programs. She reached out and turned on the hot tap, the metal squeaking slightly under her hand. Without pausing, she gave the cold tap a quarter turn. Now let's see if that plumber was worth his fifty bucks.

For a moment, nothing happened. Then, deep down underneath the floor, something rumbled. There was a rattling in the pipe that grew louder and louder as it rose up, but still no water. Then the tap coughed, the cough of an old man, of a heavy smoker. A bubble of something like saliva appeared at its lips. It coughed again and spat it out. Isabel looked down in dismay.

Whatever had been spat into the bathtub was an ugly red, the color of rust. The taps spluttered again and coughed out more of the thick, treacly stuff. It bounced off the bottom of the bath and splattered against the sides. Isabel was beginning to feel sick, and before the taps could deliver a third load of—whatever it was—into the tub, she seized hold of them and locked them both shut. She could feel the pipes rattling beneath her hands, but then it was done. The shuddering stopped. The rest of the liquid was swallowed back into the network of pipes.

But still it wasn't over. The bottom of the bath was coated with the liquid. It slid unwillingly toward the plug hole, which swallowed it greedily. Isabel looked more closely. Was she going mad or was there something *inside* the plug hole? Isabel was sure she had the plug in, but now it was half in and half out of the hole and she could see below.

There was something. It was like a white ball, turning slowly, collapsing in on itself, glistening wet and alive. And it was rising, making for the surface . . .

Isabel cried out. At the same time she leaned over and jammed the plug back into the hole. Her hand touched the red liquid and she recoiled, feeling it, warm and clinging, against her skin.

And that was enough. She reeled back, yanked a towel off the rail, and rubbed it against her hand so hard that it hurt. Then she threw open the bathroom door and ran downstairs.

Her parents were still watching television.

"What's the matter with you?" Jeremy asked.

Isabel explained what had happened, the words tumbling over one another in their hurry to get out, but it was as if her father wasn't listening. "There's always a bit of rust with a new bath," he went on. "It's in the pipes. Run the water for a few minutes and it'll go."

"It wasn't rust," Isabel said.

"Maybe the boiler's acting up again," Susan muttered.

"It's not the boiler." Jeremy frowned. He had bought

it secondhand and it had always been a sore point—
particularly when it broke down.

"It was horrible," Isabel insisted. "It was like . . ."
What had it been like? Of course, she had known all
along. "Well, it was like blood. It was just like blood.
And there was something else. Inside the plug."

"Oh, for heaven's sake!" Jeremy was irritated now,
missing his program.

"Come on! I'll come up with you . . ." Susan pushed
a pile of Sunday newspapers off the sofa—she was still
reading them even though this was Monday evening—
and got to her feet.

"Where's the TV control?" Jeremy found it in the
corner of his armchair and turned the volume up.

Isabel and her mother went upstairs, back into the
bathroom. Isabel looked at the towel lying crumpled
where she had left it. A white towel. She had wiped her
hands on it. She was surprised to see there was no trace
of a stain.

"What a lot of fuss over a teaspoon of rust!" Susan
was leaning over the bath. Isabel stepped forward and
peered in nervously. But it was true. There was a shallow puddle of water in the middle and a few grains of
reddish rust. "You know there's always a little rust in

the system," her mother went on. "It's that stupid boiler of your father's." She pulled out the plug. "Nothing in there either!" Finally, she turned on the tap. Clean, ordinary water gushed out in a reassuring torrent. No rattling. No gurgles. Nothing. "There you are. It's sorted itself out."

Isabel hung back, leaning miserably against the sink. Her mother sighed. "You were making it all up, weren't you?" she said—but her voice was affectionate, not angry.

"No, Mom."

"It seems a long way to go to get out of having a bath."

"I wasn't . . . !"

"Never mind, now. Brush your teeth and go to bed." Susan kissed her. "Good night, dear. Sleep well."

But that night Isabel didn't sleep at all.

She didn't have a bath the following night either. Jeremy Martin was out—there was a staff meeting at the school—and Susan was trying out a new Martha Stewart recipe for a dinner party the following weekend. She spent the whole evening in the kitchen.

Nor did Isabel have a bath on Wednesday. That was

three days in a row and she was beginning to feel more than uncomfortable. She liked to be clean. That was her nature, and as much as she tried washing herself using the sink, it wasn't the same. And it didn't help that her father had used the bath on Tuesday morning and her mother on Tuesday and Wednesday, and neither of them had noticed anything wrong. It just made her feel more guilty—and dirtier.

Then on Thursday morning someone made a joke at school—something about rotten eggs—and as her cheeks burned, Isabel decided enough was enough. What was she so afraid of anyway? A sprinkling of rust that her imagination had turned into . . . something else. Susan Martin was out that evening—she was at her Italian evening class—so Isabel and her father sat down together to eat the Martha Stewart crab cakes, which hadn't quite worked because they had all fallen to pieces in the pan.

At nine o'clock they went their separate ways—he to the news, she upstairs.

"Good night, Dad."

"Good night, Is."

It had been a nice, companionable evening.

And there was the bath, waiting for her. Yes. It *was*

waiting, as if to receive her. But this time Isabel didn't hesitate. If she was as brisk and as businesslike as possible, she had decided, then nothing would happen. She simply wouldn't give her imagination time to play tricks on her. So without even thinking about it, she slipped the plug into the hole, turned on the taps, and added a squirt of Body Shop avocado bubble bath for good measure. She undressed (her clothes were a useful mask, stopping her from seeing the water as it filled) and only when she was quite naked did she turn around and look at the bath. It was fine. She could just see the water, pale green beneath a thick layer of foam. She stretched out her hand and felt the temperature. It was perfect: hot enough to steam up the mirror but not so hot as to scald. She turned off the taps. They dripped as loudly as she remembered. Then she went over to lock the door.

Yet still she hesitated. She was suddenly aware of her nakedness. It was as if she were in a room full of people. She shivered. You're being ridiculous, she told herself. But the question hung in the air along with the steam from the water. It was like a nasty, unfunny riddle.

When are you at your most defenseless?

When you're naked, enclosed, lying on your back . . .
. . . *in the bath.*

"Ridiculous." This time she actually said the word. And in one swift movement, a no-going-back decision, she got in.

The bath had tricked her—but she knew it too late.

The water was not hot. It wasn't even warm. She had tested the temperature moments before. She had seen the steam rising. But the water was colder than anything Isabel had ever felt. It was like breaking through the ice on a pond on a midwinter's day. As she sank helplessly into the bath, felt the water slide over her legs and stomach, close in on her throat like a clamp, her breath was punched back and her heart seemed to stop in midbeat. The cold hurt her. It cut into her. Isabel opened her mouth and screamed as loudly as she could. The sound was nothing more than a choked-off whimper.

Isabel was being pulled under the water. Her neck hit the rim of the bath and slid down. Her long hair floated away from her. The foam slid over her mouth, then over her nose. She tried to move, but her arms and legs wouldn't obey the signals she sent them. Her bones had frozen. The room seemed to be getting dark.

But then, with one final effort, Isabel twisted around and threw herself up, over the edge. Water exploded everywhere, splashing onto the floor. Then somehow she was lying down with foam all around her, sobbing and shivering, her skin completely white. She reached out and caught the corner of a towel, pulled it over her. Water trickled off her back and disappeared through the cracks in the floorboards.

Isabel lay like that for a long time. She had been scared . . . scared almost to death. But it wasn't just the change in the temperature of the water that had done it. It wasn't just the bath—as ugly and menacing as it was. No. It was the sound she had heard as she heaved herself out and jackknifed onto the floor. She had heard it inches away from her ear, in the bathroom, even though she was alone.

Somebody had laughed.

"You don't believe me, do you?"

Isabel was standing at the bus stop with Belinda Price; fat, reliable Belinda, always there when you needed her, her best friend. A week had passed and all the time it had built up inside her, what had happened in the bathroom, the story of the bath. But still Isabel had kept it to herself. Why? Because she was afraid of being laughed at? Because she was afraid no one would believe her? Because, simply, she was afraid. In that week she had done no work . . . at school or at home. She had been told off twice in class. Her clothes and her hair were in a state. Her eyes were dark with lack of sleep. But in the end she couldn't hold it back anymore. She had told Belinda.

And now the other girl shrugged. "I've heard of haunted houses," she muttered. "And haunted castles. I've even heard of a haunted car. But a haunted bath . . . ?"

"It happened, just like I said."

"Maybe you think it happened. If you think something hard enough, it can often—"

"It wasn't my imagination," Isabel interrupted.

Then the bus came and the two girls got on, showing their passes to the driver. They took their seats on the top deck, near the back. They always sat in the same place without quite knowing why.

"You can't keep coming over to my place," Belinda said. "I'm sorry, Bella, but my mom's beginning to ask what's going on."

"I know." Isabel sighed. She had managed to go over

to Belinda's house three nights running and had showered there, grateful for the hot, rushing water. She had told her parents that she and Belinda were working on a project. But Belinda was right. It couldn't go on forever.

The bus reached the traffic light and turned onto the main road. Belinda screwed up her face, deep in thought. All the teachers said how clever she was, not just because she worked hard but because she let you see it. "You say the bath is an old one," she said at last.

"Yes?"

"Do you know where your parents got it?"

Isabel thought back. "Yes. I wasn't with them when they bought it, but it came from a place in Fulham. I've been there with them before."

"Then why don't you go and ask them about it? I mean, if it is haunted there must be a reason. There's always a reason, isn't there?"

"You mean . . . someone might have died in it or something?" The thought made Isabel shiver.

"Yes. My gran had a heart attack in the bath. It didn't kill her, though—"

"You're right!" The bus was climbing the hill now.

Muswell Hill Broadway was straight ahead. Isabel gathered her things. "I could go there on Saturday. Will you come, too?"

"My mom and dad wouldn't let me."

"You can tell them you're at my place. And I'll tell my parents I'm at yours."

"What if they check?"

"They never do." The thought made Isabel sad. Her parents never did wonder where she was, never seemed to worry about her. They were too wrapped up in themselves.

"Well . . . I don't know . . ."

"Please, Belinda. On Saturday. I'll give you a call."

That night the tub played its worst trick yet.

Isabel hadn't wanted to have a bath. During dinner she'd made a point of telling her parents how tired she was, how she was looking forward to an early night. But her parents were tired, too. The atmosphere around the table had been distinctly jagged and Isabel found herself wondering just how much longer the family could stay together. Divorce. It was a horrible word, like an illness. Some of her friends had been out of school for a week and then come back pale and miserable and had never been quite the same again. They'd caught it . . . divorce.

"Upstairs, young lady!" Her mother's voice broke into her thoughts. "I think you'd better have a bath . . ."

"Not tonight, Mom."

"Tonight. You've hardly used that bath since it was installed. What's the matter with you? Don't you like it?"

"No. I don't . . ."

That made her father twitch with annoyance. "What's wrong with it?" he asked, sulking.

But before she could answer, her mother chipped in. "It doesn't matter what's wrong with it. It's the only bath we've got, so you're just going to have to get used to it."

"I won't!"

Her parents looked at each other, momentarily helpless. Isabel realized that she had never defied them before—not like this. They were thrown. But then her mother stood up. "Come on, Isabel," she said. "I've had enough of this stupidity. I'll come with you."

And so the two of them went upstairs, Susan with that pinched, set look that meant she couldn't be argued with. But Isabel didn't argue with her. If her mother ran the bath, she would see for herself what was happening. She would see that something was wrong . . .

"Right . . ." Susan pushed the plug in and turned on the taps. Ordinary clear water gushed out. "I really don't understand you, Isabel," she exclaimed over the roar of the water. "Maybe you've been staying up too late. I thought it was only six-year-olds who didn't like having baths. There!" The bath was full. Susan tested the water, swirling it around with the tips of her fingers. "Not too hot. Now let's see you get in."

"Mom . . ."

"You're not shy in front of me, are you? For heaven's sake . . . !"

Angry and humiliated, Isabel undressed in front of her mother, letting the clothes fall in a heap on the floor. Susan scooped them up but said nothing. Isabel hooked one leg over the edge of the bath and let her toes come into contact with the water. It was hot—but not scalding. Certainly not icy cold.

"Is it all right?" her mother asked.

"Yes, Mom . . ."

Isabel got into the bath. The water rose hungrily to

greet her. She could feel it close in a perfect circle around her neck. Her mother stood there a moment longer, holding her clothes. "Can I leave you now?" she asked.

"Yes." Isabel didn't want to be alone in the bathroom, but she felt uncomfortable lying there with her mother hovering over her.

"Good." Susan softened for a moment. "I'll come and kiss you good night." She held the clothes up and wrinkled her nose. "These had better go in the wash, too."

Susan went.

Isabel lay there on her own in the hot water, trying to relax. But there was a knot in her stomach and her whole body was rigid, shying away from the cast-iron touch of the bath. She heard her mother going back down the stairs. The door of the laundry room opened. Isabel turned her head slightly and for the first time caught sight of herself in the mirror. And this time she did scream.

And screamed.

In the bath, everything was ordinary, just as it was when her mother had left her. Clear water. Her flesh a little pink in the heat. Steam. But in the mirror, in the reflection . . .

The bathroom was a slaughterhouse. The liquid in the bath was crimson and Isabel was up to her neck in it. As her hand—her reflected hand—recoiled out of the water, the red liquid clung to it, dripping down heavily, splattering against the side of the bath and clinging there, too. Isabel tried to lever herself out of the bath but slipped and fell, the water rising over her chin. It touched her lips and she screamed again, certain she would be sucked into it and die. She tore her eyes away from the mirror. Now it was just water. In the mirror . . .

Blood.

She was covered in it, swimming in it. And there was somebody else in the room. Not in the room. In the reflection of the room. A man, tall, in his forties, dressed in some sort of suit, gray face, mustache, small, beady eyes.

"Go away!" Isabel yelled. "Go away! Go away!"

When her mother found her, curled up on the floor in a huge puddle of water, naked and trembling, Isabel didn't try to explain. She didn't even speak. She allowed herself to be half carried into bed and hid herself, like a small child, under the duvet.

For the first time, Susan Martin was more worried than annoyed. That night, she sat down with Jeremy and the two of them were closer than they had been for a long time as they talked about their daughter, her behavior, the need perhaps for some sort of therapy. But they didn't talk about the bath—and why should they? When Susan had burst into the bathroom she had seen nothing wrong with the water, nothing wrong with the mirror, nothing wrong with the bath.

No, they both agreed. There was something wrong with Isabel. It had nothing to do with the bath.

The antiques shop stood on the Fulham Road, a few minutes' walk from the subway station. From the front it looked like a grand house that might have belonged to a rich family perhaps a hundred years ago: tall imposing doors, shuttered windows, white stone columns, and great chunks of statuary scattered on the pavement outside. But over the years the house had declined, the plasterwork falling away, weeds sprouting in the brickwork. The windows were dark with the dust of city life and car exhaust fumes.

Inside, the rooms were small and dark—each one filled with too much furniture. Isabel and Belinda passed through a room with fourteen fireplaces, another with half a dozen dinner tables and a crowd of empty chairs. If they hadn't known all these objects were for sale, they could have imagined that the place was still occupied by a rich madman. It was still more of a house than a shop. When the two girls spoke to each other, they did so in whispers.

They eventually found a sales assistant in a court-yard at the back of the house. This was a large, open area, filled with baths and basins, more statues, stone fountains, wrought-iron gates, and trelliswork—all sur-rounded by a series of concrete arches that made them feel that they could have been in Rome or Venice rather than a shabby corner of West London. The assistant was a young man with a squint and a broken nose. He was carrying a gargoyle. Isabel wasn't sure which of the two were uglier.

"A Victorian bath?" he muttered in response to Isabel's inquiry. "I don't think I can help you. We sell a lot of old baths."

"It's big and white," Isabel said. "With little legs and gold taps . . ."

The sales assistant set the gargoyle down. It clunked heavily against a paving stone. "Do you have the re-ceipt?" he asked.

"No."

"Well . . . what did you say your parents' name was?"

"Martin. Jeremy and Susan Martin."

"Doesn't ring a bell . . ."

"They argue a lot. They probably argued about the price."

A slow smile spread across the assistant's face. Because of the way his face twisted, the smile was oddly menacing. "Yeah. I do remember," he said. "It was delivered somewhere in North London."

"Muswell Hill," Isabel said.

"That's right." The smile cut its way over his cheekbones. "I do remember. They got the Marlin bath."

"What's the Marlin bath?" Belinda asked. She already didn't like the sound of it.

The sales assistant chuckled to himself. He pulled out a packet of ten cigarettes and lit one. It seemed a long time before he spoke again. "Jacob Marlin. It was his bath. I don't suppose you've ever heard of him."

"No," Isabel said, wishing he'd get to the point.

"He was famous in his time." The assistant blew silvery gray smoke into the air. "Before they hanged him."

"Why did they hang him?" Isabel asked.

"For murder. He was one of the those—what do you

call them?—Victorian ax murderers. Oh, yes . . ." The sales assistant was grinning from ear to ear now, enjoying himself. "He used to take young ladies home with him—a bit like Jack the Ripper. Know what I mean? Marlin would do away with them . . ."

"You mean kill them?" Belinda whispered.

"That's exactly what I mean. He'd kill them and then chop them up with an ax. In the bath." The assistant sucked at his cigarette. "I'm not saying he did it in *that* bath, mind. But it came out of his house. That's why it was so cheap. I daresay it would have been cheaper still if your mom and dad had known . . ."

Isabel turned and walked out of the antiques shop. Belinda followed her. Suddenly the place seemed horrible and menacing, as if every object on display might have some dreadful story attached to it. Only in the street, surrounded by the noise and color of the traffic, did they stop and speak.

"It's horrible!" Belinda gasped. "He cut people up in the bath and you . . ." She couldn't finish the sentence.

"I wish I hadn't come." Isabel was close to tears. "I wish they'd never bought the rotten thing."

"If you tell them—"

"They won't listen to me. They never listen to me."

"So what are you going to do?" Belinda asked.

Isabel thought for a moment. People rushed past on the pavement. Market vendors shouted their wares. A pair of policemen stopped briefly to examine some apples. It was a different world from the one they had left behind in the antiques shop. "I'm going to destroy it," she said at last. "It's the only way. I'm going to break it up. And my parents can do whatever they like . . ."

She chose a monkey wrench from her father's toolbox. It was big and she could use it both to smash and to unscrew. Neither of her parents was at home. They thought she was over at Belinda's. That was good. By the time they got back, it would all be over.

There was something very comforting about the tool, the coldness of the steel against her palm, the way it weighed so heavily in her hand. Slowly she climbed the stairs, already imagining what she had to do. Would the monkey wrench be strong enough to crack the tub? Or would she only disfigure it so badly that her parents would have to get rid of it? It didn't matter either way. She was doing the right thing. That was all she cared about.

The bathroom door was open. She was sure it had

been shut when she had glanced upstairs only minutes before. But that didn't matter either. Swinging the monkey wrench, she went into the bathroom.

The bath was ready for her.

It had filled itself to the very brim with hot water—scalding hot judging from the amount of steam. The mirror was completely misted over. A cool breeze from the door touched the surface of the glass and water trickled down. Isabel lifted the monkey wrench. She was smiling a little cruelly. The one thing the bath couldn't do was move. It could taunt her and frighten her, but now it just had to sit there and take what was coming to it.

She reached out with the monkey wrench and jerked out the plug.

But the water didn't leave the bath. Instead, something thick and red oozed out of the plug hole and floated up through the water.

Blood.

And with the blood came maggots—hundreds of them, uncoiling themselves from the plug hole, forcing themselves up through the grille and cartwheeling crazily in the water. Isabel stared in horror, then raised the monkey wrench. The water, with the blood added to it, was sheeting over the side now, cascading onto the floor. She swung and felt her whole body shake as the metal clanged into the taps, smashing the C of *cold* and jolting the pipes.

She lifted the monkey wrench, and as she did so she caught sight of it in the mirror. The reflection was blurred by the coating of steam, but behind it she could make out another shape that she knew she would not see in the bathroom. A man was walking toward her as if down a long corridor, making for the glass that covered its end.

Jacob Marlin.

She felt his eyes burning into her and wondered what he would do when he reached the mirror that seemed to be a barrier between his world and hers.

She swung with the monkey wrench—again and again. The tap bent, then broke off with the second impact. Water spurted out as if in a death throe. Now she turned her attention to the bath itself, bringing the monkey wrench crashing into the side, cracking the enamel with one swing, denting the metal with the next. Another glance over her shoulder told her that Marlin was getting closer, pushing his way toward the steam.

She could see his teeth, discolored and sharp, his gums exposed as his lips were drawn back in a grin of pure hatred. She swung again and saw—to her disbelief— that she had actually cracked the side of the bath like an eggshell. Red water gushed over her legs and feet. Maggots were sent spinning in a crazy dance across the bathroom floor, sliding into the cracks and wriggling there, helpless. How close was Marlin? Could he pass through the mirror? She lifted the monkey wrench one last time and screamed as a pair of man's hands fell onto her shoulders. The monkey wrench spun out of her hands and fell into the bath, disappearing in the murky water. The hands were at her throat now, pulling her backward. Isabel screamed and lashed out, her nails going for the man's eyes.

She only just had time to realize that it was not Marlin who was holding her but her father. That her mother was standing in the doorway, staring with wide, horror-filled eyes. Isabel felt all the strength rush out of her body like the water out of the bath. The water was transparent again, of course. The maggots had gone. Had they ever been there? Did it matter? She began to laugh.

She was still laughing half an hour later when the sound of sirens filled the room and the ambulance arrived.

It wasn't fair.

Jeremy Martin lay in the bath thinking about the events of the past six weeks. It was hard not to think about them—in here, looking at the dents his daughter had made with the monkey wrench. The taps had almost been beyond repair. As it was, they now dripped all the time and the letter C was gone forever. *Old* water, not *cold* water.

He had seen Isabel a few days before and she had looked a lot better. She still wasn't talking, but it would be a long time before that happened, they said. Nobody knew why she had decided to attack the bathtub—except maybe that fat friend of hers and she was too frightened to say. According to the experts, it had all been stress related. A traumatic stress disorder. Of course they had fancy words for it. What they meant was that it was her parents who were to blame. They argued. There was tension in the house. Isabel hadn't been able to cope and had come up with some sort of fantasy related to the bath.

In other words, it was his fault.

But was it? As he lay in the soft, hot water with the smell of pine bath oil rising up his nostrils, Jeremy Martin thought long and hard. He wasn't the one who started the arguments. It was always Susan. From the day he married her, she'd insisted on . . . well, changing him. She was always nagging him. It was like that nickname of his at school. Mouse. They never took him seriously. She never took him seriously. Well, he would show her.

Lying back with the steam all around him, Jeremy found himself floating away. It was a wonderful feeling. He would start with Susan. Then there were a couple of boys in his French class. And, of course, the headmaster.

He knew just what he would do. He had seen it that morning in a junk shop in Hampstead. Victorian, he would have said. Heavy, with a smooth wooden handle and a solid, razor-sharp head.

Yes. He would go out and buy it the following morning. It was just what he needed. A good Victorian ax . . .

Killer
Camera

The car-trunk sale took place every Saturday on the edge of Crouch End. There was a patch of empty land there; not a parking lot, not a building site, just a square of rubble and dust that nobody seemed to know what to do with. And then one summer the car-trunk sales had arrived like flies at a picnic and since then there'd been one every week. Not that there was anything very much to buy. Cracked glasses and hideous plates, moldy paperback books by writers you'd never heard of, electric kettles, and bits of hi-fi equipment that looked forty years out of date.

Matthew King decided to go in only because it was free. He'd visited the car-trunk sale before and the only thing he'd come away with was a cold. But this was a warm Saturday afternoon. He had plenty of time. And, anyway, it was there.

But it was the same old trash. He certainly wasn't

going to find his father a fiftieth birthday present here, not unless the old man had a sudden yearning for a five-hundred-piece Snow White jigsaw puzzle (missing one piece) or an electric coffeemaker (only slightly cracked) or perhaps a knitted cardigan in an unusual shade of pink (aaaagh!).

Matthew sighed. There were times when he hated living in London and this was one of them. It was only after his own birthday, his fourteenth, that his parents had finally agreed to let him go out on his own. And it was only then that he realized he didn't really have anywhere to go. Crummy Crouch End with its even crummier car-trunk sale. Was this any place for a smart, good-looking teenager on a summer afternoon?

He was about to leave when a car pulled in and parked in the farthest corner. At first he thought it must be a mistake. Most of the cars at the sale were old and rusty, as worn-out as the stuff they were selling. But this was a red Volkswagen, L-registration, bright red and shiny clean. As Matthew watched, a smartly dressed man stepped out, opened the trunk, and stood there, looking awkward and ill at ease, as if he were unsure what to do next. Matthew strolled over to him.

He would always remember the contents of the

trunk. It was strange. He had a bad memory. There was a show on TV where you had to remember all the prizes that came out on a conveyor belt and he'd never been able to manage more than two or three, but this time it stayed in his mind . . . well, like a photograph.

There were clothes: a baseball jacket, several pairs of jeans, T-shirts. A pair of Rollerblades, a Tintin rocket, a paper lampshade. Lots of books; paperbacks and a brand-new English dictionary. About twenty CDs—mainly pop, a Sony Walkman, a guitar, a box of water-color paints, a Ouija board, a Game Boy . . .

. . . and a camera.

Matthew reached out and grabbed the camera. He was already aware that a small crowd had gathered behind him and more hands were reaching past him to snatch items out of the trunk. The man who had driven the car didn't move. Nor did he show any emotion. He had a round face with a small mustache and he looked fed up. He didn't want to be there in Crouch End, at the car-trunk sale. Everything about him said it.

"I'll give you a tenner for this," someone said.

Matthew saw that they were holding the baseball jacket. It was almost new and must have been worth at least fifty dollars.

"Done," the man said. His face didn't change.

Matthew turned the camera over in his hands. Unlike the jacket, it was old, probably bought secondhand, but it seemed to be in good condition. It was a Pentax—but the X on the casing had worn away. That was the only sign of damage. He held it up and looked through the viewfinder. About twenty feet away, a woman was holding up the horrible pink cardigan he had noticed earlier. He focused and felt a certain thrill as the powerful lens seemed to carry him forward so that the cardigan now filled his vision. He could even make out the buttons—silvery white and loose. He swiveled around, the cars and the crowd racing across the viewfinder as he searched for a subject. For no reason at all he focused on a large bedroom mirror propped up against another car. His finger found the shutter release and he pressed it. There was a satisfying click; it seemed that the camera worked.

And it would make a perfect present. Only a few months before, his dad had been complaining about the pictures he'd just gotten back from their last vacation in France. Half of them had been out of focus and the rest had been so overexposed that they'd made the

Loire Valley look about as enticing as the Gobi Desert on a bad day.

"It's the camera," he'd insisted. "It's worn-out and useless. I'm going to get myself a new one."

But he hadn't. In one week's time he was going to be fifty years old. And Matthew had the perfect birthday present right in his hands.

How much would it cost? The camera felt expensive. For a start it was heavy. Solid. The lens was obviously a powerful one. The camera didn't have an automatic rewind, a digital display, or any of the other things that came as standard these days. But technology was cheap. Quality was expensive. And this was undoubtedly a quality camera.

"Will you take ten dollars for this?" Matthew asked. If the owner had been happy to take so little for the baseball jacket, perhaps he wouldn't think twice about the camera. But this time the man shook his head.

"It's worth a hundred at least," he said. He turned away to take twenty dollars for the guitar. It had been bought by a young black woman who strummed it as she walked away.

"I'll have a look at that . . ." A thin, dark-haired woman reached out to take the camera, but Matthew pulled it back. He had three twenty-dollar bills in his back pocket. Twelve weeks' worth of shoe cleaning, car washing, and generally helping around the house. He hadn't meant to spend all of it on his dad. Perhaps not even half of it.

"Will you take forty dollars?" he asked the man. "It's all I've got," he lied.

The man glared at him, then nodded. "Yes. That'll do."

Matthew felt a surge of excitement and at the same time a sudden fear. A hundred-dollar camera for forty bucks? It had to be broken. Or stolen. Or both. But then the woman opened her mouth to speak and Matthew quickly found his money and thrust it out. The man took it without looking pleased or sorry. He simply folded the notes and put them in his pocket as if the payment meant nothing to him.

"Thank you," Matthew said.

The man looked straight at him. "I just want to get rid of it," he said. "I want to get rid of it all."

"Who did it belong to?"

The man shrugged. "Students," he said—as if the one word explained it all. Matthew waited. The crowd had separated, moving on to the other stalls, and for a moment the two of them were alone. "I used to rent a couple of rooms," the man explained. "Art students. Three of them. A couple of months ago they disappeared. Just took off—owing two months' rent. Well, what do you expect! I've tried to find them, but they haven't had the decency to call. So my wife told me to sell some of their stuff. I didn't want to. But *they're* the ones who owe *me*. It's only fair . . ."

A plump woman pushed between them, snatching up a handful of the T-shirts. "How much for these?" The sun was still shining but suddenly Matthew felt cold.

. . . *they disappeared* . . .

Why should three art students suddenly vanish, leaving all their gear, including a hundred-dollar camera, behind? The landlord obviously felt guilty about selling it. Was Matthew doing the right thing, buying it? Quickly he turned around and hurried away, before either of them changed their mind.

He had just stepped through the gates and reached the street when he heard it: the unmistakable sound of shattering glass. He turned around and looked back and saw that the bedroom mirror he had just photographed with the new camera had been knocked over. At least, he assumed that was what had happened. It was lying facedown, surrounded by splinters of glass.

The owner—a short, stocky man with a skinhead haircut—bounded forward and grabbed hold of a man who had just been passing. "You knocked over my mirror!" he shouted.

"I never went near it." The man was younger, wearing jeans and a *Star Wars* T-shirt.

"I saw you! That'll be five bucks—"

"Get lost!"

And then, even as Matthew watched, the skinhead drew back his fist and lashed out. Matthew almost heard the knuckles connect with the other man's face. The second man screamed. Blood gushed out of his nose and dripped down onto his T-shirt.

Matthew drew the camera close to his chest, turned, and hurried away.

"It must be stolen," Elizabeth King said, taking the camera.

"I don't think so," Matthew said. "I told you what he said!"

"What did you pay for it?" Jamie asked. Jamie was

his younger brother. Three years younger and wildly jealous of everything he did.

"None of your business," Matthew replied.

Elizabeth pushed a lever on the camera with her fingernail and the back sprang open. "Oh, look!" she said. "There's film in here." She tilted the camera back and a Kodak cartridge fell into the palm of her hand. "It's used," she added.

"He must have left it there," Jamie said.

"Maybe you should get it developed," Elizabeth suggested. "You never know what you'll find."

"Boring family snapshots," Matthew muttered.

"It could be porn!" Jamie shouted.

"Grow up, moron!" Matthew sighed.

"You're such a nerd . . . !"

"Retard . . ."

"Come on, boys. Let's not quarrel!" Elizabeth handed the camera back to Matthew. "It's a nice present," she said. "Chris will love it. And he doesn't need to know where you got it . . . or how you think it got there."

Christopher King was an actor. He wasn't famous, although people still recognized him from a coffee commercial he'd done two years before, but he always had work. In this, the week before his fiftieth birthday, he was appearing as Banquo in Shakespeare's *Macbeth* ("the Scottish play," he called it—he said it was bad luck to mention the piece by name). He'd been murdered six nights—and one afternoon—a week for the past five weeks and he was beginning to look forward to the end of the run.

Both Matthew and Jamie liked it when their father was in a London play, especially if it coincided with summer vacation. It meant they could spend quite a bit of the day together. They had an old Labrador, Polonius, and the four of them would often go out walking on Hampstead Heath. Elizabeth King worked part-time in a dress shop, but if she was around she'd come, too. They were a close, happy family. The Kings had been married for twenty years.

Secretly, Matthew was a little shocked about how much money he had spent on the camera, but by the time the birthday arrived, he had managed to put it behind him and he was genuinely pleased by his father's reaction.

"It's great!" Christopher exclaimed, turning the camera in his hands. The family had just finished breakfast and were still sitting around the table in the kitchen.

"It's exactly what I wanted. Automatic exposure *and* a light meter! Different apertures . . ." He looked up at Matthew, who was beaming with pleasure. "Where did you get it from, Matt? Did you rob a bank?"

"It was secondhand," Jamie announced.

"I can see that. But it's still a great camera. Where's the film?"

"I didn't get any, Dad . . ." Matthew remembered the film he'd found in the camera. It was on the table by his bed. Now he cursed himself. Why hadn't he thought to buy some new film? What good was a camera without film?

"You haven't opened my present, Dad," Jamie said.

Christopher put down the camera and reached for a small, square box, wrapped in Power Rangers paper. He tore it open and laughed as a box of film tumbled onto the table. "Now that was a great idea," he exclaimed.

Cheapskate, Matthew thought, but wisely said nothing.

"Now, how does it go in . . . ?"

"Here. Let me." Matthew took the camera from his father and opened the back. Then he tore open the box and started to lower the film into place.

But he couldn't do it.

He stopped.

And slid into the nightmare.

It was as if his family—Christopher and Elizabeth sitting at the breakfast table, Jamie hovering at their side—had become a photograph themselves. Matthew was suddenly watching them from outside, frozen in another world. Everything seemed to have stopped. At the same time he felt something that he had never felt in his life—a strange tingling at the back of his neck as, one after another, the hairs stood on end. He looked down at the camera, which had become a gaping black hole in his hands. He felt himself falling, being sucked into it. And once he was inside, the back of the camera would be a coffin lid that would snap shut, locking him in the terrible darkness . . .

"Matt? Are you all right?" Christopher reached out and took the camera, breaking the spell, and Matthew realized that his whole body was trembling. There was sweat on his shoulders and in the palms of his hands. What had happened to him? What had he just experienced?

"Yes. I'm . . ." He blinked and shook his head.

"Are you getting a summer cold?" his mother asked. "You've gone quite pale."

"I . . ."

There was a loud snap. Christopher held up the camera. "There! It's in!"

Jamie climbed onto his chair and stuck one leg out like a statue, showing off. "Take me!" he called out. "Take a picture of me!"

"I can't. I haven't got a flash."

"We can go out in the garden!"

"There's not enough sun."

"Well, you've got to take something, Chris," Elizabeth said.

In the end, Christopher took two pictures. It didn't matter what the subjects were, he said. He just wanted to experiment.

First of all, he took a picture of a tree, growing in the middle of the lawn. It was the cherry tree that Elizabeth had planted while he was appearing in Chekhov's *The Cherry Orchard* just after they were married. It had flowered every year since.

And then, when Jamie had persuaded Polonius, the Labrador, to waddle out of his basket and into the garden, Christopher took a picture of him as well.

Matthew watched all this with a smile but refused to take part. He was still feeling sick. It was as if he had been half-strangled or punched in the pit of his stomach. He reached out and poured himself a glass of apple juice. His mother was probably right. He must be coming down with flu.

But he forgot about it later when two more actors from "the Scottish play" stopped over and they all went out for an early lunch. After that, Christopher caught a bus into town—it was a Wednesday and he had to be at the theater by two—and Matthew spent the rest of the afternoon playing computer games with Polonius asleep at the foot of his bed.

It was two days later that his mother noticed it.

"Look at that!" she exclaimed, gazing out of the kitchen window.

"What's that?" Christopher had been sent a new play and he was reading it before his audition.

"The cherry tree!"

Matthew walked over to the window and looked out. He saw at once what his mother meant. The tree was about ten feet tall. Although the best of the blossom was over, it had already taken on its autumn colors, a great burst of dark red leaves fighting for attention on the delicate branches. At least, that was how it had been the day before.

Now the cherry tree was dead. The branches were bare, the leaves brown and shriveled, scattered over the lawn. Even the trunk seemed to have turned gray and the whole tree was bent over like a sick, old man.

"What's happened?" Christopher opened the kitchen door and walked out into the garden. Elizabeth followed him. He reached the tree and scooped up a handful of the leaves. "It's completely dead!" he exclaimed.

"But a tree can't just . . . die." Matthew had never seen his mother look so sad and he suddenly realized that the cherry must have been more than a tree to her. It had grown alongside her marriage and her family. "It looks as if it's been poisoned!" she muttered.

Christopher dropped the leaves and wiped his hand on his sleeve. "Perhaps it was something in the soil," he said. He pulled Elizabeth toward him. "Cheer up! We'll plant another one."

"But it was special. *The Cherry Orchard* . . ."

Christopher put an arm around his wife. "At least I took a picture of it," he said. "It means we've got something to remember it by."

The two of them went back into the house, leaving Matthew alone in the garden. He reached out and ran a finger down the bark of the tree. It felt cold and slimy to the touch. He shivered. He had never seen anything that looked quite so . . . dead.

At least I took a picture of it . . .

Christopher's words echoed in his mind. He suddenly felt uneasy—but he didn't know why.

The accident happened the next day.

Matthew wasn't up yet. Lying in bed, he heard first the sound of the front door crashing open—too hard—and then the voices echoing up the stairs toward him.

"Liz! What is it? What's the matter?"

"Oh, Chris!" Matthew froze. His mother never cried. Never. But she was crying now. "It's Polonius . . ."

"What happened?"

"I don't know! I don't understand it!"

"Lizzie, he's not . . ."

"He is. I'm sorry. I'm so sorry . . ." That was all she could say.

In the kitchen, Christopher made tea and listened to the cold facts. Elizabeth had walked down into Crouch End to get the newspaper and mail some letters. She had taken Polonius with her. As usual, the Labrador had padded after her. She never put him on a leash. He was well trained. He never ran into the road, even if he saw a cat or a squirrel. The truth was that, at nearly twelve years old, Polonius hardly ever ran at all.

But today, for no reason, he had suddenly walked off the sidewalk. Elizabeth hadn't even seen him until it was too late. She had opened her mouth to call his name when the Land Rover had appeared, driving too fast around the corner. All the cars drove too fast on Wolseley Road. Elizabeth had closed her eyes at the last moment. But she had heard the yelp, the terrible thump, and she had known that Polonius could not have survived.

At least it had been quick. The driver of the Land Rover had been helpful and apologetic. He had taken the dog to the vet . . . to be buried or cremated or whatever. Polonius was gone. He had been with the family since he was a puppy and now he was gone.

Lying in bed, Matthew listened to his parents talking, and although he didn't hear all of it, he knew enough. He rested his head on the pillow, his eyes brimming with tears. "You took a picture of him," he muttered to himself. "A picture is all we have left."

And that was when he knew.

At the car-trunk sale, Matthew had taken a picture of a mirror. The mirror had smashed.

His father had taken a picture of the cherry tree. The cherry tree had died.

Then he'd taken a picture of Polonius . . .

Matthew turned to one side, his cheek coming into contact with the cool surface of the pillow. And there it was, where he had left it, on the table by his bed. The film that he had found inside the camera when he bought it. The film that had already been exposed.

That afternoon, he took it to the drugstore and had it developed.

There were twenty-four pictures in the packet.

Matthew had bought himself a Coke in a café in Crouch End and now he tore the packet open, letting the glossy pictures slide out onto the table. For a moment he hesitated. It felt wrong, stealing this glimpse into somebody else's life . . . like a Peeping Tom. But he had to know.

The first ten pictures only made him feel worse.

They showed a young guy, in his early twenties, and somehow Matthew knew that this was the owner of the camera. He was kissing a pretty blond girl in one picture, throwing a baseball in another.

Art students. Three of them . . .

The man at the car-trunk sale had rented part of his house to art students. And this must be them. Three of them. The camera owner. The blond girl. And another guy, thin, with long hair and uneven teeth.

Matthew shuffled quickly through the rest of the pictures.

An exhibition of paintings. A London street. A railway station. A beach. A fishing boat. A house . . .

The house was different. It was like nothing Matthew had ever seen before. It stood, four stories high, in the ruins of a garden, slanting out of a tangle of nettles and briars with great knife blades of grass stabbing at the brickwork. It was obviously deserted, empty. Some of the windows had been smashed. The black paint was peeling in places, exposing brickwork that glistened like a suppurating wound.

Closer. A cracked gargoyle leered at the camera, arching out over the front door. The door was a massive slab of oak, its iron knocker shaped like a pair of baby's arms with the hands clasped.

Six people had come to the house that night. There was a picture of them, grouped together in the garden. Matthew recognized the three students from art school. Now they were all dressed in black shirts, black jeans. Two more men and another girl, all about twenty, stood behind them. One of the men had raised his arms and was grimacing, doing a vampire impersonation. They were all laughing. Matthew wondered if a seventh person had taken the picture or if it had been set to automatic. He turned over the next photograph and was taken into the house.

Click. A vast entrance hall. Huge flagstones and, in the distance, the rotting bulk of a wooden staircase twisting up to nowhere.

Click. The blond girl drinking red wine. Drinking it straight from the bottle.

Click. A guy with fair hair holding two candles. Behind him another guy holding a paintbrush.

Click. The flagstones again, but now they've painted a white circle on them and the guy with fair hair is adding words. But you can't read the words. They've been wiped out by the reflection from the flash.

Click. More candles. Flickering now. Placed around the circle. Three members of the group holding hands.

Click. They're naked! They've taken off their clothes. Matthew can see everything, but at the same time he sees nothing. He doesn't believe it. It's madness . . .

Click. A cat. A black cat. Its eyes have caught the flash and have become two pinpricks of fire. The cat has sharp, white teeth. It is snarling, writhing in the hands that hold it.

Click. A knife.

Matthew closed his eyes. He knew now what they were doing. At the same time he remembered the other object that the man had been selling at the car-trunk sale. He had noticed it at the time but hadn't really thought about it. The Ouija board. A game for people who like to play with things they don't understand. A game for people who aren't afraid of the dark. But Matthew was afraid.

Sitting there in the café with the photographs spread out in front of him, he couldn't bring himself to believe it. But there could be no escaping the truth. A group of students had gone to an abandoned house. Perhaps they'd taken some sort of book with them; an old book of spells . . . they could have found it in an antiques shop. Matthew had once seen something like that in the shop where his mother worked: an old, leather-bound book with yellowing pages and black, splattery handwriting. A grimoire, she'd called it. The people in the photograph must have found one somewhere, and tired of the Ouija board, they'd decided to do something more dangerous, more frightening. To summon up . . .

What?

A ghost? A demon?

Matthew had seen enough horror films to recognize what the photographs showed. A magic circle. Candles. The blood of a dead cat. The six people had taken it all very seriously—even stripping naked for the ritual. And they had succeeded. Somehow Matthew knew that the ritual had worked. That they had raised . . . something. And it had killed them.

They disappeared. Just took off . . .

The man at the car-trunk sale had never seen them again. Of course they'd returned to his house, to wherever it was they rented. If they hadn't gone back, the camera would never have been there. But after that, something must have happened. Not to one of them. But to all of them.

The camera . . .

Matthew looked down at the prints. He had worked his way through the pile, but there were still three or four pictures left. He reached out with his fingers to separate them, but then stopped. Had the student who owned the camera taken a picture of the creature, the thing, whatever it was they had summoned up with their spells? Was it there now, on the table in front of him? Could it be possible . . . ?

He didn't want to know.

Matthew picked up the entire pile and screwed them up in his hands. He tried to tear them but couldn't. Suddenly he felt sick and angry. He hadn't wanted any of this. He had just wanted a birthday present for his father and he had brought something horrible and evil into the house. One of the photographs slipped through his fingers and . . .

. . . something red, glowing, two snake eyes, a huge shadow . . .

. . . Matthew saw it out of the corner of his eye even as he tried not to look at it. He grabbed hold of the picture and began to tear it, once, twice, into ever-smaller pieces.

"Are you all right, love?"

The waitress had appeared from nowhere and stood over the table looking down at Matthew. Matthew half smiled and opened his hand, scattering fragments of the photograph. "Yes . . ." He stood up. "I don't want these," he said.

"I can see that. Shall I put them in the trash for you?"

"Yes. Thanks . . ."

The waitress swept up the crumpled photographs and the torn pieces and carried them over to the trash can. When she turned around again, the table was empty. Matthew had already gone.

Find the camera. Smash the camera. The two thoughts ran through his mind again and again. He would explain it to his father later. Or maybe he wouldn't. How could he tell him what he now knew to be true?

"You see, Dad, this guy had the camera and he used it in some sort of black-magic ritual. He took a picture of a demon and the demon either killed him or frightened him away and now it's *inside* the camera. Every time you take a picture with the camera, you kill whatever you're aiming at. Remember the cherry tree? Remember Polonius? And there was this mirror, too . . ."

Christopher would think he was mad. It would be better not even to try to explain. He would just take the camera and lose it. Perhaps at the bottom of a canal. His parents would think someone had stolen it. It would be better if they never knew.

He arrived home. He had his own keys and let himself in.

He knew at once that his parents had gone out. The coats were missing in the hall, and apart from the sound of vacuuming coming from upstairs, the house felt empty. As he closed the front door, the sound of the vacuum cleaner stopped and a short, round woman appeared at the top of the stairs. Her name was Mrs. Bayley and she came in twice a week to help Elizabeth with the cleaning.

"Is that you, Matthew?" she called down. She relaxed when she saw him. "You mom said to tell you she'd gone out."

"Where did she go?" Matthew felt the first stirrings of alarm.

"Your dad took her and Jamie up to Hampstead Heath. And that new camera you bought him. He said he wanted to take their picture . . ."

And that was it. Matthew felt the floor tilt underneath him and he slid back, his shoulders hitting the wall.

The camera.

Hampstead Heath.

Not Mom! Not Jamie!

"What's the matter?" Mrs. Bayley came down the stairs toward him. "You look like you've seen a ghost!"

"I have to go there!" The words came out as a gabble. Matthew forced himself to slow down. "Mrs. Bayley. Have you got your car? Can you give me a lift?"

"I still haven't done the kitchen . . ."

"Please! It's important!"

There must have been something in his voice. Mrs. Bayley looked at him, puzzled. Then she nodded. "I can take you up if you like. But the Heath's a big place. I don't know how you're going to find them . . ."

She was right, of course. The Heath stretched all the way from Hampstead to Highgate and down to Gospel Oak, a swath of green that rose and fell with twisting paths, ornamental lakes, and thick clumps of woodland. Walking on the Heath, you hardly felt you were in London at all, and even if you knew where you were going, it was easy to get lost. Where would they have gone? They could be anywhere.

Mrs. Bayley had driven him down from Highgate in her rusting Fiat Panda and was about to reach the first main entrance when he saw it, parked next to a bus stop. It was his father's car. There was a sticker in the back window—LIVE THEATER MAKES LIFE BETTER—and the bright red letters jumped out at him. Matthew had always been a little embarrassed by that stupid line. Now he read the words with a flood of relief.

"Stop here, Mrs. Bayley!" he shouted.

Mrs. Bayley twisted the steering wheel and there was the blare of a horn from behind them as they swerved into the side of the road. "Have you seen them?" she asked.

"Their car. They must be up at Kenwood . . ."

Kenwood House. It was one of the most beautiful sights of the Heath; a white, eighteenth-century building on a gentle rise, looking down over a flat lawn and a lake. It was just the sort of place where Christopher might have gone for a walk . . .

Gone to take a picture.

Matthew scrambled out of the car, slamming the

door behind him. Already he could imagine Elizabeth and Jamie with their backs to the house. Christopher standing with the camera. "A little closer. Now smile . . ." His finger would stab downward—and then what? Matthew remembered the cherry tree, colorless and dead. Polonius, who had never stepped into the road before. The mirror, smashing at the car-trunk sale. A gush of blood from the fight it had provoked. Even as he ran along the pavement and swung through the first entrance to the Heath, he wondered if he wasn't mad, if he hadn't imagined the whole thing. But then he remembered the pictures: the empty house, the candles.

The shadow. Two burning red eyes . . .

And Matthew knew that he was right, that he had imagined none of it, and that he had perhaps only minutes in which to save his father, his mother, his younger brother.

If it wasn't too late already.

Christopher, Elizabeth, and Jamie weren't at Kenwood. They weren't on the terrace, or on the lawn. Matthew ran from one end of the house to the other, pushing through the crowds, ignoring the cries of protest. He thought he saw Jamie in the ornamental gardens and pounced on him—but it was another boy, nothing like his brother. The whole world seemed to have smashed (like the mirror at the car-trunk sale) as he forced himself on, searching for his family. He was aware only of the green of the grass, the blue of the sky, and the multicolored pieces, the unmade jigsaw, of the people in between.

"Mom! Dad! Jamie!" He shouted their names as he ran, hoping against hope that if he didn't see them, they might hear him. He was half-aware that people were looking at him, pointing at him, but he didn't care. He swerved around a man in a wheelchair. His foot came down in a bed of flowers. Somebody shouted at him. He ran on.

And just when he was about to give up, he saw them. For a moment he stood there, his chest heaving, the breath catching in his throat. Was it really them, just standing there? They looked as if they had been waiting for him all along.

But had he reached them in time?

Christopher was holding the camera. The lens cap was on. Jamie was looking bored. Elizabeth had been talking, but seeing Matthew, she broke off and gazed at him, astonished.

"Matthew . . . ?" She glanced at Christopher. "What are you doing here? What's the matter . . . ?"

Matthew ran forward. It was only now that he realized he was sweating, not just from the effort of running but from sheer terror. He stared at the camera in his father's hand, resisting the impulse to tear it away and smash it. He opened his mouth to speak, but for a moment no words came. He forced himself to relax.

"The camera . . ." he rasped.

"What about it?" Christopher held it up, alarmed.

Matthew swallowed. He didn't want to ask the question. But he had to. He had to know. "Did you take a picture of Mom?" he asked.

Christopher King shook his head. "She wouldn't let me," he said.

"I'm too much of a mess," Elizabeth added.

"What about Jamie?"

"What about me?"

Matthew ignored him. "Did you take a picture of him?"

"No." Christopher smiled, perplexed. "What is all this, Matthew? What's the matter?"

Matthew held up his hands. "You haven't taken a picture of Jamie? You haven't taken a picture of Mom?"

"No."

Then—the horrible thought. "Did you let them take a picture of you?"

"No." Christopher laid a hand on Matthew's shoulder. "We only just got here," he said. "We haven't taken any pictures of each other. Why is it so important anyway? What are you doing here?"

Matthew felt his knees go weak. He wanted to sink onto the grass. He felt the breeze rippling past his cheeks and a great shout of laughter welled up inside him. He had arrived in time. Everything was going to be all right.

Then Jamie spoke. "I took a picture," he said.

Matthew froze.

"Dad let me!"

"Yes." Christopher smiled. "It's the only picture we've taken."

"But . . ." Just four words. But once they were spoken, his life would never be the same. "What did you take?"

Jamie pointed. "London."

And there it was. The entire city of London. They were standing on a hill and it lay there, spread out before them. You could see it all from here. St. Paul's

Cathedral. The Post Office Tower. Nelson's Column. Big Ben. That's why the Kings had come here.

For the view.

"London . . . ?" Matthew's throat was dry.

"I got a great picture."

"London . . . !"

The sun had disappeared. Matthew stood watching as the clouds closed in and the darkness rolled toward the city.

Light
Moves

I suppose my story begins with the death of a man I never met. His name was Ethan Sly and he was a journalist, the racing correspondent for the *Ipswich News* with his own column, which was called *Sly's Eye*. He was, apparently, a thirty-a-day man—cigarettes, that is—and when he wasn't smoking he was eating, and when he wasn't eating he was drinking.

So nobody was very surprised when, at the ripe old age of forty-two, Ethan had a huge heart attack and dropped dead. In fact, nobody even noticed for a couple of hours. He'd been working at his desk, typing up his tips for the Grand National, when that poor, overworked organ (his heart) had decided that enough was enough. The doctor said that it had probably happened too fast for him to feel any pain. Certainly, when they found him he just looked mildly surprised.

I learned all this because my dad worked on the

same newspaper. I've always been a bit embarrassed by this. You see, he writes the cooking column. Why cooking? Why not football or crime or even the weather report? I know I'm probably sexist and Dad's told me a hundred times that most of the famous chefs are men, but still . . .

Anyway, he was there when they cleared out Ethan's office and that's how I ended up with the computer. And that's when all the trouble began.

Dad came back home with it the day after the funeral. He was carrying it in a big cardboard box and for a crazy moment I thought it must be a puppy or a kitten or something like that. It was the way he was cradling it in his arms, almost lovingly. He set it down gently on the kitchen table.

"Here you are, Henry," he said. "This is for you."

"What is it?" Claire asked. She's my little sister, nine years old, heavily into Barbie and boy bands. We don't get along.

"It's for Henry," my dad repeated. "You always said you wanted to be a writer. This is to help you get started."

I had said—once—that I wanted to be a writer. I'd

just heard how much Jeffrey Archer earned. Since then the idea had stuck, and now whenever Dad introduced me to anyone, he said I was going to write. Parents are like that. They like labels.

I opened the box.

The computer was old and out-of-date. You could tell just from the way that the white plastic had gone gray. The keyboard was so grubby you could hardly read some of the letters and the plastic knob had fallen off the DELETE button, leaving a metal prong showing through. There were sticky brown rings all over the hard drive where the last owner must have stood his coffee mugs while he was working. It had a color screen and a Pentium processor but no 3-D accelerator . . . which meant I could kiss all the best games good-bye.

"What's that?" My mom had come into the kitchen and was looking at the computer in dismay. We live in a modern house in a development just outside Ipswich and my mom likes to keep it clean. She has a part-time job in a shoe shop and a full-time job as a housewife and mother. She never sits still. She's always hovering—dusting, polishing, or washing. The cooking, of course, she leaves to Dad.

"It's a computer," I said. "Dad gave it to me."

"Where did you get it?" She scowled. "It needs a wipe-down."

"What did you get *me*?" Claire whined.

"It's for Henry. To help him with writing," Dad said, ignoring her. "They were clearing out poor old Ethan's office this morning and a whole lot of stuff was going begging. I got the computer."

"Thanks, Dad," I said, although I wasn't entirely sure about it. "Does it work?"

"Of course it works. Ethan was using it the morning he . . ." But then he shrugged and fell silent.

I carried the computer up to my room and made a space for it on my desk, but I didn't turn it on then and I'll tell you why. I suppose it was kind of my dad to think of me and I know he meant well, but I didn't like it. It was such an ugly old machine with its gray coiling wires and heavy sockets. Although I had tucked it away in the corner, it seemed to dominate the room. Do you know what I mean? I didn't want to look at it, but at the same time I couldn't keep my eyes off it. And I had a nasty feeling that the empty, dark green glass monitor . . . well, I almost felt that it was staring back.

I had tea. I did my homework. I talked on the telephone to Leo (my best friend). I kicked a soccer ball around the garden and finally I had a bath and went to bed. It sounds silly but the truth is I'd put off going back to my room as long as I could. I kept on thinking of Ethan Sly. Dead and rotting in his grave. And just forty-eight hours before, his nicotine-stained fingers had been pattering across the keyboard that now sat waiting on my desk. A dead man's toy. The thought made me shiver.

I fell asleep quickly. I'm normally a heavy sleeper, but I woke up that night. Suddenly my eyes were wide open and I could feel the cool of the pillow under my head. What had woken me up? There was no sound in the room except . . . now I could hear a low humming noise; soft and insistent and strange. Then I realized that there was a green glow in the room. It had never been there before. It was illuminating the movie posters on my walls—not enough to make the words readable but enough to show up the pictures. I turned my head, feeling the bones in my neck click as they rotated on my spine. My left cheek touched the pillow. I looked across the room.

The computer was on. That was what was making the humming sound. The screen was lit up with a single word in large capital letters stretching across the center.

CASABLANCA

That made no sense to me at all. Casablanca. A city in North Africa. The title of an old film that always made my grandmother cry. Who had typed it on the screen and why? I was more annoyed than puzzled. Obviously my dad had come into my room and turned the computer on while I was asleep. I suppose he wanted to check that it worked. But I was fussy about who came into my room. It was my private place and Mom and Dad usually respected that. I didn't mind him fixing the computer. But I'd have preferred it if he'd asked.

I was too tired to get out of bed and turn it off. Instead I closed my eyes and turned my head away again to go back to sleep. But I didn't sleep. It was as if someone had thrown a bucket of ice water over me.

This is what I had seen even though my eyes had

refused to believe it. This is what I was seeing now.

The computer wasn't plugged in.

The plug was lying on the carpet with the cord curled around it, a good six inches away from the socket. But the computer was still on. I put two and two together and decided I had to be dreaming. What other possibility could there be? I shut my eyes and went back to sleep.

I forgot all about the computer the next morning. I'd overslept (as usual) and I was late for school for the second time that week. It was all just a mad scramble to get into my clothes, into the bathroom before Claire, and into school before they locked the gates. After that it was the usual school routine: math, French, history, science . . . with each lesson melting into the next in the early summer sun. But then something happened and suddenly school was forgotten and the computer was right back in my mind.

It was just before the last class and I was walking down the corridor and Mr. Priestman (biology) and Mr. Thompson (English) were walking the other way. Now everybody knew that Mr. Priestman was a bit on the wild side; down at the pub at lunchtime, smoking in the bathroom since they'd made the staff room a no-smoking area, and off to the betting shop between lessons. Well, he was grinning from ear to ear as he came out of his classroom and the other teacher must have asked him what he was so pleased about because this was the fragment of conversation that I heard.

"A hundred and fifty bucks." That was the Priest.

"What was that, then? A horse?" Mr. Thompson asked.

"Yeah. The two o'clock at Newbury. Casablanca came in at fifteen to one."

Casablanca.

A horse.

Ethan Sly's computer.

I don't know how I managed to get through the last class—it would have to be religious studies, wouldn't it?—but as soon as school was over, I found my friend Leo and poured the whole thing out to him. Leo is the same age as me, fourteen, and lives on the next block. He's dark and foreign-looking—his mother came from Cyprus—and he's the smartest boy in our class.

"All right," he said when I'd finished. "So the ghost of this racing journalist . . ."

". . . Ethan Sly . . ."

". . . came back last night and haunted your Apple."

"It's not an Apple. It's a Zircon. Or Zincom. Or something . . ."

"He haunted your computer and told you the result of a race that was happening today?"

"Yes, Leo. Yes. What do you think?"

Leo thought for a moment. "I think you've had a bit too much sun."

Maybe Leo isn't as smart as people think.

That night I did my homework at double speed, wolfed down my supper, and cut out my usual argument with Claire. I went up to my room as soon as I could, closed the door, and plugged in the computer. There was a switch on the front. I pressed it, then sat back and waited.

The screen lit up and a line of text stretched itself across the glass.

Zincom System. Base memory 640K. 00072K extended.

It was just the usual computer jargon—nothing unusual about that. The screen flickered a couple of times and I found myself holding my breath, but then the software finished booting itself and clicked into an ordinary word-processing program; the electronic equivalent of a blank page. I typed my name on the screen.

HENRY MARSH

The letters sat there doing nothing. I typed a line of text, even though I felt uneasy doing it.

HELLO, MR. SLY. ARE YOU THERE?

Again, nothing happened and I started wondering if I wasn't behaving like an idiot. Maybe Leo was right. Maybe I had dreamed the whole incident. On the screen, the little cursor was blinking, waiting for my next input. I reached out and turned it off.

But the computer didn't turn off.

I had cut the power. The whole thing should have shut down, but even as I sat there staring, two words glowed on the screen in front of me. There really was something ghostly about the letters. They didn't seem to be projected onto the glass but hung behind it, sus-pended in the darkness.

MILLER'S BOY

That was the name of a horse if ever I'd heard one.

I reached out for a sheet of paper, and as I did so, I noticed that my hand was shaking. I was actually terrified, but I suppose I was too fascinated by what was happening to notice. And something else was already stirring in my mind. The computer had already predicted the winner of one race. Priestman had won a hundred and fifty dollars on Casablanca. And now here was a second horse. Maybe there would be others. Suppose I were to put money on them myself? There was no limit to the amount I could make.

I wrote the name down on the paper. At the same time the letters began to fade on the screen as if it knew they were no longer needed. A moment later they had gone.

I tracked down Leo during the first break at school the next day. He listened to what I had to say with his usual, serious face, but then he shook his head.

"Henry . . ." he began in a voice that told me what was about to follow.

"I'm not afraid and I'm not making this up," I interrupted. "Look . . ." I had bought the *Sun* newspaper on the way to school and now I opened it at the back, where the races were listed. I stabbed at the page with a finger. "There it is," I said triumphantly. "The four-forty Bunbury Fillies Handicap at Chester. Number five. Miller's Boy."

Leo peered at the newspaper. But he couldn't argue. There it was in black and white.

"The odds are nine to two," he said.

"That's right. So if we put two dollars on it, we'll get nine dollars back."

"If it wins."

"Of course it'll win. That's the whole point."

"Henry, I don't think—"

"Why don't we go down to the betting shop after school? We can go there on the way home." Leo looked doubtful. "We don't have to go in," I went on. "But it can't hurt to find out."

"No." Leo shook his head. "You can go if you want to, but I'm not coming. I think it's a bad idea."

But of course he came. Why else do you think he's my best friend?

We went as soon as school was over. The betting shop was in a shabby, unfriendly neighborhood, the sort of place where there's always graffiti on the walls and litter in the streets. The only times I passed it were on the bus and nothing would have normally made me want to stop there. It was part of a series of three shops and the funny thing was that you couldn't see into any of them. On the left was a liquor store, its window covered by steel mesh. On the right was a smoke-filled café with its window coated in grease. The betting shop didn't have a window. It just had a sheet of glass painted to look like a racetrack. The door was open, but there were plastic strips hanging down to stop people from looking in.

There was a television on inside and fortunately it was turned up high enough for us to be able to hear the commentary. Leo and I hung about on the sidewalk trying to look innocent as the four-twenty Fulford Handicap came to its close.

"... and it's Lucky Liz from Maryland ... Lucky Liz as they come to the finishing line ... it's Lucky Liz ... Lucky Liz ... then Maryland, then the favorite, Irish Cream ..."

Now, even as I was hearing this, a thought was forming in my mind. I shoved my hand into my pocket and found exactly what I knew was there. Two dollars. I'd washed the car, mowed the lawn, and cleared the table twice for that. Slave labor! But I was thinking of what Leo had said. If I put two dollars on Miller's Boy,

I'd get nine dollars back when it won. I took the money out.

"Put it away!" Leo must have read my mind. "You said we were only coming to look. Anyway, you're too young to bet. They wouldn't even let you in."

And that was when Bill Garrett appeared.

Bill was famous at our school. For five years he had terrorized staff and pupils alike, never doing enough to get himself expelled but always walking close to the line. The fire that had destroyed the gymnasium had always been put down to him although nobody could ever prove anything, just like the theft of two hundred dollars from the Kosovo relief fund. It was said that when he left, age sixteen, with no qualifications whatsoever, the teachers had thrown a party that had lasted the whole night. For a while after that, he had hung around the school gates, occasionally latching onto some of the younger kids for their lunch money. But he had soon gotten bored with that and hadn't been seen for a while.

But here he was, strolling out of the café with a cigarette between his lips and an ugly look in his eyes. He must have been eighteen by now, but smoking had stunted his growth. His body was thin and twisted and he smelled. He had black curly hair that fell over one eye like seaweed clinging to a rock. Leo coughed loudly and began to edge away, but it was too late to run.

"What are you two doing here?" Garrett asked, recognizing our uniform.

"We're lost . . ." Leo began.

"No we're not," I said. I looked Garrett straight in the eye, hoping he wouldn't thump me before I got to the end of the sentence. "We want to put a bet on a horse," I explained.

That amused him. He smiled, revealing a set of jagged teeth, stained with nicotine. "What horse?" he asked.

"Miller's Boy. In the four-forty at Chester." Leo was making huge eyes at me, but I ignored him. "I want to put on two dollars." I held out the money for Garrett to see.

"Two dollars?" He sneered. Suddenly his hand lashed out, his palm slapping up beneath my outstretched fingers. The two bills flew into the air. His hand whipped out and grabbed them. I bit my lip, annoyed with myself. They were gone and I knew it.

Garrett waved the bills in his hand. "Shame to waste it on a horse," he said. "You can buy me a pint of beer."

"Let's get out of here," Leo muttered. He was just glad we were still alive.

"Wait a minute." I was determined to see this through. "Miller's Boy in the four-forty," I said. "It's going to win. Put the money on the horse and I'll let you keep half of it. Four-fifty each . . ."

"Henry . . . !" Leo groaned.

But I'd caught Garrett's interest. "How can you be so sure it'll win?"

"I have a friend . . ." I searched for the right words. "He knows about horses. He told me."

"Miller's Boy?"

"I promise you, Garrett." Inspiration struck. I held up my watch, noticing that the time was 4:35. It was now or never. "If it loses, I'll give you my watch," I said.

Leo rolled his eyes.

Garrett considered. You could almost see his thoughts reflected in his eyes as they churned around slowly in what passed for his brain. "All right," he said at last. "You wait here. And if you move you'll be sorry."

He loped into the betting shop, the plastic strips falling across behind him. As soon as he had gone, Leo turned to me.

"Let's run!" he gasped.

"He'd catch us."

"We could catch a bus."

"He knows where to find us. School—"

"I knew we shouldn't have come here." The sadder Leo becomes, the funnier he looks. Right now I didn't know whether to laugh or cry. "What happens if the horse doesn't win?"

"It'll win," I muttered. "It has to."

The plastic strips parted and Garrett appeared holding a blue betting ticket. "I just got it in time," he announced. "The race is about to start."

"And they're off . . . !" The sound from the television echoed out onto the street as the three of us stood there, Leo and me not knowing quite where to look. I wanted to get closer to the door, but at the same time I didn't want to seem too eager, so I stayed where I was. I could hardly hear any of the commentary and the bits I did hear didn't sound too good. It seemed that a horse called Jenny Wren had taken an early lead. Borsalino was coming up behind. I didn't even hear Miller's Boy mentioned.

But then at the very end, when the commentator's voice was at its most frantic, the magic words finally reached me.

"And it's Miller's Boy coming up on the inside. Miller's Boy! He's overtaken Borsalino and now he's moving in on Jenny Wren. Miller's Boy . . . can he do it?"

A few seconds later it was all over. Miller's Boy had come in first by a head. Bill Garrett looked at me long and hard. "Wait here," he commanded. He went back into the shop.

Leo grimaced. "Now we're in real trouble," he said.

"What do you mean?" I retorted. "The horse won."

"That's exactly what I mean. You wait and see . . ."

Garrett came out of the betting shop. There was a smile on his lips, but it wasn't a pleasant one. It's how you'd imagine a snake would smile at a rabbit. "What's your name?" he asked.

"Henry Marsh."

He held out a hand. There were three dollar bills in the palm. "Here you are, Henry," he said. "Three for you and six for me. That seems fair, doesn't it?"

It didn't seem fair at all, but I wasn't going to argue.

"This friend of yours . . ." Garrett had lit another cigarette. He blew cold blue smoke into the air. "You think I could meet him?"

"He's very shy," I said.

"In the racing business, is he?"

"He used to be." That was true, anyway.

Garrett placed a hand on my shoulder. His fingers dug into my collarbone, making me wince. "It seems you and me, we need each other," he said. His voice was friendly, but his fingers were digging deep. "You get the tips, but you're too young to place the bets . . ."

"I don't think there will be any more tips," I whimpered.

"Well, if there are, you make sure you keep in touch."

"I will, Garrett."

His hand left my shoulder and clouted me across the chin hard enough to make my eyes water. "I'm Mr. Garrett now," he explained. "I'm not at school anymore."

He turned and walked into the liquor store. I guessed he was going to spend the six dollars he had just won.

"Let's go," Leo muttered.

I didn't need prompting. Together we ran to the bus stop just in time to catch a bus home. I don't think

I'd ever been so glad to feel myself on the move.

That night the computer woke me up again. This time the screen carried three words.

TEA FOR TWO

I buried my head in the pillow, trying to blot it out, but the words still burned in my mind. I'm not sure how I felt just then. Part of me was depressed. Part of me was frightened. But I was excited, too. What was happening was new and strange and fantastic. And it could still make me rich. I could be a millionaire a thousand times over. Just thinking of that was enough to keep me awake all night. It would be like winning the pools every day for the rest of my life.

I didn't tell Leo about the horse. He hardly spoke to me at school the next day and I got the feeling that he didn't want to know. I had thought about telling my mom and dad, but had decided against it—at least for the time being. It was my computer, but if I told them, they'd probably take it away and I wasn't ready for that. Not yet.

Bill Garrett was waiting for me when I came out of

school. I was on my own—Leo had gotten a part in the school play and had stayed behind to rehearse. At first I ignored him, walking toward the bus stop like I always did. But I wasn't surprised when he fell into step beside me. And the truth is, I wasn't even sorry. Because, you see, Garrett had been right the day before. He'd told me I needed him. And I did.

He was friendly enough. "I was wondering if you'd had any more tips," he said.

"I might have," I replied, trying to keep the tremble out of my voice.

"Might have?" I thought he'd turn around and punch me then. But he didn't.

"How much money have you got?" I asked him.

He dug into his pockets and pulled out a soiled five-dollar bill, three singles, and a handful of change. "About eight bucks," he said. At a glance I could see it was closer to ten, but as I told you, math wasn't Garrett's strong point.

"I could turn that into . . ." I'd already checked the odds and now I made a mental calculation. "One hundred and eighty-five dollars," I said.

"What?"

"How much will you give me?"

"Out of a hundred and eighty-five?" He considered. "I'll let you have thirty."

"I want a hundred."

"Wait a minute . . ." The ugly look was back on his face, although I'm not sure it had ever left it.

"That still leaves you with eighty-five," I said. "You put the stake down, I'll tell you the name of the horse."

"What happens if it loses."

"Then I'll save up and pay you back."

We were some way from the school by now, which was just as well. It wouldn't have done me any good to be seen talking to Garrett. He sneered at me in his own special way. "How do you know I'll pay you the money if it does win?" he asked.

"If you don't, I won't give you any more tips." I had it all worked out. At least, that's what I thought. Which only goes to show how wrong you can be.

Garrett nodded slowly. "All right," he said. "It's a deal. What's the name of the horse?"

"Tea for Two." Even as I spoke the words I knew that there could be no going back now. I was in this up to my neck. "It's running in the four-fifty at Carlisle," I said. "The odds are fifteen to one. It's the outsider. You can put on ten bucks of your own and another three from me." I gave him the money I had won the day before.

"Tea for Two?" Garrett repeated the words.

"Come to school on Monday with the winnings and maybe I'll have another tip for you."

Garrett gave me an affectionate clip on the ear. It was still stinging as he scuttled off down the sidewalk and leaped onto a bus.

Tea for Two romped home easily. I heard the result on the radio later that evening and went to bed with a grin that stretched from ear to ear. Seeing me so cheerful, my mom decided I must be in love and Claire spent a whole hour teasing me. Well, I'd show her when I was a multimillionaire! That night the computer stayed blank, but I wasn't worried. Maybe Ethan still took the weekend off. He'd be back. For once I was actually looking forward to school and Monday morning. One hundred dollars. Put that on another horse at twenty-five to one and I'd be talking thousands.

But I didn't have to wait until Monday morning to see Garrett again. He came over the next day. He brought Leo with him. One look at the two of them and I knew I was in trouble.

Leo had a black eye and a bloody nose. His clothes

were torn and his whole face was a picture of misery. As for Garrett, he was swaggering and stalking around like a real king of the castle. I'd forgotten just how bad his reputation was. Well, I was learning the truth now and at the worst possible time. Dad was at the newspaper. Mom was taking Claire to her dancing lesson. I was in the house alone.

"Where is it?" Garrett demanded, pushing Leo through the open front door.

"What?" I asked him. But I knew.

Garrett was in the house now. I wondered if I could make a dash for the upstairs phone and call the police before he broke several of my bones. It seemed unlikely. He slammed the door.

"I'm sorry . . ." Leo began.

"It had to be something special," Garrett explained. "I knew, you see. Nobody can predict winners. Not twice in a row. Not for certain. So there had to be some sort of trick." He lit a cigarette. My mom would kill me when she smelled the smoke. If Garrett didn't do it first. "I knew you'd never tell me," he went on. "So I popped over and visited your friend. Took him out for a little chat. Well, he didn't want to tell me neither, so I had to rough him up a little bit. Made him cry, didn't I."

"There was nothing I could do," Leo whispered.

"This is my fault," I said. Right then I would have given Garrett the computer just to get him out of the house.

"So then sissy-boy starts telling me this story about a ghost and a computer," Garrett went on, puffing smoke. "You know . . . I hit him some more when he told me that. I didn't believe him. But he insisted and you know what? I began to think it must be true because when I threatened to pull his teeth out, he still insisted." Garrett turned on me. "Is it true?"

"Yes." There seemed no point in lying.

"Where is it?"

"Upstairs. In my room. But if you go up there, I'll call the police."

"The police?" He laughed. "You invited me in."

He took two steps toward the stairs and I hurried over, blocking his way. Now a streak of crimson crept into his face and his eyes took on the dead look of a police Identikit picture. "I know your parents are out," he hissed. "I saw them go. You get out of my way or I'll put you in the hospital. You wait and see what I'll do."

"He means it," Leo rasped.

"It's my computer!" I cried.

Garrett threw a handful of crumpled bills at me. "No. You sold it to me for a hundred dollars. Remember?" He grinned. "It's my computer now. You're too young to gamble anyway. It's against the law. You ought to be ashamed . . ."

He pushed past me. There was nothing I could do. Leo looked on miserably and I felt a bitter taste in my mouth. This was all my fault. How could I have been so stupid?

"Leo . . ." I began. But there was nothing I could say. I just hoped that we would still be friends when this was all over.

"You'd better go up," Leo said.

I hurried upstairs. Garrett had already found my room and was sitting at my desk in front of the computer. He had turned it on and was waiting as the system booted itself. I stood in the doorway, watching.

"All right," Garrett muttered. He balled his fist and struck down at the keyboard. A tangle of letters appeared on the screen. "Come on, come on, Mr. Ghost!" He slapped the side of the monitor. "What have you got for me? Don't keep me waiting!" He hit the keyboard again. More letters appeared.

DBNOYEawES . . .

"Come on! Come on!" Garrett clasped the monitor in two dirty hands and pressed his face against the glass. "You want to end up in the junkyard? Give me a name."

I was certain nothing would happen. I had never asked for a horse's name to come up. It had just happened. And I had never been as greedy as this, although I realized with a sick feeling in my stomach that given time, I might well have become as hungry and horrible as Garrett was now. I was sure nothing would happen. But I was wrong.

The tangle of letters faded away. Two words took their place.

LIGHT MOVES

Garrett stared at the screen as if it was only now that he really believed what Leo had told him. The cigarette fell out of his lips and he giggled. His whole body was shaking. "Light Moves." He rolled the words on his tongue. "Light Moves. Light Moves." He seemed to notice me for the first time. "Does this thing give you the odds?" he asked.

"No," I said. I was defeated. I just wanted him to go. "I get them in the paper."

"I'll get them at the betting shop." Garrett stood up. His hand curled around the cord and he yanked the plug out of the wall. The screen went blank. Then he scooped up the entire computer, holding it against his chest. "I'll see you," he said. "Enjoy the hundred bucks."

I followed him back down the stairs. Perhaps I could have stopped him, but the truth is that I didn't want to. I just wanted him to go.

Leo opened the front door.

"Good-bye, suckers," Garrett shouted.

He ran out and over the road. There was a squeal of tires and a terrible crash. Leo and I stared at each other, then ran outside. And even now I can still see what I saw then. It's like a photograph printed into my mind.

Garrett had been hit by a large white van that had come to a halt a few yards from our front door. The driver was already out of the cab, looking down in horror. Garrett was lying in a pool of blood that was already widening around his head. His arms and legs were splayed out, so that he looked as if he were trying to swim across the tarmac of the road. But he wasn't moving. Not even to breathe.

The computer, which he had been carrying when he was hit, was smashed beyond repair. All the king's horses and all the king's men wouldn't put Zincom together again. Glass from the monitor was all over the road. The casing around the hard drive had split open and there were valves and wires everywhere—electronic spaghetti.

All of that was horrible, but do you know what was worse? It was the name on the side of the moving van. I saw it then and I see it just as clearly now.

G. W. FAIRWEATHER MOVING CO.

And beneath that, in large red letters:

LIGHT MOVES

The
Night
Bus

Nick Hancock and his brother, Jeremy, knew they were in trouble but what they couldn't agree on was whose fault it was. Jeremy blamed Nick, of course. Nick blamed Jonathan Saunders. And they both knew that when they finally got home—if they ever got home—their dad would blame them. But whoever was guilty, the fact was that they were stuck in the middle of London. It was five minutes to midnight. And they should have been home twenty-five minutes ago.

It was a Saturday night—and not just any Saturday night. This was October 31. Halloween. The two of them had been invited to a party in central London, just off Holborn. Even getting permission to go had been hard work. Nick was seventeen and was allowed out on his own. His younger brother, Jeremy, was just twelve, although it was true that in another week he'd be a teenager himself. The party was being given by their cousin and that was what probably changed their parents' minds. Anybody else's party would be drugs, alcohol, and vomit . . . at least, that was how they saw it. But this was family. How could they say no?

John Hancock, the boys' father, had finally agreed. "All right," he said. "The two of you can go. But I want you home by eleven-thirty . . . no arguments! Has Jonathan been invited?"

Jonathan Saunders lived just down the road. The three of them all went to the same school.

"Fine. I'll take the three of you. His mom or dad can bring you back. I'll give them a call. And, Nick—you look after your brother. I just hope I'm not going to regret this . . ."

It had all gone horribly wrong. John Hancock had driven the three boys all the way into town. It was about a forty-minute journey from Richmond, where they all lived, out on the western edge of the city. John, who worked as a copywriter in one of the main advertising agencies, usually took the subway. But how could he take three boys across London on public transport when one of them was dressed up as a devil, one as a vampire, and the last (Jonathan) as Frankenstein, complete with a bolt going through his neck?

He had dropped them off at the house near Holborn and it had been a great party. The trouble came at the end of it, at eleven o'clock. Jonathan had said it was time to go. Nick and Jeremy had wanted to stay. And what with the noise of the music and the darkness and the crowds of other kids, they had somehow gotten their wires crossed.

Jonathan had left without them.

His mother, who had come to pick the three of them up, had cheerfully driven off into the night, taking Jonathan but leaving the two other boys behind. Catherine Saunders was like that. She was a writer, a novelist who was always dreaming of her next plot. She was the sort of person who could drive to work only to find she'd forgotten the car. Scatty—that was her nickname. Maybe, at the end of the day, the blame was hers.

And this was the end of the day. It was five to twelve and Nick, dressed as the devil, and Jeremy, as Count Dracula, were feeling very small and stupid as they walked together through Trafalgar Square in the heart of London.

"We shouldn't have left," Jeremy said, miserably.

"We had to. If Uncle Colin had seen us, he'd have

called Dad and you know what that would have meant. Grounded for a month."

"Instead of which we'll be grounded for a year . . ."

"We'll get home . . ."

"We should have been there twenty minutes ago!"

They should, of course, have taken a taxi—but there were no free taxis around. They had thought about the subway. But somehow they'd missed the Holborn and Covent Garden stations and found themselves in Trafalgar Square, in the shadow of Nelson's Column, before they knew where they were. Surprisingly, there weren't that many people around. Perhaps it was too late for the theatergoers, who would already be well on their way home, and too early for the clubbers, who wouldn't even think about home until dawn. A few people glanced in the boys' direction as they made their way around the stone lions that guarded the square, but quickly looked away. After all, what do you say to Dracula and the devil at five to twelve on a Saturday night?

"What are we going to do?" Jeremy complained. It felt like he'd been walking forever. He was cold and his feet were aching.

"The night bus!" Nick spoke the words even as he

saw the bus in question, parked at the far corner of the square, opposite the National Gallery.

"Where?"

"There!"

Nick pointed and there it was, an old-fashioned red bus with a hop-on, hop-off platform at the back and the magical word RICHMOND printed in white letters on the panel above the driver's cabin. The bus was the 227B. Its other destinations were printed underneath: ST. MARK'S GROVE, PALLISER ROAD, FULHAM PALACE ROAD, LOWER MILL HILL ROAD, and CLIFFORD AVENUE. At least two of the names were familiar to Nick. The bus was heading west. And they had enough money for the fare.

"Come on!" Jeremy had already broken into a run, his vampire cloak billowing behind him. Nick tightened his grip on his pitchfork and ran after his younger brother, at the same time clinging on to his horns, which were slipping off his head.

They reached the bus, climbed on, and took a seat about halfway along the lower deck. It was only when they were sitting down that Nick became aware that there were no lights on the bus, no other passengers, no driver, and no conductor. With a sinking feeling he realized that this was one bus that wasn't going anywhere—

at least not in the near future. Next to him, Jeremy was sitting back panting with his eyes half-closed. He looked at his watch. Eleven fifty-nine and counting. Ten seconds to midnight. Maybe it would be better to try again for a taxi, he decided. A taxi would have to drive through Trafalgar Square sooner or later.

"Jerry . . ." he said.

And, at the same moment, the lights came on, the engine rumbled into life, the bell rang, and the bus lurched forward.

Nick looked up, slightly alarmed. The bus had been empty a few seconds ago, he was sure of it. But now he could see the hunched-over shoulders and dark hair of a driver, sitting in the cabin. And there was a conductor on the platform, dressed in a crumpled gray uniform that looked at least ten years out-of-date, feeding a paper spool into his ticket machine.

Nick and Jeremy were still the only passengers.

"Jerry . . . ?" he whispered.

"What?"

"Did you see the driver get on?"

"What driver?" Jeremy was half-asleep.

Nick looked out of the window as the bus turned up

Haymarket and made its way toward Piccadilly Circus. They passed a second bus stop with a few people waiting, but the night bus didn't stop. Nor did the people waiting seem to notice it going past. Nick felt the first prickles of unease. There was something dreamlike about this whole journey: the empty bus that wasn't stopping, the driver and conductor appearing out of nowhere, even Jeremy and himself, wearing these ridiculous costumes, traveling through London in the middle of the night.

The conductor walked up the bus toward them. "Where to?" he demanded.

Now that Nick could see the man close up, he felt all the more uneasy. The conductor looked more dead than alive. His face was quite white, with sunken eyes and limp black hair hanging down. He was frighteningly thin. There seemed to be almost no flesh at all on his hands, which were clasped around the ticket machine; not one of the newfangled ones that worked electronically but an old-fashioned thing with a wheel that you had to crank to spit the tickets out. But then the whole bus was completely out-of-date: the pattern on the seats, the shape of the windows, the cord suspended from the ceiling that you pulled to ring the bell, even the posters on the walls advertising products he had never heard of.

"Where to?" the conductor asked. He had a voice that seemed to echo before it had even left his mouth.

"Two to Richmond," Nick said.

The conductor looked at him more closely. "I haven't seen you before," he said.

"Well . . ." Nick wasn't sure what to say. "We don't go out this late very often."

"You're very young," the conductor said. He glanced at Jeremy, who was now completely asleep. "Is he your brother?"

"Yes."

"So how did you both go?"

"I'm sorry?"

"How did you depart? What was it that"—the conductor coughed politely—". . . took you?"

"My dad's car," Nick replied, mystified.

"Tragic." The conductor sighed and shook his head. "So where are you going?"

"Richmond, please."

"Lower Grove Road, I suppose. All right . . ." The

conductor's hand rattled around in a circle and a double ticket jerked out of the machine. He handed it to Nick. "That'll be a dime."

"I'm sorry?" Nick was mystified. He handed the conductor a dollar bill and the man squinted at it distastefully.

"New currency," he muttered. "I still haven't gotten used to it. All right . . ." He reached into his pocket and pulled out a handful of change, including several large pennies and even a threepenny piece. The last time Nick had seen one of those, it had been in an antiques shop. But he didn't dare complain. Nor had he mentioned that they didn't actually want to go to Lower Grove Road. He didn't even know where it was. He didn't say anything. The conductor walked back to the platform and left him on his own.

The bus drove around Hyde Park Corner, down through Knightsbridge, and on through South Kensington. At least Nick recognized the roads and knew they were heading in the right direction. But the bus hadn't stopped; not once. Nobody had gotten on, not even when it was waiting at the red traffic light near Harrods. Jeremy was asleep, snoring lightly. Nick was sitting still, counting the minutes. He just wanted to be in Richmond. No matter how furious his parents would be when he finally arrived, he wanted to get back home.

And then, on the other side of Kensington, just past the Virgin Cinema on Fulham Road, the bus finally pulled in. "St. Mark's Grove," the conductor called out. Nick looked out of the window. There was a tall, black, metal grille on the other side of the road and a sign that he couldn't quite read in the darkness. A group of people had been waiting just in front of it, and as he watched they crossed over the road and got onto the bus. The conductor pulled the cord twice and they moved off again.

Four men and three women had gotten on. They were all extremely well dressed, and Nick assumed they must have all come from the same dinner party. Or perhaps they'd been to the opera. Two of the men were wearing black ties with wing collars. One also had a white scarf and an ebony walking stick. The women were in long dresses, though they wore no jewelry. They were all fairly elderly, perhaps in their sixties—but then, just as the bus picked up speed, a fifth man suddenly ran to catch up with it, reached out a hand, and pulled himself onto the moving platform. Nick gasped. This was a much younger man, a motorcyclist still dressed in his leathers and carrying his helmet. But at some time he must have been involved in a terrible accident. There was a livid scar running down the side of his face and part of his head had crumpled inward like a punctured football. The man had staring eyes and a huge grin that had nothing to do with humor. The scar had wasted his flesh, pulling one side of his lip back to expose a row of heavy, yellowish teeth. He was also dirty and smelled; the sour smell of old, damp earth. Nick wanted to stare at him, but he forced himself to look away. The motorcyclist plopped himself down on a seat a few places behind him. Looking out of the corner of his eye, Nick could just make out his reflection in the glass of the window.

Curiously, the smartly dressed people seemed quite happy to have the motorcyclist in their midst.

"You almost missed it!" one of them exclaimed, nodding at the bus.

"Yeah." The other side of his mouth twitched and for a moment the smile on his face looked almost natural. "I got up late."

Got up late? Nick wondered what he meant. It was, after all, a quarter past twelve at night.

"Seven tickets to Queensmill Road," one of the women told the conductor. The handle cranked around four times, spitting out a length of white ticket.

"Queensmill Road!" the motorcyclist exclaimed. "That's near where I had my accident." He touched his wounded head with his finger, although to Nick, watching all this in the reflection of the window, it looked as if he actually put his finger through the wound and *into his head.* "I collided with a bookmobile," he explained.

"Did you get booked for bad driving?" the man with the silk scarf asked, and the entire company roared with laughter at the joke.

The bus stopped for a second time about five minutes later.

"Palliser Road," the conductor called out.

At least a dozen people were waiting at the stop and they had clearly all been to the same Halloween party. They were in a lively mood as they got onto the night bus, chatting among themselves and wearing a bizarre assortment of costumes. Nick couldn't help looking over his shoulder as they took the seats all around them. There were two women dressed in eerie green robes like ghosts. There were two skeletons. A boy only a few years older than Nick himself had a knife jutting out from between his shoulders and crimson blood trickling from the corner of his mouth. An older couple had chosen, for some reason, to wear Victorian dress complete with top hat and tails for the man and a flowing ball gown for the woman. Although it wasn't raining outside, both of them were dripping wet. The man noticed Nick staring at him. "Last time I take a vacation on the *Titanic*!" he exclaimed. Nick looked the other way, embarrassed.

The people from the first bus stop soon fell into conversation with the people from the second stop and the atmosphere on the bus became quite partylike itself.

"Sir Oswald! I haven't seen you for what . . . ? Thirty years? You look terrible!"

"Barbara, isn't it? Barbara Bennett! How is your husband? Still alive? Oh—I *am* sorry to hear it."

"Yes, I took the family skiing for Christmas. We had a marvelous time except unfortunately I had a massive heart attack . . ."

"Actually, I'm popping down to Putney to see the Fergusons. Lovely couple. Both blown up in the war . . ."

This went on for the next half hour. The other passengers ignored Nick and he was grateful for it.

Although he was completely surrounded by them, he felt somehow different from them. He couldn't quite explain how. Perhaps it was the fact that they all seemed to know one another. They just somehow had more in common.

The night bus stopped three more times. At Queensmill Road, where the seven partygoers got off. At Lower Mill Hill Road. And finally at Clifford Avenue. By the time it left this third stop, the bus was completely full, with people standing in the corridor and on the platform. The last person to get on was more peculiar than any of them. He seemed to have just escaped from a fire. His clothes were charred and in tatters. Smoke was drifting up from his armpits and he could only nod his head in apology as the conductor tapped him on the shoulder and pointed to the "No Smoking" sign.

If anything, the party atmosphere had intensified. All around Nick there were people talking so loudly that he could no longer hear the engine, while the passengers on the upper deck had broken into song, a chorus of "John Brown's body lies a-mold'ring in the grave," which seemed to cause them great merriment. Nick tried not to stare, but he couldn't help himself. As the bus approached the shops on the outskirts of Richmond, a huge, fat woman dressed, bizarrely, in a green surgical gown and sitting next to a small, bald man suddenly turned around and blinked at him.

"What are you looking at?" she demanded.

"I wasn't . . ." Nick was completely tongue-tied. "I'm sorry. It's just that I'm very late. And my parents are going to kill me!"

"It's a bit late for that, isn't it?"

"I don't know what you mean."

"Well, that's your funeral. Your funeral!" The woman roared with laughter and nudged the bald man so hard that he fell off his seat.

Laughter echoed through the night bus. There was more singing upstairs. A man in a three-piece suit muttered a quiet "Excuse me" and brushed a maggot off his knee. The woman next to him held a handkerchief to her nose while the woman behind her appeared to pull her nose off and hold it to her handkerchief.

Nick had had enough. The bus was approaching the center of the town. He recognized the shops. It slowed down for a red light and that was when he decided. He grabbed hold of Jeremy, waking him up.

"Come on!" he hissed.

"What?"

"We're here!"

Half dragging his brother, Nick got to his feet and began to push his way to the back of the bus. The light was still red, but he knew it would change any second now. The other passengers didn't try to stop him, but they seemed surprised that he should be trying to get off.

"You can't leave here!" one of them exclaimed.

"We're not there yet!"

"What are you doing?"

"Come back!"

The light turned green. The bus moved forward.

"Stop!"

"Stop him!"

The conductor, standing at the back of the platform, lunged toward Nick, and for a second he felt fingers as cold as ice clamp around his arm. "Jump!" he shouted. Jeremy jumped off the moving bus and Nick, clinging to his brother with one hand, was pulled with him. The conductor cried out and released him. And then they were both sprawling on the road while the night bus thundered on, rattling down the high street and on into the shadows beyond.

"What was all that about?" Jeremy said, pulling himself to his feet.

"I don't know," Nick muttered. He knelt where he was, watching as the night bus turned a corner and disappeared, a last chorus of "John Brown" hanging like some invisible creature in the air before swooping away and racing after it.

"I've twisted my ankle," Jeremy groaned.

"It doesn't matter." Nick got up and went over to his brother. "We're home."

"You are the most irresponsible, disobedient, selfish children I've ever met! Do you realize I was two inches away from calling the police about you? Your mother and I were sick with worry. This is the last time you go to a party on your own. In fact, it's the last time you go to any party at all! I can't believe you could be so stupid . . ."

It was Sunday morning, breakfast, and John Hancock was still in a rage. Of course he'd been waiting for the boys when they got home, cold and exhausted, at ten to one. That night he'd rationed himself to ten minutes' shouting, but after a good night's sleep it seemed he was going to rage on until lunch. In his heart, Nick couldn't blame him. His parents had been scared—that was the truth of it. Admittedly, he was seventeen and could look after himself, but Jeremy was just twelve. And there were lots of weirdos out on the streets. Everyone knew that.

Weirdos . . .

"I want you to tell me more about how you got home," his mother said. Rosemary Hancock was a quiet, sensible woman who was used to stepping in between the father and his sons when arguments flared . . . which they often did in the small, crowded household. She managed a bookshop in Richmond and Nick noticed she had two books with her now. One was a history of London. The other was a map book. She had brought them to the table along with the croissants and coffee.

"They already told us." John scowled.

Rosemary ignored him. "You said you took the 227B bus," she said. "An old-fashioned bus. Did it look like this?" She showed Nick a photograph in the book. It showed a bus just like the one he had been on.

"What does it matter what the bus looked like?" John said.

"Yes. It was just like that," Jeremy interrupted. "With the open door at the back."

"And the conductor gave you old coins?"

"Yes." Nick had left the coins beside his bed. In the daylight they had looked more than old. Some of them were rusty and coated in some sort of slime. Just looking at them had made him shudder, although he couldn't say quite why.

"Do you remember where the bus stopped?" Rosemary asked. She closed the book. "You said it went to Clifford Avenue and Lower Mill Hill Road."

"Yes." Nick thought back. "It stopped in Fulham first. St. Peter's Grove or something. And then at Palliser Road. And then—"

"Would it have been Queensmill Road?" Rosemary asked.

Nick stared at her. "Yes. How do you know?"

"What are you going on about?" John demanded. "What does it matter what the bus looked like or where it went?"

"It's just that there is no 227B bus," Rosemary replied. "I called London Transport this morning while you were out getting the croissants. There is a bus that goes from Trafalgar Square to Richmond, but it's the N9." She tapped the book. "And the bus that the boys described, the one I showed them in the photograph . . . it's an old Routemaster. They haven't built buses like that for thirty years and there certainly aren't any on the road."

"Well then, how . . . ?" John turned to look at Nick.

But Nick's eyes were fixed on his mother. The blood was draining from his face. He could actually feel it being sucked down his neck. "But you knew the route," he said.

"I don't know exactly what's going on here," Rosemary began. "Either you two boys have made the whole thing up or . . . I don't know . . . I suppose it must have been a practical joke or something."

"Go on," Nick said. He reached for his orange juice and took a sip. His mouth had gone dry.

"Well, it seems that last night you two did a tour of West London's cemeteries." She opened the map book and pointed. "St. Mark's Grove, just off the Fulham Road . . ."

Nick remembered the tall metal grille and the sign.

". . . that's Brompton Cemetery. Hammersmith Cemetery is on Palliser Road. Fulham Cemetery . . .

that's on the Fulham Palace Road, but it's opposite Queensmill Road. Putney Cemetery is on Lower Mill Hill Road, and Clifford Avenue, where you say you saw that man who seemed to be smoldering or on fire—well, that's Mortlake Crematorium."

She closed the book.

Jeremy was sitting in his seat, a piece of croissant halfway to his lips.

John Hancock stood up. "Of course it was a practical joke," he said. "Now you'd better help me get Nick off the floor. He seems to have fainted."

Harriet's
Horrible
Dream

What made the dream so horrible was that it was so *vivid*. Harriet actually felt that she was sitting in a movie theater, rather than lying in bed, watching a film about herself. And although she had once read that people dream only in black-and-white, her dream was in full Technicolor. She could see herself wearing her favorite pink dress and there were red bows in her hair. Not, of course, that Harriet would have *dreamed* of having a black-and-white dream. Only the best was good enough for her.

Nonetheless, this was one dream that she wished she wasn't having. Even as she lay there with her legs curled up and her arms tight against her sides, she wished that she could wake up and call for Fifi—her French nanny—to go and make the breakfast. This dream, which could have gone on for seconds but at the same time seemed to have stretched through the whole night, was a particularly horrid one. In fact, it was more of a nightmare. That was the truth.

It began so beautifully. There was Harriet in her pink dress, skipping up the path of their lovely house just outside Bath, in Wiltshire. She could actually hear herself singing. She was on her way back from school, and a particularly good day it had been, too. She had been first in the class in spelling, and even though she knew she had cheated—peeking at the words that she had hidden in her pencil case—she had still enjoyed going to the front of the class to receive her merit mark. Naturally, Jane Wilson (who had come second) had said some nasty things, but Harriet had gotten her back, "accidentally" spilling a glass of milk over the other girl during lunch.

She was glad to be home. Harriet's house was a huge, white building—nobody in the school had a bigger house than she did—set in a perfect garden complete with its own stream and miniature waterfall. Her brand-new bicycle was leaning against the wall outside the front door, although perhaps she should have put it in the garage as it had been left out in the rain for a week now and had already begun to rust. Well, that was Fifi's fault. If the nanny had put it away for her, it would be all right now. Harriet thought about complaining to her mother. She had a special face for when things went wrong and a way of squeezing out buckets of tears. If she complained hard enough, perhaps Mommy would sack Fifi. That would be fun. Harriet had already managed to get four nannies sacked. The last one had only been there three weeks!

She opened the front door and it was then that things began to go wrong. Somehow she knew it even before she realized what was happening. But of course that was something that was often the case in dreams. Events happened so quickly that you were aware of them before they actually arrived.

Her father was home from work early. Harriet had already seen his Porsche parked in the driveway. Guy Hubbard ran an antiques shop in Bath, although he had recently started dabbling in other businesses, too. There was a property he was developing in Bristol, and something to do with time-share apartments in Majorca. But antiques were his main love. He would tour the country visiting houses, often where people had recently died. He would introduce himself to the widows and take a look around, picking out the treasures with a practiced eye. "That's a nice table," he would say. "I could give you fifty dollars for that. Cash in hand. No questions asked. What do you say?" And later on that same table would turn up in his shop with a price tag for five hundred or even five thousand dollars. This was the secret of Guy's success. The people he dealt with never had any idea how much their property was worth. But he did. He once said he could smell a valuable piece even before he saw it.

Right now he was in the front living room, talking to his wife in a low, unhappy voice. Something had gone wrong. Terribly wrong. Harriet went over to the door and put her ear against the wood.

"We're finished," Guy was saying. "Done for. We've gone belly-up, my love. And there's nothing we can do."

"Have you lost it all?" his wife was saying. Hilda Hubbard had once been a hairdresser, but it had been years since she had worked. Even so, she was always complaining that she was tired and took at least six vacations a year.

"The whole bloody lot. It's this development. Jack and Barry have cleared out. Skipped the country. They've taken all the money and they've left me with all the debts."

"But what are we going to do?"

"Sell out and start again, old girl. We can do it. But the house is going to have to go. And the cars . . ."

"What about Harriet?"

"She'll have to move out of that fancy school for a start. It's going to be a public school from now on. And that cruise the two of you were going on. You're going to have to forget about that!"

Harriet had heard enough. She pushed open the door and marched into the room. Already her cheeks had gone bright red and she had pressed her lips together so tightly that they were pushing out, kissing the air.

"What's happened?" she exclaimed in a shrill voice. "What are you saying, Daddy? Why can't I go on the cruise?"

Guy looked at his daughter unhappily. "Were you listening outside?" he demanded.

Hilda was sitting in a chair, holding a glass of whiskey. "Don't bully her, Guy," she said.

"Tell me! Tell me! Tell me!" Harriet had drawn herself up as if she was about to burst into tears. But she had already decided she wasn't going to cry. On the other hand, she might try one of her earsplitting screams.

Guy Hubbard was standing beside the fireplace. He was a short man with black, slicked-back hair and a small mustache. He was wearing a checked suit with a red handkerchief poking out of the top pocket. He and Harriet had never really been close. In fact, Harriet spoke to him as little as possible and usually only to ask him for money.

"You might as well know," he said. "I've just gone bankrupt."

"What?" Harriet felt the tears pricking her eyes despite herself.

"Don't be upset, my precious baby doll—" Hilda began.

"*Do* be upset!" Guy interrupted. "There are going to be a few changes around here, my girl. I can tell you that. You can forget your fancy clothes and your French nannies . . ."

"Fifi?"

"I fired her this morning."

"But I liked her!" The tears began to roll down Harriet's cheeks.

"You're going to have to start pulling your weight. By the time I've paid off all the debts, we won't have enough money to pay for a tin of beans. You'll have to get a job. How old are you now? Fourteen?"

"I'm twelve!"

"Well, you can still get a paper route or something. And, Hilda, you're going to have to go back to hair. Cut and blow-dry at thirty bucks a shot." Guy took out a cigarette and lit it, blowing blue smoke into the air. "We'll buy a house in Bletchly or somewhere. One bedroom is all we can afford."

"So where will I sleep?" Harriet quavered.

"You can sleep in the bath."

And that was what did it. The tears were pouring now—not just out of Harriet's eyes but also, more revoltingly, out of her nose. At the same time she let out one of her loudest, shrillest screams. "I won't! I won't! I won't!" she yelled. "I'm not leaving this house and I'm not sleeping in the bath. This is all your fault, Daddy. I hate you and I've always hated you and I hate Mommy, too, and I am going on my cruise and if you stop me I'll report you to social services and the police and I'll tell everyone that you steal things from old ladies and you never pay any taxes and you'll go to prison and see if I care!"

Harriet was screaming so loudly that she had almost suffocated herself. She stopped and sucked in a great breath of air, then turned on her heel and flounced out of the room, slamming the door behind her. Even as she went, she heard her father mutter, "We're going to have to do something about that girl."

But then she was gone.

And then, as is so often the way in dreams, it was the next day, or perhaps the day after, and she was sitting at the breakfast table with her mother, who was eating a bowl of low-fat granola and reading the *Sun* when her father came into the kitchen.

"Good morning," he said.

Harriet ignored him.

"All right," Guy said. "I've listened to what you had to say and I've talked things over with your mother and it does seem that we're going to have to come to a new arrangement."

Harriet helped herself to a third crumpet and smothered it in butter. She was being very prim and ladylike, she thought. Very grown up. The effect was only spoiled when melted butter dribbled down her chin.

"We're moving," Guy went on. "But you're right.

There isn't going to be room for you in the new setup. You're too much of a little miss."

"Guy . . ." Hilda muttered disapprovingly.

Her husband ignored her. "I've spoken to your uncle Algernon," he said. "He's agreed to take you."

"I don't have an Uncle Algernon," Harriet sniffed.

"He's not really your uncle. But he's an old friend of the family. He runs a restaurant in London. The Sawney Bean. That's what it's called."

"That's a stupid name for a restaurant," Harriet said.

"Stupid or not, it's a big hit. He's raking it in. And he needs a young girl like you. Don't ask me what for! Anyway, I've telephoned him today and he's driving down to pick you up. You can go with him. And maybe one day when we've sorted ourselves out—"

"I'll miss my little Harry-Warry!" Hilda moaned.

"You won't miss her at all! You've been too busy playing bridge and having your toes manicured to look after her properly. Maybe that's why she's turned into such a spoiled little so-and-so. But it's too late now. He'll be here soon. You'd better go and pack a bag."

"My baby!" This time it was Hilda who began to cry, her tears dripping into her granola.

"I'll take two bags," Harriet said. "And you'd better

give me some pocket money, too. Six months in advance!"

Uncle Algernon turned up at midday. After what her father had said, Harriet had expected him to drive a Rolls-Royce or at the very least a Jaguar and was disappointed by her first sight of him, rattling up the drive in a rather battered white van with the restaurant name, SAWNEY BEAN, written in bloodred letters on the side.

The van stopped and a figure got out, almost impossibly, from the front seat. He was so tall that Harriet was unsure how he had ever managed to fit inside. As he straightened up, he was much taller than the van itself, his bald head higher even than the antenna on the roof. He was also revoltingly thin. It was as if a normal human being had been put on a rack and stretched. His legs and his arms, hanging loose by his side, seemed to be made of elastic. His face was unusually repulsive. Although he had no hair on his head, he had big, bushy eyebrows that didn't quite fit over his small, glistening eyes. His skin was roughly the same shape. He was wearing a black coat with a fur collar around his neck and gleaming black shoes that squeaked when he walked.

Guy Hubbard was the first one out to greet him.

"Hello, Archie!" he exclaimed. The two men shook hands. "How's business?"

"Busy. Very busy." Algernon had a soft, low voice that reminded Harriet of an undertaker. "I can't hang around, Guy. I have to be back in town by lunch. Lunch!" He licked his lips with a wet, pink tongue. "Fully booked today. And tomorrow. And all week. Sawney Bean has been more successful than I would ever have imagined."

"Packing 'em in, I bet."

"You could say that."

"So have you got it, then?"

Algernon smiled and reached into the pocket of his coat, pulling out a crumpled brown envelope, which he handed to Guy. Harriet watched, puzzled, from the front door. She knew what brown envelopes meant where her father was concerned. This man, Algernon, was obviously giving him money—and lots of it from the size of the envelope. But he was the one who was taking her away to look after her. So shouldn't Guy have been paying *him*?

Guy pocketed the money.

"So where is she?" Algernon asked.

"Harriet!" Guy called.

Harriet picked up her two suitcases and stepped out of the house for the last time. "I'm here," she said. "But I hope you're not expecting me to travel in that perfectly horrid little van . . ."

Guy scowled. But it seemed that Algernon hadn't heard her. He was staring at her with something in his eyes that was hard to define. He was certainly pleased by what he saw. He was happy. But there was something else. Hunger? Harriet could almost feel the eyes running up and down her body.

She put the suitcases down and grimaced as he ran a finger along the side of her face. "Oh, yes," he breathed. "She's perfect. First-class. She'll do very well."

"What will I do very well?" Harriet demanded.

"None of your business," Guy replied.

Meanwhile, Hilda had come out onto the driveway. She was trembling and, Harriet noticed, refused to look at the new arrival.

"It's time to go," Guy said.

Algernon smiled at Harriet. He had dreadful teeth. They were yellow and uneven and—worse—strangely pointy. They were more like the teeth of an animal. "Get in," he said. "It's a long drive."

Hilda broke out in fresh tears. "Aren't you going to kiss me good-bye?" she wailed.

"No," Harriet replied.

"Good-bye," Guy said. He wanted to get this over with as soon as possible.

Harriet climbed into the van while Algernon placed her cases in the back. The front seat was covered in cheap plastic and it was torn in places, the stuffing oozing through. There was also a mess on the floor; candy-bar wrappers, old invoices, and an empty cigarette pack. She tried to lower the window, but the handle wouldn't turn.

"Good-bye, Mommy! Good-bye, Dad!" she called through the glass. "I never liked it here and I'm not sorry I'm going. Maybe I'll see you again when I'm grown up."

"I doubt it . . ." Had her father really said that? That was certainly what it sounded like. Harriet turned her head away in contempt.

Algernon had climbed in next to her. He had to coil his whole body up to fit in and his head still touched the roof. He started the engine up and a moment later the van was driving away. Harriet didn't look back. She didn't want her parents to think she was going to miss them.

The two of them didn't speak until they had reached the M4 motorway and begun the long journey east toward the city. Harriet had looked for the radio, hoping to listen to music. But it had been stolen, the broken wires hanging out of the dashboard. She was aware of Algernon examining her out of the corner of his eye even as he drove, and when this became too irritating, she finally spoke.

"So tell me about this restaurant of yours," she said.

"What do you want to know?" Algernon asked.

"I don't know . . ."

"It's very exclusive," Algernon began. "In fact, it's so exclusive that very few people know about it. Even so, it is full every night. We never advertise, but word gets around. You could say that it's word of mouth. Yes. Word of mouth is very much what we're about."

There was something creepy about the way he said that. Once again his tongue slid over his lips. He smiled to himself, as if at some secret joke.

"Is it an expensive restaurant?" Harriet asked.

"Oh, yes. It is the most expensive restaurant in

London. Do you know how much dinner for two at my restaurant would cost you?"

Harriet shrugged.

"Five hundred dollars. And that's not including the wine."

"That's crazy!" Harriet scowled. "Nobody would pay that much for a dinner for two."

"My clients are more than happy to pay. You see . . ." Algernon smiled again. His eyes never left the road. "There are people who make lots of money in their lives. Film stars and writers. Investment bankers and businessmen. They have millions and millions of dollars and they have to spend it on something. These people think nothing of spending a hundred dollars on a few spoonfuls of caviar. They'll spend a thousand dollars on a single bottle of wine! They go to all the classiest restaurants and they don't care how much they pay as long as their meal is cooked by a famous cook, ideally with the menu written in French and all the ingredients flown, at huge expense, from all around the world. Are you with me, my dear?"

"Don't call me 'my dear,' " Harriet said.

Algernon chuckled softly. "But of course there comes

a time," he went on, "when they've eaten everything there is to be had. The best smoked salmon and the finest filet mignon. There are only so many ingredients in the world, my dear, and soon they find they've tasted them all. Oh, yes, there are a thousand ways to prepare them. Pigeon's breast with marmalade and foie gras. But there comes a time when they feel they've had it all. When their appetites become jaded. When they're looking for a completely different eating experience. And that's when they come to Sawney Bean."

"Why did you give the restaurant such a stupid name?" Harriet asked.

"It's named after a real person," Algernon replied. He didn't seem ruffled at all even though Harriet had been purposefully trying to annoy him. "Sawney Bean lived in Scotland at the start of the century. He had unusual tastes . . ."

"I hope you're not expecting me to work in this restaurant."

"To work?" Algernon smiled. "Oh, no. But I do expect you to appear in it. In fact, I'm planning to introduce you at dinner tonight . . ."

The dream shifted forward and suddenly they were

in London, making their way down the King's Road, in Chelsea. And there was the restaurant! Harriet saw a small, white-bricked building with the name written in red letters above the door. The restaurant had no window and there was no menu on display. In fact, if Algernon hadn't pointed it out, she wouldn't have noticed it at all. He hit the turn signal and the van turned into a narrow alley, running behind the building.

"Is this where you live?" Harriet asked. "Is this where I'm going to live?"

"For the next few hours," Algernon replied. He pulled up at the end of the alley in a small courtyard surrounded on all sides by high brick walls. There was a row of garbage cans and a single door, sheet metal with several locks. "Here we are," he said.

Harriet got out of the van, and as she did so the door opened and a short, fat man came out, dressed entirely in white. The man seemed to be Japanese. He had pale orange skin and slanting eyes. There was a chef's hat balanced on his head. When he smiled, three gold teeth glinted in the afternoon light.

"You got her!" he exclaimed. He had a strong Oriental accent.

"Yes. This is Harriet." Algernon had once again unfolded himself from the van.

"Do you know how much she weigh?" the chef asked.

"I haven't weighed her yet."

The chef ran his eyes over her. Harriet was beginning to feel more and more uneasy. The way the man was examining her . . . well, she could almost have been a piece of meat. "She very good," he murmured.

"Young and spoiled," Algernon replied. He gestured at the door. "This way, my dear."

"What about my suitcases?"

"You won't need those."

Harriet was nervous now. She wasn't sure why, but it was not knowing that made her feel all the worse. Perhaps it was the name. Sawney Bean. Now that she thought about it, she *did* know it. She'd heard that name on a television show or perhaps she'd read it in a book. Certainly she knew it. But how . . . ?

She allowed the two men to lead her into the restaurant and flinched as the solid metal door swung shut behind her. She found herself in a gleaming kitchen, all white-tiled surfaces, industrial-size cookers, and gleaming pots and pans. The restaurant was closed. It was about three o'clock in the afternoon. Lunch was over. It was still some time until dinner.

She became aware that Algernon and the chef were staring at her silently, both with the same excited, hungry eyes. Sawney Bean! *Where* had she heard the name?

"She perfect," the chef said.

"That's what I thought," Algernon agreed.

"A bit fatty perhaps . . ."

"I'm not fat!" Harriet exclaimed. "Anyway, I've decided I don't like it here. I want to go home. You can take me straight back."

Algernon laughed softly. "It's too late for that," he said. "Much too late. I've paid a great deal of money for you, my dear. And I told you, we want you here for dinner tonight."

"Maybe we start by poaching her in white wine," the chef said. "Then later tonight with a béarnaise sauce . . ."

And that was when Harriet remembered. Sawney Bean. She had read about him in a book of horror stories.

Sawney Bean.

The cannibal.

She opened her mouth to scream, but no sound came out. Of course it's impossible to scream when you're having a bad dream. You try to scream, but your mouth won't obey you. Nothing will come out. That was what was happening to Harriet. She could feel the scream welling up inside her. She could see Algernon and the chef closing in on her. The room was spinning, the pots and pans dancing around her head, and still the scream wouldn't come. And then she was sucked into a vortex and the last thing she remembered was a hand reaching out to support her so she wouldn't bruise herself, wouldn't damage her flesh when she fell.

Mercifully, that was when she woke up.

It had all been a horrible dream.

Harriet opened her eyes slowly. It was the most delicious moment of her life, to know that everything that had happened *hadn't* happened. Her father hadn't gone bankrupt. Her parents hadn't sold her to some creep in a white van. Fifi would still be there to help her get dressed and serve up the breakfast. She would get up and go to school and in a few weeks' time she and her mother would leave on their Caribbean cruise. She was annoyed that such a ridiculous dream should have frightened her so much. On the other hand, it had seemed so realistic.

She lifted a hand to rub her forehead.

Or tried to.

Her hands were tied behind her. Harriet opened her eyes wide. She was lying on a marble slab in a kitchen. A huge pot of water was boiling on a stove. A Japanese chef was chopping onions with a glinting stainless-steel knife.

Harriet opened her mouth.

This time she was able to scream.

Scared

Gary Wilson was lost. He was also hot, tired, and angry. As he slogged his way through a field that looked exactly the same as the last field and exactly the same as the one ahead, he cursed the countryside, his grandmother for living in it, and above all his mother for dragging him from their comfortable London house and dumping him in the middle of it. When he got home he would make her suffer, that was for sure. But where exactly was home? How had he managed to get so lost?

He stopped for the tenth time and tried to get his bearings. If there had been a hill he would have climbed it, trying to catch sight of the pink cottage where his grandmother lived. But this was Suffolk, the flattest country in England, where county lanes could lie perfectly concealed behind even the shortest length of grass and where the horizon was always much farther away than it had any right to be.

Gary was fifteen years old, tall for his age, with the permanent scowl and narrow eyes of the fully qualified school bully. He wasn't heavily built—if anything, he was on the thin side—but he had long arms, hard fists, and he knew how to use them. Maybe that was what made him so angry now. Gary liked to be in control. He knew how to look after himself. If anyone had seen him stumbling around an empty field in the middle of nowhere, they'd have laughed at him. And of course he'd have had to pay them back.

Nobody laughed at Gary Wilson. Not at his name, not at his place in class (always last), not at the acne that had recently exploded across his face. Generally people avoided him, which suited Gary fine. He actually enjoyed hurting other kids, taking their lunch money or ripping pages out of their books. But scaring them was just as much fun. He liked what he saw in their eyes. They were scared. And Gary liked that best of all.

About a quarter of the way across the field, Gary's foot found a pothole in the ground and he was sent sprawling with his hands outstretched. He managed to save himself from falling, but a bolt of pain shot up his leg as his ankle twisted. He swore silently, the four-letter word that always made his mother twitch nervously in her chair. She had long since stopped trying to talk him out of using bad language. He was as tall as her now and he knew that in her own, quiet way, she was scared of him, too. Sometimes she would try to reason with him, but for her, the time of telling had long since passed.

He was her only child. Her husband—Edward Wilson—had been a clerk at the local bank until one day, quite suddenly, he had fallen over dead. It was a massive heart attack, they said. He was still holding his date stamp in one hand when they found him. Gary had never gotten along with his father and hadn't really missed him—particularly when he realized that he was now the man of the house.

The house in question was a two-up, two-down, part of a terrace in Notting Hill Gate. There were insurance policies and the bank provided a small pension so Edith Wilson was able to keep it. Even so, she'd had to go back to work to support Gary and herself . . . no need to ask which of the two was the more expensive.

Vacations abroad were out of the question. As much as Gary whined and complained, Edith Wilson couldn't find the money. But her mother lived on a farm in Suffolk and twice a year, in the summer and at

Christmas, the two of them made the two-hour train journey up from London to Pye Hall just outside the little village of Earl Soham.

It was a glorious place. A single track ran up from the road past a line of poplar trees and a Victorian farmhouse and on through a gap in the hedge. The track seemed to come to an end here, but in fact it twisted and continued on to a tiny, lopsided cottage painted a soft Suffolk pink in a sea of daisy-strewn grass.

"Isn't it beautiful?" his mother had said as the taxi from the station had rattled up the lane. A couple of black crows swooped overhead and landed in a nearby field.

Gary had sniffed.

"Pye Hall!" His mother had sighed. "I was so happy here once."

But where was it?

Where was Pye Hall?

As he crossed what he now realized was a quite enormous field, Gary found himself wincing with every step. He was also beginning to feel the first stirrings of . . . something. He wasn't actually scared. He was too angry for that. But he was beginning to wonder just how much farther he would have to walk before he knew where he was. And how much farther *could* he walk? He swatted at a fly that was buzzing him and went on.

Gary had allowed his mother to talk him into coming, knowing that if he complained hard enough she would be forced to bribe him with a handful of CDs—at the very least. Sure enough, he had passed the journey from Liverpool Street to Ipswich listening to *Heavy Metal Hits* and had been in a good enough mood to give his grandmother a quick peck on the cheek when they arrived.

"You've grown so much," the old lady had exclaimed as he slouched into a battered armchair beside the open fireplace in the front room. She always said that. She was so boring.

She glanced at her daughter. "You're looking thinner, Edith. And you're tired. You've got no color at all."

"Mother, I'm fine."

"No, you're not. You don't look well. But a week in the country will soon sort you out."

A week in the country! As he limped onward and onward through the field, swatting again at the wretched fly that was still circling his head, Gary thought longingly of concrete roads, bus stops, traffic lights, and hamburgers. At last he reached the hedge that divided this field from the next and he grabbed at it, tearing at the leaves with his bare hands. Too late, he saw the nettles behind the leaves. Gary yowled, bringing his clenched hand to his lips. A string of white bumps rose up, scattered across the palm and the insides of his fingers.

What was so great about the country?

Oh, his grandmother went on about the peace, the fresh air, all the usual rubbish spouted by people who wouldn't even recognize a crosswalk if they saw one. People with no life at all. The flowers and the trees and the birds and the bees. Yuck!

"Everything is different in the country," she would say. "You float along with time. You don't feel time rushing past you. You can stand out here and imagine how things were before people spoiled everything with their noise and their machines. You can still feel the magic in the countryside. The power of Mother Nature. It's all around you. Alive. Waiting . . ."

Gary had listened to the old woman and sneered. She was obviously getting senile. There was no magic in the countryside, only days that seemed to drag on forever and nights with nothing to do. Mother Nature?

That was a good one. Even if the old girl *had* existed—which was unlikely—she had long ago been finished off by the cities, buried under miles of concrete motorway. Driving along the M25 at 100 mph with the roof open and the CD player on full blast . . . to Gary, *that* would be real magic.

After a few days lazing around the house, Gary had allowed his grandmother to persuade him to go for a walk. The truth was that he was bored by the two women and, anyway, out in the fields he would be able to smoke a couple of the cigarettes he had bought with money stolen from his mother's handbag.

"Make sure you follow the footpaths, Gary," his mother had said.

"And don't forget the country code," his grandmother had added.

Gary remembered the country code all right. As he ambled away from Pye Hall, he picked wildflowers and tore them to shreds. When he came to a gate he deliberately left it open, smiling to himself as he thought of the farm animals that might now wander onto the road. He drank a Coke and flung the crumpled can into the middle of a meadow full of buttercups. He half snapped the branch off an apple tree and left it dangling there. He smoked a cigarette and threw the butt, still glowing, into the long grass.

And he had stayed off the footpath. Perhaps that hadn't been such a good idea. He was lost before he knew it. He was tramping through a field, crushing the crop underfoot, when he realized that the ground was getting soft and mushy. His foot broke through the corn or whatever it was and water curled over his shoe, soaking into his sock. Gary grimaced, thought for a moment, and decided to go back the way he had come . . .

Only the way he had come was somehow no longer there. It should have been. He had left enough landmarks after all. But suddenly the broken branch, the Coke can, and the torn-up plants had vanished. Nor was there any sign of the footpath. In fact, there was nothing at all that Gary recognized. It was very odd.

That had been over two hours ago.

Since then, things had gone from bad to worse. Gary had made his way through a small wood (although he was sure there hadn't been a wood anywhere near Pye Hall) and had managed to scratch his shoulder and gash his leg on a briar. A moment later he had backed into a tree that had torn his favorite jacket, a black-and-white-striped blazer that he had shoplifted from a thrift shop in Notting Hill Gate.

He had managed to get out of the wood—but even that hadn't been easy. Suddenly he had found a stream blocking his path and the only way to cross it had been to balance on a log that was lying in the middle. He had almost done it, too, but at the last minute the log had rolled under his foot, hurling him backward into the water. He had stood up spluttering and swearing. Ten minutes later he had stopped to have another cigarette, but the whole pack was sodden, useless.

And now . . .

Now he screamed as the insect, which he had assumed was a fly but that in fact was a wasp, stung him on the side of the neck. He pulled at his damp and dirty Bart Simpson T-shirt, squinting down to see the damage. Out of the corner of his eye he could just make out the edge of a huge, red swelling. He shifted his weight onto his bad foot and groaned as fresh pain shuddered upward. Where was Pye Hall? This was all his mother's fault. And his grandmother's. They were the ones who'd suggested the walk. Well, they'd pay for it. Perhaps they'd think twice about how lovely the countryside was when they saw their precious cottage go up in smoke.

And then he saw it. The pink walls and slanting chimneys were unmistakable. Somehow he had found his way back. He had only one more field to cross and he'd be there. With a stifled sob, Gary set off. There was a path of sorts going around the side of the field, but he wasn't having any of that. He walked straight across the middle. It had only just been sown. Too bad!

This field was even bigger than the one he had just crossed and the sun seemed to be hotter than ever. The soil was soft and his feet sank into it. His ankle was on fire, and every step he took, his legs seemed to get heavier and heavier. The wasp wouldn't leave him alone either. It was buzzing around his head, round and round, the noise drilling into his skull. But Gary was too tired to swat at it again. His arms hung lifelessly in their sockets, his fingertips brushing against the legs of his jeans. The smell of the countryside filled his nostrils, rich and deep, making him feel sick. He had walked now for ten minutes, maybe longer. But Pye Hall was no closer. It was blurred, shimmering on the edge of his vision. He wondered if he was suffering from sunstroke. Surely it hadn't been as hot as this when he set out?

Every step was becoming more difficult. It was as if his feet were trying to root themselves in the ground. He looked back (whimpering as his collar rubbed the wasp sting) and saw with relief that he was exactly halfway across the field. Something ran down his cheek and dripped off his chin—but whether it was sweat or a tear he couldn't say.

He couldn't go any farther. There was a pole stuck in the ground ahead of him and Gary seized hold of it gratefully. He would have to rest for a while. The ground was too soft and damp to sit on, so he would rest standing up, holding on to the pole. Just a few minutes. Then he would cross the rest of the field.

And then . . .

And then . . .

When the sun began to set and there was still no sign of Gary, his grandmother called the police. The officer in charge took a description of the lost boy and that same night they began a cross-country search that would go on for the next five days. But there was no trace of him. The police thought he might have gotten into a car with a stranger. He might have been abducted. But nobody had seen anything. It was as if the countryside had taken him and swallowed him up, one policeman said.

Gary watched as the police finally left. He watched as his mother carried her suitcase out of Pye Hall and got into the taxi that would take her back to Ipswich station and her train to London. He was glad to see that she had the decency to cry, mourning her loss. But he couldn't help feeling that she looked rather less tired and rather less ill than she had when she arrived.

Gary's mother did not see him. As she turned around in the taxi to wave good-bye to her mother and Pye Hall, she did notice that this time there were no crows. But then she saw why. They had been scared away by a figure that was standing in the middle of a field, leaning on a stick. For a moment she thought she recognized its torn black-and-white jacket and the grimy Bart Simpson T-shirt. But she was probably confused. It was best not to say anything.

The taxi accelerated past the new scarecrow and continued down past the poplar trees to the main road.

A Career
in Computer
Games

It was just a card like all the others, in the window of
his local newsstand, but right from the start Kevin
knew the job had to be for him. He was sixteen years
old and just out of school and there were two things
about him that were absolutely true. He had no experience and no qualifications.

Kevin loved games. His pocket computer had gone
to school with him every day of the last year, even
though it was against school rules, and when it was finally confiscated by a weary teacher in the middle of a
geography lesson (just as he'd been about to find the

last gold star in Moon Quest), he'd gone straight out and bought another one—this time with a color screen—and had spent the rest of the term playing with that.

Every day when he got home he threw his bag into the corner, ignoring his homework, and either booted up his dad's laptop for a game of Brain Dead or Blade of Evil or plugged in his own for a quick session of Road Kill 2. Kevin's bedroom was piled high with computer magazines and posters. It would also be true to say that he had never actually met most of his best friends. He simply exchanged messages with them on the Internet—mainly hints for games, the secret codes, and shortcuts.

And that wasn't the end of it. On Saturdays, Kevin would take the bus into London and lose himself in the arcades. There was one, right in the heart of Piccadilly, that was three floors high and absolutely crammed with all the latest equipment. Kevin would go up the escalator with his pockets bulging with quarters. To him, there was no sound in the world sweeter than a brand-new coin rolling into a slot. By the end of the day, he would stagger home with empty pockets, an empty head, and a dazed smile on his face.

The result of all this was that Kevin had finally left

school with no knowledge of anything at all. He had failed all his exams—the ones that he'd even bothered to show up for, that is. College was obviously out of the question—he couldn't even have spelled it. And, as he was already discovering, job opportunities for people as ignorant as him were few and far between.

But he wasn't particularly worried. Since the age of thirteen, he'd never been short of money and he saw no reason why this shouldn't continue. Kevin was the youngest of four children living in a large house in Camden Town, North London. His father, a quiet, sad-looking man, did the night shift in a bakery and slept for most of the day, so that the two of them never met. His mother worked in a shop. He had a brother in the army. A married sister and another brother training to be a taxi driver. He himself was a thief. And he was good at it.

For that was how he'd gotten the money to buy himself all the computer equipment and games. That was how he paid for the arcades in town. He'd started with shoplifting—the local supermarket, the corner shops, the bookshop, and the drugstore on the High Street. Then he'd met some other kids who'd taught him the riskier—but more profitable—arts of car theft and burglary. There was a pub he knew in Camden Town where he could get five dollars for a car radio, twenty for a decent stereo or video camera, and no questions asked. Kevin had never been caught. And the way he saw it, provided he was careful, he never would be.

Kevin had been passing the newsstand on his way to the pub when he saw the notice. Jobs—that is, honest jobs—didn't interest him. But there was something about the advertisement that did. The "highest salary and bonus" bit for a start. But it wasn't just that. He knew he was fit. He'd sprinted away from enough smashed car windows and broken back doors to know that. He was certainly enthusiastic, at least when it came to computer games. Of course he might be wasting his time—if they wanted someone to do programming or anything like that. But . . .

Why not. Why the hell not?

And that was how, three days later, he found himself outside an office on Rupert Street, in the middle of Soho. He had come to meet a Miss Toe. That was what she had called herself. Kevin had called her from a pay phone and he'd been so pleased to get an interview that for once he hadn't vandalized the phone. Now, though, he wasn't so sure. The address that she had given him belonged to a narrow, red-brick building squeezed in between a cake shop and a tobacconist. It was so narrow, in fact, that he'd walked past it twice before he found where it was. It was also very old, with dusty windows and the sort of front door you'd expect to find on a dungeon. There was a small brass plaque beside this. Kevin had to lean down to read it.

GALACTIC GAMES LTD

It wasn't a good start. In all the magazines he'd read, Kevin had never heard of anyone called Galactic Games. And now that he thought of it, what sort of computer-game company would be advertising in the window of a newsstand in Camden Town? What sort of computer company would have a crummy office like this?

He almost decided to go. He'd actually turned around and walked away before he changed his mind. Now that he was here, he might as well go in. After all, he'd paid for a ticket on the subway (even if he had cheated and bought a child's fare). He had nothing else to do. It would probably be a laugh, and if nobody was looking, he might be able to cop an ashtray.

He rang the bell.

"Yes?" The voice at the other end of the intercom was high-pitched, a bit singsong.

"My name's Kevin Graham," he said. "I've come about the job."

"Oh, yes. Please come straight up. The first floor."

The door buzzed and he pushed it open and went in. A narrow flight of stairs in a dark, empty corridor led up. Kevin was liking this less and less. The stairs were crooked. The whole place felt about a hundred years old. And all sound from the street had disappeared from the moment the heavy door had swung shut behind him. Once again he thought about turning around, but it was too late. A door opened at the top of the stairs, spilling a golden light into the gloom. A figure appeared, looking down at him.

"Please. This way . . ."

Kevin reached the door and saw that it had been opened by a small, Japanese-looking woman wearing a plain black dress with black high-heeled shoes that tilted her forward as if she were about to fall flat on her face. Her face, what he could see of it, was round and pale. Black sunglasses covered her eyes. And she really was small. Her head barely came up to his chin.

"So who are you?" he asked.

"I am Miss Toe," she said. She had a strange accent. It wasn't Japanese, but it certainly wasn't English. And as she spoke she left the tiniest of gaps between each word. "I—am—Miss—Toe. We—spoke—on—the—telephone." She closed the door.

Kevin found himself in a small office with a single desk, bare but for a single phone and with a single chair behind it. There was nothing else in the room. The walls, recently painted white, didn't have one picture on them, not even a calendar. So much for stealing, he thought to himself. There wasn't anything to take.

"Mr. Go will see you now," she said.

Miss Toe and Mr. Go in Soho. Kevin wanted to laugh, but for some reason he couldn't. It was too weird.

Mr. Go was sitting in an office next to Miss Toe's. It was like walking through a mirror. His room was exactly the same as hers, with bright white walls, one desk, one telephone, but two chairs. Mr. Go was the same size as his assistant and also wore dark glasses. He was dressed in a sweater that was slightly too small for him and a pair of cords that was slightly too big. As he stood up his movements were jerky and he, too, left gaps between his words.

"Please, come in," Mr. Go said, seeing Kevin at the door. He smiled, revealing a row of teeth with more silver than white. "Sit down!" He gestured at the chair and Kevin took it, feeling more suspicious by the minute. There was definitely something odd here. Something not quite right. Mr. Go reached into his desk and took out a square of paper—some sort of form. Kevin's reading was no great shakes and anyway the paper was upside down, but as far as he could tell the form wasn't written in English. The words were made up of pictures rather than letters and seemed to go down rather than across the page. It had to be Japanese, he supposed.

"What is your name?" Mr. Go asked him.

"Kevin Graham."

"Age?"

"Sixteen."

"Address?"

Kevin gave it.

"You've left school?"

"Yeah. A couple of months ago."

"And tell me please. Did you get good grades?"

"No." Kevin was angry now. "Your ad said no

qualifications needed. That's what it said. So why are you wasting my time asking me?"

Mr. Go looked up sharply. It was impossible to tell with the dark glasses covering his eyes, but he seemed to be pleased. "You're quite right," he said. "Quite right. Yes. Qualifications are not required. Not at all. But can you supply references?"

"What do you mean?" Kevin was lounging in his chair. He had decided he didn't care if he got the job or not—and he didn't want this ridiculous Jap to think he did.

"References from your teachers. Or your parents. Or former employers. To tell me what sort of person you are."

"I've never had an employer," Kevin said. "My teachers would just give you a load of rubbish. And my parents can't be bothered. Shove the references! Who needs them anyway?"

Even as he spoke the words, he knew that the interview was probably over. But there was something about the empty room and the small, doll-like man that unnerved him. He wanted to go. To his surprise, Mr. Go smiled again and nodded his head vigorously.

"Absolutely!" he agreed. "The references can indeed be shoved. Although you have only been in my office for a matter of some twenty-nine and a half seconds, I can already see your character for myself. And my dear Kevin—I may call you Kevin?—I can see that it is exactly the sort of character we require. Exactly!"

"What is this place?" Kevin demanded.

"Galactic Games," Mr. Go replied. "The finest game inventors in the universe. Certainly the most advanced this side of the Milky Way. We've won many, many awards for Smash Crash Slash 500. And our new, advanced version (we call it Smash Crash Slash 500 Plus) is going to be even better."

"Smash Crash Slash?" Kevin wrinkled his nose. "I've never heard of it."

"It hasn't been marketed yet. Not in this . . . area. But we want you to work on this game. In this game. And if you're game, the job's yours."

"How much do you pay?" Kevin demanded.

"Two thousand a week plus car plus health care plus funeral package."

"Funeral package?"

"It's just an extra we throw in—not, of course, that you'll need it." Mr. Go took out a golden pen and scribbled a few notes on the piece of paper, then spun it around so that it faced Kevin. "Sign here," he said.

Kevin took the pen. It was curiously heavy. But for a moment he hesitated. "Two thousand a week," he repeated.

"Yes."

"What sort of car?"

"Any car you want."

"But you haven't told me what I have to do. You haven't told me anything about the job . . ."

Mr. Go sighed. "All right," he said. "Right. Right. Right. Never mind. We'll find someone else."

"Wait a minute . . ."

"If you're not interested!"

"I am interested." Kevin had caught the smell of money. Two thousand dollars a week and a car! What did it matter if Mr. Go seemed to be completely mad and if he'd never heard of either the company or the game . . . what was it called? Bash Smash Dash. He quickly searched for a clear space on the sheet of paper and scribbled his name.

Kevin Graham . . .

But the strange thing was that as the pen traveled across the page it seemed to become red-hot in his hand. It only lasted for a second or two, as long as it took him to form his signature, but no sooner was it done than he cried out and dropped the pen, curling his fingers and holding them up as if to find burn marks. But there was nothing. Mr. Go picked up the pen. It was quite cool again. He popped it back into his pocket and slid the sheet of paper back to his side of the desk.

"Well, that's it," he said. "Welcome to Smash Crash Slash 500 Plus."

"When do I start?" Kevin asked.

"You already have." Mr. Go stood up. "We'll be in touch with you very soon," he said. He gestured. "Please. Show yourself out."

Kevin was going to argue. Part of him even thought of punching the little man in the nose. That would show him! But his hand was still smarting from the pen and he very much wanted to get out, back onto the street. Maybe he'd walk over to the Piccadilly arcade. Or maybe he'd just go home and go to bed. Whatever he did, he didn't want to stay here.

He left the room the way he had come.

Miss Toe was no longer in her office, but the door was open on the other side and he walked out. And that was when he noticed something else strange. The door was glowing. It was as if there was a neon strip built into the frame. As he walked through it the light danced in his eyes, dazzling him.

"What on earth . . . ?" he muttered to himself.

He didn't stop walking until he got home.

There weren't many people around as Kevin turned onto the street where he lived. It was half past three and most of the mothers would be picking their kids up from school or in the kitchens preparing tea. The ones who weren't at work themselves, of course. Cranwell Grove was actually a crescent; a long, quiet road with Victorian terraced houses standing side by side all the way around. About half the buildings belonged to a housing association and Kevin's father had been lucky enough to get the one at the very end of the row, three floors high, stained glass in the front door, and ivy growing up the side. Kevin didn't like it there, of course. He argued with the neighbors. (Why did they have to get so uptight about their cat? He'd only thrown the one brick at it . . .) And it was *too* quiet for his taste. Too boring and middle class. He'd rather have had his own place.

He had just reached the front door when he saw the

man walking toward him. He wouldn't normally have taken any notice of anyone walking down Cranwell Grove, but there were two things about this man that struck him as odd. The first was that he was wearing a suit. The second thing was the speed at which he was walking; a fast, deliberate pace. He was heading for Kevin's house. There could be no doubt of it.

Kevin's first thought was that this was a plainclothes policeman. With his hand resting on the key, which was already in the lock, his mind raced back over the past few weeks. He'd robbed a car stereo from a BMW parked on Camden Road. And then there'd been that bottle of gin that he had slipped out of the liquor store near the station. But neither time had anyone seen him. Could his face have been caught by a video camera? Even if it had been, how had they managed to find him?

The man was closer now, close enough for Kevin to see his face. He shivered. The face was round and expressionless, the mouth a single, horizontal line, the eyes as lifeless as marbles. The man seemed to have had some sort of surgery, plastic surgery that had left him with more plastic than skin. Even his hair could have been painted on.

The man stopped. He was about fifty feet away.

"What do you . . . ?" Kevin began.

The man pulled out a gun.

Kevin stared—more amazed than actually frightened. He had seen guns on television a thousand times. People shot one another all the time in plays and films. But this was different. This man, this total stranger, was just ten paces away. He was standing in Cranwell Grove and he was holding . . .

The man brought up the weapon and aimed it. Kevin yelled out and ducked. The man fired. The bullet slammed into the door, inches above his head, shattering the wood.

Real bullets!

That was his first, insane thought. This was a real gun with real bullets. His second thought was even more horrible.

The man was aiming again.

Somehow, when Kevin ducked, he'd managed to hold on to the key. It was above his head now, his fingers still clinging around it. Hardly knowing what he was doing, he turned the key in the lock and almost cried with relief as he felt the door open behind him. He leaned back and virtually tumbled in as the man fired a second shot, this one snapping into the wall and spitting fragments of sand and brickwork into his face.

He landed with a thud on the hall carpet, twisted around, jerked the key out, and slammed the door. For a moment he lay there, panting, his heart beating so hard that he could feel it pushing against his chest. This wasn't happening to him. *What* wasn't happening to him? He tried to collect his thoughts. Some lunatic had escaped from an asylum and had wandered into Cranwell Grove, shooting anything that moved. No. That wasn't right. Kevin remembered how the man had walked toward him. He had been heading straight for Kevin. There was no question about it. It was him the man wanted to kill.

But why? Who was he? Why him?

He heard the sound of feet moving outside. The man hadn't given up! He was getting closer. Desperately, Kevin looked around him. Was he alone in the house?

"Mom!" he called. "Dad!"

No answer.

He saw the telephone. Of course, he should have thought of it at once. There was a dangerous lunatic outside and he'd wasted precious seconds when he should have been calling the police. He snatched up the receiver, but before he had even dialed the first nine, there was a volley of shots that seemed to explode all around him. He stared in horror. From his side, it looked as if the door was tearing itself apart, but he knew it was the man out on the sidewalk, shooting out the lock. Even as he watched, the door handle and lock shuddered and ricocheted onto the carpet. The door swung open.

Kevin did the only thing he could think of. With a shout, he snatched up the table on which the telephone had stood and swung it around in a great arc. And he was lucky. Just as the table reached the door, the man appeared, stepping into the hall. The table smashed right into his face and he fell backward, crumpling in a heap.

Kevin stood where he was, catching his breath. He was stunned, the gunshots still ringing in his ears, his head reeling. What was he going to do? Oh, yes. Call the police. But the telephone had fallen when he had picked up the table and there it was, smashed on the floor. There was a second phone in his parents' bedroom, but that was no use. The door would be locked. His mother had locked it ever since she'd found him stealing from her handbag.

But there *was* a telephone. A pay phone at the end of the street. Better to go there than stay in the house because the man he'd just hit wouldn't stay unconscious forever. Better not to be around when he woke up. Kevin stepped over the body and went out.

And stopped.

A second man was walking toward him, and what was odd, what made it all so nightmarish, was that this man was identical to the first. Not just similar—exactly the same. They could have been two dummies out of the same store window. Kevin almost giggled at the thought—but it was true. The same dark suit. The same plastic, empty face. The same measured pace. And now the man was reaching into his jacket for . . .

. . . the same heavy, silver-plated gun.

"Go away!" Kevin screamed. He lurched backward into the house just as the man fired off a shot, the bullet drilling through the stained-glass window in the front door and smashing a picture that hung in the hall.

This time Kevin was defenseless. He had already used the telephone table, and apart from his mother's umbrella, there was nothing else in sight. He had to get away. That was the only thing to do. He was unarmed.

Defenseless. He had just been attacked by a lunatic and now it seemed that the lunatic had a twin brother.

Whimpering to himself, Kevin crossed the hall and ran up the stairs, stumbling as he tried to keep his eyes on the front door. He was aware of a sudden shadow and then the man were there, stepping into the opening and firing at the same time. The bullet shot over Kevin's shoulder. Kevin screamed and jumped out of the window.

He hadn't opened it first. Glass and wood exploded all around him, almost blinding him as he fell through the air and landed on all fours on the roof below. There was a lean-to next to the kitchen at the top of the garden and that was where he was now. His wrist was hurting and he saw that he had cut himself. Bright red blood slid over the gap between his thumb and index finger. Grimacing, he pulled a piece of glass out of the side of his arm. He was just glad he hadn't broken an arm or a leg.

Because he was going to need them.

From where Kevin was standing—or crouching, rather—he had a view of all the back gardens, not just of the houses in Cranwell Grove but those of Addison

Road, which ran parallel to it. Here everything was green, precise rectangles of lawn separated by crumbling walls and fences and punctuated with greenhouses, sheds, garden furniture, and barbecues. He had no time to enjoy the view. Even as he straightened up he saw them: half a dozen more men with guns, all of them identical to the two he had already encountered. They were making their way through the gardens, hoisting themselves over the fences, marching across the lawns.

"Oh, no . . ." he began.

Behind him, the man who had broken through his front door appeared at the shattered window and took aim. Kevin somersaulted forward and landed on his own back lawn, a fall that knocked his breath away and left him dizzy and confused. The man at the window fired. The bullet whacked into a sunflower, chopping it in half. Kevin got to his feet and ran to the far end of the garden, hurled himself over the fence, and tumbled, with a furious yell, into his neighbor's goldfish pond.

He was soaking wet. His shoulder was bruised, his wrist stung from the broken glass, and he was feeling sick and disoriented, but sheer terror drove him on. It suddenly occurred to him that from the moment the nightmare had begun, nobody had said a word. There were at least eight men in suits pursuing him, but none of them had spoken. And despite the sounds of gunfire on a quiet summer afternoon, none of the residents of Cranwell Grove had come to see what was happening. He had never felt more utterly alone.

Dripping water, Kevin crossed his neighbor's garden and then vaulted over the wall into the next garden along. This one had a gate and he pushed through it, emerging into a narrow alleyway that led back to the road. Limping now—he must have twisted his ankle in the fall from the window—he ran to the end, just in time to hop onto a bus that was pulling out of a stop. Gratefully, he sank into his seat. As the bus picked up speed he looked back out of the window. Four of the men in suits—or maybe it was four new ones—had appeared in Cranwell Grove and stood in a crowd in the middle of the road. Four shop dummies from The Gap, Kevin thought. Despite everything, he felt a surge of pleasure. Whoever they were, he had beaten them. He had left them behind.

And that was when he heard the motorcycles.

They roared out of nowhere, overtaking the four men in suits and pounding up the road toward the bus.

There were about nine of them; huge machines, all glinting metalwork and fat, black tires. The nine riders were dressed in uniform mauve leather, covering them from head to toe. Their heads were covered by silver helmets with black glass completely hiding their faces.

"Oh, God . . ." Kevin whispered.

Nobody on the bus seemed to have noticed him. Despite the fact that he was dirty, his clothes soaked, his hair in disarray, and his face covered in sweat, the other passengers were completely ignoring him. Even the bus conductor walked straight past him with a vacant smile.

What was happening to him?

What was going on?

The first of the motorbikes drew level with the bus. The rider reached behind him and pulled a weapon out of a huge holster slung across his shoulders. Kevin gazed through the window, his mouth dropping. The rider had produced some sort of bazooka, a weapon at least ten feet long and as thick as a tree trunk. Kevin whimpered. He reached up to pull the stop cord. The motorcyclist fired.

There was an explosion so loud that several windows shattered. An elderly woman with a newspaper was propelled out of her seat. Kevin saw her hurtle through the air from the very front of the bus to the back, where she landed and cheerfully went on reading. The bus careered to the left, mounted the sidewalk, and crashed into the window of a supermarket. Kevin covered his eyes and screamed. He felt the world spinning around him as the wheels of the bus screeched and slid across the supermarket floor. Something soft hit him on the shoulder and he opened one eye to glimpse an avalanche of toilet paper cascading down on him through the hole that the biker had blasted in the bus. The bus was still moving, drilling through the interior of the supermarket. It smashed through breakfast cereals, dairy products, and baked goods, skidded into soft drinks and frozen vegetables, and finally came to a halt in dog food.

Kevin opened his other eye, grateful that it was still there. He was covered in broken glass, fallen plaster, dust, and toilet paper. The other passengers were still sitting in their seats, gazing out of the windows and looking only mildly surprised that the driver had decided to take a shortcut through a supermarket.

"What's the matter with you?" Kevin screamed. "Can't you see what's going on?"

Nobody said anything. But the old lady who had been rocketed out of her seat turned a page and smiled at him vaguely.

Outside the supermarket, the motorcycles waited, parked in a perfect semicircle. The drivers dismounted and began to walk toward what was left of the window. Kevin let out a sob and got shakily to his feet. He just had time to throw himself out of the wreckage of the bus before the whole vehicle disappeared in a barrage of explosions, the bazookas ripping it apart as if it were nothing more than a large red paper box.

How he got out of the supermarket he would never know. In all the dust and the confusion, he could barely see and the noise of the bazookas had utterly deafened him. All he knew was that somehow he had to survive. He leaped over the cheese counter—but not quite far enough. One foot plopped down in a loose Camembert and he was nearly thrown flat on his back. There was a door on the other side and he reeled through it, dragging a foot that not only hurt but that now smelled of ripe French cheese. There was a storeroom on the other side and a loading bay beyond that. Two men in white coats were unloading a delivery of fresh meat. They ignored him.

Fresh meat. Suddenly Kevin knew how it felt.

Somehow he made it to Camden High Street, dodging up alleyways and crouching behind parked cars, desperately looking out for men in black suits and men on motorbikes. Three yellow helicopters were buzzing overhead now and somehow, just looking at them, he knew they were part of it, too. Perhaps it was intuition. Or perhaps it was the fact that they had KILL KEVIN GRAHAM written in red letters on their sides. But he knew they were the enemy. They were looking for him.

He had two more narrow escapes.

One of the bikers spotted him outside Waterstones and fired off a rocket that just missed him, completely destroying the bookshop and littering the High Street with a blizzard of burning pages. He was almost killed a few seconds later by one of the helicopters firing an air-to-ground heat-seeking missile. It should have locked onto Kevin's body heat and disintegrated him in a single, vast explosion, but he was lucky. He had been standing next to an electronics store and the missile was confused at the last moment by the electric fires on display. It snaked over his shoulder and into the shop, utterly destroying it and three other buildings in the same arcade, and although Kevin was blown several yards away by the force of the blast, he wasn't seriously hurt.

By the time the clock struck nine, there was nothing left on the High Street that you could actually call high. Most of the shops had been reduced to piles of rubble. The bus stops and streetlamps had been snapped in half, mailboxes uprooted, and prefabricated offices defabricated and demolished. And when the clock did strike nine, it was itself struck by a thermonuclear warhead, fired by one of the helicopters, and blown to smithereens. At least the mauve-suited bikers were nowhere to be seen. It would have been impossible to drive up Camden High Street in anything but a tractor. There wasn't much street left—just a series of huge holes. On the other hand, their place had now been taken by a swarm of green-and-silver flying dragons with scorpion tails, razor-sharp claws, and searchlight eyes. The dragons were incinerating anything that moved. But nothing was moving. Night had fallen and Camden Town with it.

Kevin Graham was squatting in one of the bomb craters. His clothes were rags—his jeans missing one entire leg—and his body was streaked with blood, fresh and dry. There was a cut over his eye and a bald patch at the back of his head where a large part of his hair had been burned off. His eyes were red. He had been crying. His tears left dirty tracks down his cheeks. He was lying underneath a mattress that had been blown out of a furniture store. He was grateful for it. It hid him from the helicopters and from the dragons. It was the only soft thing left in his world.

He must have fallen asleep because the next thing he knew, it was light. The morning sun had risen and everything around him was silent. With a shiver, he heaved the mattress off him and stood up. He listened for a moment, then climbed out of the crater.

It was true. The nightmare was over. The armies that had spent the whole day trying to kill him had disappeared. He stretched his legs, feeling the warm sun on his back, and gazed around him at the smoldering mess that had once been a prosperous North London suburb. Well, that didn't matter. To hell with Camden Town. He was alive!

And he had finally worked out what he had to do.

He had to make his way back into town and find the offices of Galactic Games. He had to tell Mr. Go that it had all been a mistake, that he didn't want a career in computer games, that he wasn't interested in Smash Crash Slash 500, even if it was the most popular game in the universe. And he believed that now. He just wondered from which part of the universe Mr. Go had come.

That was what he would do. Mr. Go would understand. He'd tear up the contract and it would all be over.

Kevin took a step forward and stopped.

Overhead, he heard a sound like thunder. For a moment it filled the air—a strange rolling, booming, followed by a pause and then a metallic crash.

A summer storm?

At the far end of the battlefield, a man in a black suit appeared and began to walk toward him.

Kevin felt his legs turn to jelly. His eyes watered and a sob cracked in his throat. He knew that sound all right. He knew it all too well.

The sound of an arcade.

And someone, somewhere, had just put in another coin.

The Man
with the
Yellow
Face

I want to tell you how it happened. But it's not easy. It's all a long time ago now, and even though I think about it often, there are still things I don't understand. Maybe I never did.

Why did I even go into the machine? What I'm talking about is one of those instant photograph booths. It was on Platform One at York station—four shots for $2.50. It's probably still there now if you want to go and look at it. I've never been back, so I can't be sure. Anyway, there I was with my uncle and aunt, waiting for the train to London, and we were twenty minutes early and I had about three dollars on me, which was all that was left of my pocket money. I could have gone back to the kiosk and bought a comic, another bar of chocolate, a puzzle book. I could have gone into the café and bought Cokes all around. I could have just hung on to it. But maybe you know the feeling when you've been on vacation and your mom has given you a certain amount to spend. You've just got to spend it. It's almost a challenge. It doesn't matter what you spend it on. You've just got to be sure it's all gone by the time you get home.

Why the photographs? I was thirteen years old then and I suppose I was what you'd call good-looking. Girls said so, anyway. Fair hair, blue eyes, not fat, not thin. It was important to me how I looked—the right jeans, the right sneakers, that sort of thing. But it wasn't crucial to me. What I'm trying to say is, I didn't take the photographs to pin on the wall or to prove to anyone what a movie star I was.

I just took them.

I don't know why.

It was the end of a long weekend in York. I was with my uncle and aunt because, back in London, my mom and dad were quietly and efficiently arranging their divorce. It was something that had been coming for a long time and I wasn't bothered by it anymore, but even so, they'd figured it would upset me to see the moving men come in. My father was moving out of the house and into an apartment, and although my mother was keeping most of the furniture, there was still *his* piano, *his* books and pictures, *his* computer, and the old wardrobe that he had inherited from *his* mother. Suddenly everything was his or hers. Before it had simply been ours.

Uncle Peter and Aunt Anne had been drafted in to keep me diverted while it all happened and they'd chosen York, I suppose, because it was far away and I'd never been there before. But if it was a diversion, it didn't really work. Because while I was in York Minster or walking around the walls or being trundled through the darkness in the Viking Museum, all I could think about was my father and how different everything would be without him, without the smell of his cigarettes and the sound of the out-of-tune piano echoing up the stairs.

I was spoiled that weekend. Of course, that's something parents do. The guiltier they feel, the more they'll spend, and a divorce, the complete upheaval of my life and theirs, was worth plenty. I had twenty dollars to spend. We stayed in a hotel, not a bed-and-breakfast. Whatever I wanted, I got.

Even four useless photographs of myself from the photo booth on Platform One.

Was there something strange about that photo

booth? It's easy enough to think that now, but maybe even then I was a little . . . scared. If you've been to York you'll know that it's got a proper, old station with a soaring roof, steel girders, and solid red brickwork. The platforms are long and curve around, following the rails. When you stand there you almost imagine that a steam train will pull in. A ghost train, perhaps. York is both a medieval and a Victorian city; enough ghosts for everyone.

But the photo booth was modern. It was an ugly metal box with its bright light glowing behind the plastic facings. It looked out of place on the platform—almost as if it had landed there from outer space. It was in a strange position, too, quite a long way from the entrance and the benches where my uncle and aunt were sitting. You wouldn't have thought that many people would have come to this part of the platform. As I approached it I was suddenly alone. And maybe I imagined it, but it seemed that a sudden wind had sprung up, as if blown my way by an approaching train. I felt the wind, cold against my face. But there was no train.

For a moment I stood outside the photo booth, wondering what I was going to do. One shot for the front of my school notebook. A shot for my father—he'd be seeing more of it now than he would of me. A silly, cross-eyed shot for the fridge . . . Somewhere behind me, the PA system sprang to life.

"The train now approaching Platform Two is the ten forty-five to Glasgow, stopping at Darlington, Durham, Newcastle . . ."

The voice sounded far away. Not even in the station. It was like a rumble coming out of the sky.

I pulled back the curtain and went into the photo booth.

There was a circular stool that you could adjust for height and a choice of backgrounds—a white curtain, a black curtain, or a blue wall. The people who designed these things were certainly imaginative. I sat down and looked at myself in the square of black glass in front of me. This was where the camera was, but looking in the glass, I could only vaguely see my face. I could make out an outline; my hair falling down over one eye, my shoulders, the open neck of my shirt. But my reflection was shadowy and, like the voice on the PA, distant. It didn't look like me.

It looked more like my ghost.

Did I hesitate then, before I put the money in? I think I did. I didn't want these photographs. I was wasting my money. But at the same time I was here now and I might as well do it. I felt hemmed in, inside the photo booth, even though there was only one flimsy curtain separating me from the platform. Also, I was nervous that I was going to miss the train even though there were still fifteen minutes until it arrived. Suddenly I wanted to get it over with.

I put in the coins.

For a moment nothing happened and I thought the photo booth might be broken. But then a red light glowed somewhere behind the glass, deep inside the machine. A devil eye, winking at me. The light went out and there was a flash accompanied by a soft, popping sound that went right through my head.

The first picture had caught me unawares. I was just sitting there with my mouth half-open. Before the machine flashed again, I quickly adjusted the stool and twisted my features into the most stupid face I could make. The red eye blinked, followed by the flash. That one would be for the fridge. For the third picture, I whipped the black curtain across, leaned back, and smiled. The picture was for my father and I wanted it to be good. The fourth picture was a complete disaster.

I was pulling back the curtain, adjusting the stool, and trying to think of something to do when the flash went off and I realized I'd taken a picture of my left shoulder with my face—annoyed and surprised—peering over the top.

That was it. Those were the four pictures I took.

I went outside the photo booth and stood there on my own, waiting for the pictures to develop. Three minutes according to the notice on the side. Nobody came anywhere near and once again I wondered why they had put the machine so far from the station entrance. Farther up the platform, the station clock ticked to 10:47. The second hand was so big that I could actually see it moving, sliding over the Roman numerals. Doors slammed on the other side of a train. There was the blast of a whistle. The 10:45 to Glasgow shuddered out of the station, a couple of minutes late.

The three minutes took an age to pass. Time always slows down when you're waiting for something. I watched the second hand of the clock make two more complete circles. Another train, without any carriages, chugged backward along a line on the far side of the station. And meanwhile the photo booth did . . . nothing. Maybe there were wheels turning inside, chemicals splashing, spools of paper unfolding. But from where I was standing it just looked dead.

Then, with no warning at all, there was a whir and a strip of white paper was spat out of a slot in the side. My photographs. I waited until a fan had blown the paper dry, then pried it out of its metal cage. Being careful not to get my fingers on the pictures themselves, I turned them over in my hand.

Four pictures.

The first. Me looking stupid.

The second. Me out of focus.

The fourth. Me from behind.

But the third picture, in the middle of the strip, wasn't a picture of me at all.

It was a picture of a man, and one of the ugliest men I had ever seen. Just looking at him, holding him in my hand, sent a shiver all the way up my arm and around the back of my neck. The man had a yellow face. There was something terribly wrong with his skin, which seemed to be crumpled up around his neck and chin, like an old paper bag. He had blue eyes, but they had sunk back, hiding in the dark shadows of his eye sockets. His hair was gray and stringy, hanging lifelessly over his forehead. The skin here was damaged, too, as if someone had drawn a map on it and then rubbed it out, leaving just faint traces. The man was leaning back against the black curtain and maybe he was smiling. His lips were certainly stretched in something like a smile, but there was no humor there at all. He was staring at me, staring up from the palm of my hand. And I would have said his face was filled with raw horror.

I almost crumpled up the photographs then and there. There was something so shocking about the man that I couldn't bear to look at him. I tried to look at the three images of myself, but each time my eyes were drawn down or up, so that they settled only on him. I closed my fingers, bending them over his face, trying to blot him out. But it was too late. Even when I wasn't looking at him, I could still see him. I could still feel him looking at me.

But who was he and how had he gotten there? I walked away from the machine, glad to be going back to where there were people, away from that deserted end of the platform. Obviously the photo booth *had* been broken. It must have muddled up my photographs with those of whoever had visited it just before me. At least, that's what I tried to tell myself.

My uncle Peter was waiting for me at the bench. He seemed relieved to see me.

"I thought we were going to miss the train," he said. He ground out the Gauloise he'd been smoking. He was as bad as my father when it came to cigarettes. High-tar French. Not just damaging your health. Destroying it.

"So let's see them," Aunt Anne said. She was a pretty, rather nervous woman who always managed to sound enthusiastic about everything. "How did they come out?"

"The machine was broken," I said.

"The camera probably cracked when it saw your face." Peter gave one of his throaty laughs. "Let's see . . ."

I held out the strip of film. They took it.

"Who's this?" Anne tried to sound cheerful, but I could see that the man with the yellow face had disturbed her. I wasn't surprised. He'd disturbed me.

"He wasn't there," I said. "I mean, I didn't see him. All the photographs were of me—but when they were developed, he was there."

"It must have been broken," Peter said. "This must be the last person who was in there."

Which was exactly what I had thought. Only now I wasn't so sure. Because it had occurred to me that if there was something wrong with the machine and everyone was getting photographs of someone else, then surely the man with the yellow face would have appeared at the very top of the row: one photograph of him followed by three of me. Then whoever went in next would get one picture of me followed by three of them. And so on.

And there was something else.

Now that I thought about it, the man was sitting in exactly the same position that I'd taken inside the photo booth. I'd pulled the black curtain across for the third photograph and there it was now. I'd been leaning back and so was he. It was almost as if the man had some-how gotten into the machine and sat in a deliberate parody of me. And maybe there was something in that smile of his that was mocking and ugly. It was as if he were trying to tell me something. But I didn't want to know.

"I think he's a ghost," I said.

"A ghost?" Peter laughed again. He had an annoy-ing laugh. It was loud and jagged, like machine-gun fire. "A ghost in a platform photo booth?"

"Peter . . . !" Anne was disapproving. She was worried about me. She'd been worried about me since the start of the divorce.

"I feel I know him," I said. "I can't explain it. But I've seen him somewhere before."

"Where?" Anne asked.

"I don't know."

"In a nightmare?" Peter suggested. "His face does look a bit of a nightmare."

I looked at the picture again even though I didn't want to. It was true. He did look familiar. But at the same time I knew that despite what I'd just said, it was a face I'd never seen before.

"The train now arriving at Platform One . . ."

It was the train announcer's voice again, and sure enough there was our train, looking huge and somehow menacing as it slid around the curve of the track. And it was at that very moment, as I reached out to take the photographs, that I had the idea that I shouldn't get on the train because the man with the yellow face was going to be on it, that somehow he was dangerous to me, and that the machine had sent me his picture to warn me.

My uncle and aunt gathered up our weekend bags.

"Why don't we wait?" I said.

"What?" My uncle was already halfway through the door.

"Can't we stay a little longer? In York? We could take the train this afternoon . . ."

"We've got to get back," my aunt said. As always, hers was the voice of reason. "Your mother's going to be waiting for us at the station, and anyway, we've got reserved seats."

"Come on!" Uncle Peter was caught between the platform and the train, and with people milling around us, trying to get in, this obviously wasn't the best time or place for an argument.

Even now I wonder why I allowed myself to be pushed, or persuaded, into the train. I could have turned around and run away. I could have sat on the platform and refused to move. Maybe if it had been my mother and father there, I would have done that, but then, of course, if my mother and father had only managed to stay together in the first place, none of it would have happened. Do I blame them? Yes. Sometimes I do.

I found myself on the train before I knew it. We had seats quite near the front and that also played a part in what happened. While Uncle Peter stowed the cases up on the rack and Aunt Anne fished in her shopping bag for magazines, drinks, and sandwiches, I took the seat next to the window, miserable and afraid without knowing why.

The man with the yellow face. Who was he? A psychopath perhaps, released from a mental hospital, traveling to London with a knife in his raincoat pocket. Or a terrorist with a bomb, one of those suicide bombers you read about in the Middle East. Or a child killer. Or some sort of monster . . .

I was so certain I was going to meet him that I barely even noticed as the train jerked forward and began to move out of the station. The photographs were still clasped in my hand and I kept on looking from the yellow face to the other passengers in the carriage, expecting at any moment to see him coming toward me.

"What's the matter with you?" my uncle asked. "You look like you've seen a ghost."

I was expecting to. I said nothing.

"Is it that photograph?" Anne asked. "Really, Simon, I don't know why it's upset you so much."

And then the ticket collector came. Not a yellow face at all but a black one, smiling. Everything was normal. We were on a train heading for London and I had allowed myself to get flustered about nothing. I took the strip of photographs and bent it so that the yellow face disappeared behind the folds. When I got back to London, I'd cut it out. When I got back to London.

But I didn't get back to London. Not for a long, long time.

I didn't even know anything was wrong until it had happened. We were traveling fast, whizzing through green fields and clumps of woodland when I felt a slight lurch, as if invisible arms had reached down and pulled me out of my seat. That was all there was at first, a sort of mechanical hiccup. But then I had the strange sensation that the train was flying. It was like a plane at the end of the runway, the front of the train separating from the ground. It could only have lasted a couple of seconds, but in my memory those seconds seem to stretch out forever. I remember my uncle's head turning, the question forming itself on his face. And my aunt, perhaps realizing what was happening before we did, opening her mouth to scream. I remember the other passengers; I carry snapshots of them in my head. A mother with two small daughters, both with ribbons in their hair. A man with a mustache, his pen hovering over the *Times* crossword. A boy of about my own age, listening to a Walkman. The train was almost full. There was hardly an empty seat in sight.

And then the smash of the impact, the world spinning upside down, windows shattering, coats and suitcases tumbling down, sheets of paper whipping into my face, thousands of tiny fragments of glass swarming into me, the deafening scream of tearing metal, the sparks and the smoke and the flames leaping up, cold air rushing in, and then the horrible rolling and shuddering that was like the very worst sort of amusement-park ride, only this time the terror wasn't going to stop, this time it was all for real.

Silence.

They always say there's silence after an accident and they're right. I was on my back with something pressing down on me. I could only see out of one eye. Something dripped onto my face. Blood.

Then the screams began.

It turned out that some kids—maniacs—had dropped a concrete pile off a bridge outside Grantham. The train hit it and derailed. Nine people were killed in the crash and a further twenty-nine were seriously injured. I was one of the worst of them. I don't remember anything more of what happened, which is just as well, as my car caught fire and I was badly burned before my uncle managed to drag me to safety. He was hardly hurt in the accident, apart from a few cuts and bruises. Aunt Anne broke her arm.

I spent many weeks in the hospital and I don't remember much of that either. All in all, it was six months before I was better, but "better" in my case was never what I had been before.

This all happened thirty years ago.

And now?

I suppose I can't complain. After all, I wasn't killed, and despite my injuries, I enjoy my life. But the injuries are still there. The plastic surgeons did what they could, but I'd suffered third-degree burns over much of my body and there wasn't a whole lot they could do. My hair grew back, but it's always been gray and rather lifeless. My eyes are sunken. And then there's my skin.

I sit here looking in the mirror.

And the man with the yellow face looks back.

The
Monkey's
Ear

The story began, as so many stories do, in the *souk*—or covered market—of Marrakesh. It has been said that there are as many stories in the *souk* as there are products, and if you have ever lost yourself in the dozens of covered walkways jammed on all sides with the hundreds of shops and little stalls groaning under the weight of thousands of objects from trinkets and spice bottles to carpets and coffee beans, you will realize that this must add up to more stories than could be told in a hundred and one nights or even a hundred and one years.

The Beckers had come to Morocco on vacation and had found themselves in the *souk* of Marrakesh only because they had accepted a free tour to go there. All the hotels offered free tours. The idea, of course, was to get the tourists to spend their money once they get to the market. But it wasn't going to work this time . . . not with the Beckers.

"It's too hot here," Brenda Becker was complaining. "And all these flies! We shouldn't have come! I said I didn't want to come. And anyway it's not as if there's anything to buy. All this foreign muck . . ." She swatted at a fly buzzing around her plump, rather sunburned face. "Why can't we just find a branch of Marks and Spencer?" she moaned.

Her husband, Brian Becker, gritted his teeth and followed behind her. It seemed to him that he was always one step behind her, like Prince Philip and the frigging Queen. It was certainly true that she ruled over everything he did. That was why he enjoyed his job so much—he worked as a traffic cop. First of all, it got him away from her. But also it meant that, at least when he was out in the street, he was in charge.

A salesman in torn jeans and a grubby T-shirt came up to him, showing off a string of beads. Brian waved a tired hand. "Go away!" he shouted. "Buzz off, Bozo!" He stopped and wiped the sweat off his forehead where it had dripped through what was left of his hair. Brian Becker was a small, weedy man with a thin face and slightly orange skin. He had lost his hair before he was twenty, and even now he was embarrassed by the sight of his head, bald and speckled like an egg. That was another good thing about being a traffic cop. He liked the uniform. It made him feel smart, particularly the cap, which disguised his baldness. He often wore the cap at home, in bed and even in the bath. But dressed as he was now, in shorts that were much too wide for his spindly legs and a brilliant shirt festooned with flowers (Brenda had chosen it for him before they left), he looked simply ridiculous.

A twelve-year-old boy, walking just beside Brian, completed the family. This was Bart Becker, their only child. Bart had been fortunate in that he had inherited neither his father's looks nor his mother's excessive weight. He was slim, with a pale face and fair hair that rose over his forehead rather like his favorite comic-book hero, Tintin. He was the only one of the three who was enjoying his time in the *souk*. The jumble of colors, the rich smells, and the shouts of the traders woven in with the distant wail of pipes and drums all seemed mysterious and exciting to him. Perhaps the main difference between Bart and his parents was that from a very early age he had enjoyed reading books. He loved stories and to him life was a constant adventure. To his

parents it was simply something they had to get
through.

"We're lost!" Brenda exclaimed. "This is all your
fault, Brian. I want to go back to the hotel."

"All right! All right!" Brian licked his lips and looked
around him. The trouble was that here, in the middle of
the *souk*, every passageway looked much like the next
one and he had long ago lost any sense of direction.
"It's that way," he said, pointing.

"We just came from there!"

"Did we?"

"You're an idiot, Brian. My mother always said it
and I should have listened to her. We're lost and we're
never going to get out of this wretched place."

"All right! All right!" Brian was forever repeating
the same two words. "I'll ask someone."

There was a shop to one side selling antique daggers
and pieces of jewelry. As Brenda had already pointed
out—several times—everything in the *souk* was probably fake. Most of it was no more antique than her own
artificial hip. But this stall was different. The knives
looked somehow a little more deadly and the jewels
glowed just a little more brightly. And there was something else. The very building itself, dark and crooked,

seemed older than the rest of the *souk*, as if it had been there first and the rest of the market had slowly grown around it.

They went in. As they passed through the door all the sounds of the *souk* were abruptly shut off. They found themselves standing on a thick carpet in a cave-like room with the smell of sweet mint tea hanging in the air.

"There's nobody here!" Brenda exclaimed.

"Look at this! This is wicked!" Bart had found a long, curving sword. The hilt was encrusted with dark green stones and the blade was stained with what could have been dried blood.

"Don't touch it, Bart!" Brenda snapped. "It's dirty."

"And we'll have to pay for it if you break it," Brian added.

A curtain hanging over the door rippled and a young boy appeared. He must have been about the same age as Bart, but he was shorter, with very dark skin, black hair, and a round, slightly feminine face. He would have been handsome but for the fact that one of his eyes had a large sty, forcing it into a squint, and this made him look almost sinister.

"Good morning. You want buy?" His English was

heavily accented and singsong. He had probably learned it parrot-fashion from his parents.

"We're not here to buy, thank you very much," Brenda said.

"We're looking for the way out. The exit." Brian jerked his thumb in the direction of the door. "Go to the hotel. Taxi!"

"We have fine jewelry," the boy replied. "Nice necklace for lady. Or maybe you like carpet?"

"We don't want jewelry or carpets," Brian replied angrily. "We want to go home!"

"This is useless, Brian!" Brenda muttered.

"I sell you something very special!" The boy looked around him and his eyes settled on a wrinkled object lying on a shelf. It was brown and curved, half-wrapped in moldy tissue paper. "I sell you this!" He took it and placed it on the counter.

"We don't want it," Brian said.

"It's revolting," Brenda agreed.

"What is it?" Bart asked.

The boy leered. "It is my uncle's," he said. "The monkey's ear. It is very old. Very powerful. Very secret."

"What does it do?" Bart asked.

"Don't encourage him, Bart," his mother said.

But it was too late. The boy ignored her. "The monkey's ear gives four wishes," he said. He counted on his fingers as if checking his English. "One. Two. Three. Four. You say to the ear what you want and you get. Very rare! But also very cheap! I give you good price . . ."

"We don't want it," Brenda insisted.

Bart reached out and took it. The ear nestled in the palm of his hand. It seemed to be made of leather, but there were a few hairs on the back. The inside of the ear was black and felt like plastic. He rather hoped it was plastic. He didn't particularly want to imagine that he was holding a real ear, severed from a real monkey.

"Four wishes," the boy repeated. "One. Two. Three. Four."

"Let's get out of here," Brenda said.

"No. I want it!" Bart looked up at his parents. "You said I could have something from the *souk* and I want this!"

"But why?" A trickle of sweat dripped off Brian's chin and he wiped it with the cuff of his shirt. "What do you want it for?"

"I just want it. I think it's cool . . ."

"Brian . . . ?" Brenda began, using her special tone of voice. She always used it when she was about to explode.

"How much do you want for it?" Brian asked.

"A thousand dirhem," the boy replied.

"A thousand dirhem? That's . . . That's . . ." Brian tried to work it out.

"It's too much," Brenda cut in. "It's more than fifty dollars."

"Will you take five hundred dirhem?" Bart asked.

"Seven hundred," the boy replied.

"Come on, Bart." Brian grabbed hold of his son's arm. "We didn't come in to buy anything. We just wanted to find the way out!"

"Six hundred!" Bart insisted. He wasn't quite sure why he wanted the monkey's ear, but now that he had decided on it, he was determined to have his way.

"Yes. Is deal. Six hundred." The boy rapidly folded the monkey's ear in its dirty wrapping and held it out.

Brian grimaced, then counted out the notes. "That's still twenty bucks," he complained. "It seems a lot to pay for a bit of rubbish . . ."

"You promised," Bart said. He'd actually worked

out that the price was nearer thirty dollars, but thought it better not to say.

They left the shop and within minutes they had once again disappeared into the swirl of the *souk*. Back in the shop, the curtain had moved for a second time and an enormously fat man had come in, dressed in traditional white robes that reached down to his sandals. The man had popped out to buy some Turkish Delight and was licking the last traces from his fingers as he sat down behind the counter. He glanced at the boy, who was still counting the money. The man frowned and the two of them began to talk in their own language so that even if the Beckers had been there, they wouldn't have understood a word that was said.

"Some tourists came in, Uncle. Stupid English tourists. They gave me six hundred dirhem!"

"What did you sell them?"

"The monkey's ear."

The man's eyes widened. He stood up quickly and went over to the shelf. One look told him all he needed to know. *"You sold them the monkey's ear!"* he exclaimed. *"Where are they? Where did they go?"* He grabbed hold of the boy and drew him closer. *"Tell me!"*

"They've left! I thought you'd be pleased, Uncle! You told me that the monkey's ear was worthless. You said it was—"

"I said we couldn't sell it! We mustn't sell it! The monkey that the ear was taken from was sick. You have no idea of the danger! Quickly, you son of a goat! You must find the tourists. You must give them back their money. You must get it back . . ."

"But you said—"

"Find them! Go now! In the name of Allah, let's pray it's not too late!" The man pushed the boy out of the shop. *"Search everywhere!"*

The boy ran out into the *souk*. The man sank back into his seat, his head buried in his hands.

It was already too late. The Beckers had managed to find their way out and were by now in a taxi on the way back to their hotel. And two days later they left Marrakesh. The monkey's ear went with them.

The Beckers lived in a modern bungalow in Stanmore, a sprawling suburb to the north of London. They had been home for a week when Brenda stumbled on the monkey's ear. She was cleaning Bart's bedroom. Brenda had a strange way of cleaning. Somehow it always involved searching every drawer and cupboard, reading Bart's diary and letters, and generally poking around wherever she could. She was the sort of mother who always believed the worst of her child. She was sure he kept secrets from her. Perhaps he had started smoking. Or perhaps he was gay. Whatever he was hiding, she was determined to be the first to find out.

As usual, though, she had found nothing. She had come upon the monkey's ear underneath a pile of Tintin comics and she carried it downstairs in order to prove a point.

Bart had just gotten home from school. Brian had also gotten back from work. He'd had a disappointing day. Although he'd been out in the street for nine hours, he'd issued only 307 parking tickets, far short of his record. He was sitting in the kitchen, still wearing his uniform and precious cap, eating a fish-sticks sandwich. Bart was also at the table, doing his homework.

"I see you've still got this filthy thing," Brenda exclaimed.

"Mom . . ." Bart began. He knew his mother must have been looking through his room.

"We paid all that money for it and you've just

shoved it in a drawer." She sniffed indignantly. "It's a complete waste. We should never have bought it."

"It's not true," Bart protested. "I took it to school and showed everyone. They thought it was creepy."

"Have you made any wishes?" Brian giggled. "You could wish yourself first in your class. It would make a pleasant change."

"No." Bart had almost forgotten what the boy with the sty had said, but the truth was that he would have been too embarrassed to make a wish using the monkey's ear. It would be like saying he believed in fairies or Santa Claus. He had wanted the ear because it was strange and ugly. Not because he thought it could make him rich.

His father must have been reading his mind. "It's all just rubbish," he said. "A monkey's ear that gives you wishes! That's just a load of baloney!"

"That's not true!" Bart couldn't stop himself from arguing with his father. He did it all the time. "We had a story in school this week. It was exactly the same . . . except it wasn't a monkey's ear. It was a monkey's paw. And it wasn't as good as an ear because it only gave you three wishes, not four."

"So what happened in the story?" Brian asked.

"We haven't finished it yet." This wasn't actually true. Their English teacher had finished the story— which had been written by someone called W. W. Jacobs—but it had been a hot day and Bart had been daydreaming, so he hadn't heard the end.

Brian took the ear from his wife and turned it over in his hand. He wrinkled his nose. The ear was soft and hairy and felt warm to the touch. "It would be bloody marvelous if it worked," he said.

"What would you wish for, Dad?" Bart asked.

Brian held the ear up between his finger and thumb. He raised his other hand for silence. "I wish for a Rolls-Royce!" he exclaimed.

"What a lot of nonsense!" his wife muttered.

The doorbell rang.

Brian stared at Brenda. Brenda sniffed. "I'll get it," Bart said.

He went to the door and opened it. Of course there wasn't going to be a Rolls-Royce there. He didn't expect that for a minute. Even so, he was a little disappointed to discover that he was right, that the street was empty apart from a small Japanese man holding a brown paper bag.

"Yes?" Bart said.

"This is 15 Green Lane?"

"Yes." That was their address.

The Japanese man held up the paper bag. "This is the takeout you ordered."

"We didn't order any takeout . . ."

Brenda had come into the hall behind Bart. "Who is it?" she asked.

"It's someone saying we ordered takeout," Bart told her.

Brenda glanced at the Japanese man with distaste. She didn't like foreign food, and for that matter, she didn't like foreigners either. "You've got the wrong house," she said. "We don't want any of that here."

"Fifteen Green Lane," the Japanese man insisted. "Sushi for three people."

"Sushi?"

"It's all paid for." The man thrust the bag into Bart's hand, and before anyone could say anything, he had turned and walked away.

Bart carried the bag into the kitchen. "What is it?" his father asked.

"It's Japanese takeout," Bart said. "He said it was sushi . . ."

Brian frowned. "There isn't a Japanese takeout around here."

"He said it was already paid for," Brenda said.

"Well, we might as well have it, then."

None of the Beckers had ever eaten sushi before. When they opened the bag they found a plastic box containing three sets of chopsticks and twelve neat rolls of rice stuffed with crabmeat and cucumber. Brian picked up one of the pieces with his fingers and ate it. "Disgusting!" he announced.

"I'll give it to the cat," Brenda said.

Brian sighed. "Just for a minute there, I thought that stupid monkey's ear had actually worked," he said. "I thought you'd open the door and find I'd won a brand-new Rolls-Royce in a competition or something. Wouldn't that have been great!"

"A Rolls-Royce would be a stupid wish anyway," Brenda said. "We could never afford to drive it. Just think of the insurance!"

"What would you wish for, Mom?" Bart asked.

"I don't know . . ." Brenda thought for a minute. "I'd probably wish for a million dollars. I'd wish I could win the lottery."

"All right, then!" Brian held up the monkey's ear for a second time. "I wish for a ton of money!"

But nothing happened. The doorbell didn't ring. Nor did the telephone. When the lottery was drawn later that evening (it was a Wednesday), Brian hadn't even gotten one number right. He went to bed as poor and as frustrated as he had been when he woke up.

There was, however, one strange event the next day. Brian was out on his rounds and had just given a parking ticket to an old retiree and was on his way down to the station where he knew he would find at least a dozen illegally parked cars when he came upon a woman leaning under the hood of a small white van. Brian smiled to himself. The van had stopped on a yellow line. He reached for his ticket machine.

"You can't park there!" he exclaimed in his usual way.

The woman straightened up and closed the hood. She was young and rather pretty—younger and prettier, certainly, than Brenda. "I'm very sorry," she said. "My van broke down. I'm just on my way to the market. But I've managed to fix it. You're not going to give me a ticket, are you?"

"Well . . ." Brian pretended to think about it, but in fact he had no real reason to ticket her, not if she was about to move. "All right," he said. "I'll let you off this time."

"You're very kind." The woman reached into the van and took a small tin off the front seat. The tin had a yellow-and-black label with the words ELM CROSS FARM printed on the front. "Let me give you this," she said. "To thank you."

"What is it?" Brian wasn't supposed to accept gifts, but he was intrigued.

"It's what I sell at the market," the woman explained. "I have a small farm in Hertfordshire. I keep bees. And this is our best honey. It's really delicious. I hope you enjoy it."

"Well, I don't know . . ." Brian began. But the woman had already gotten back into the van and a moment later she drove off.

The honey was delicious. Brian and Bart ate it for tea that evening, although Brenda, who was on a diet, refused. She was in a bad mood. The washing machine had broken that afternoon and the repairman had said it would cost ninety dollars to fix. "I don't know where

I'm going to find the cash," she said. Her eye fell on the monkey's ear that was still lying on the sideboard where they had left it the night before. "I notice we didn't get a single penny from that stupid thing," she said. "If only it did have the power to grant wishes. I'd have a new washing machine for a start. And a new house. And a new husband, too, for that matter . . ."

"What's wrong with me?" Brian complained.

"Well, you haven't got much of a job. You don't earn enough. You pick your nose in bed. And I always think it's a shame you lost your hair. You looked much more handsome when you were younger."

It was a particularly nasty thing to say. Brenda knew that Brian was sensitive about his appearance, but whenever she was in a bad mood, she always took it out on him.

Brian scowled. He snatched up the monkey's ear. "I wish I had my hair again," he cried.

"You're wasting your time," Brenda muttered. "You're bald now and you'll be bald until you die. In fact, that ear's got more hair on it than you have!"

That night the weather changed. Although it had been a beautiful day, by the time the Beckers went to bed, the clouds had rolled in and the wind had risen and just before midnight there was a sudden, deafening rumble of thunder. Brenda was jerked out of her sleep. "What was that?" she whimpered.

There was a second boom of thunder. At the same time the clouds opened and a torrent of rain crashed down, rattling on the roof and driving into the windows with such force that the glass shivered in the frames. The wind became stronger. The trees along Green Lane bent and twisted, then jerked crazily as whole branches were torn off and thrown across the street. Lightning flickered in the air. Somewhere a burglar alarm went off. Dogs howled and barked. The wind screamed and the rain hammered into the house like machine-gun bullets.

"What's going on?" Brenda cried.

Brian went over to the window in his pajamas, but he could hardly see anything. The rain was lashing at the glass, a solid curtain that seemed to enshroud the bungalow. "It's gone crazy!" he exclaimed.

"But the weather forecast didn't say anything about rain!"

"The weather forecast was wrong!" There was an explosion above Brian's head and something red and solid hurtled past, disintegrating on the front drive.

"What was that?"

"It's the bloody chimney! The whole place is coming down!"

In fact, the bungalow stood up to the storm, but the following morning at breakfast, the Beckers realized that they were going to have to pay for more than a new washing machine. The storm had torn off the chimney and part of the roof. Brian's car had been blown over onto its side. His rock garden was missing. All the fish had been sucked out of his fishpond and his garden fence was somewhere on the other side of London.

Curiously, theirs was the only house that seemed to have been damaged. It was as if the storm had descended on them and them alone.

"I just don't understand it!" Brenda wailed. "What's going on? Why us? What have we done to deserve this?"

"It was a blooming hurricane!" Brian said. "A hurricane! That's what it was!"

Bart had been listening to his parents in silence, but Brian's last words somehow reminded him of something. A hurricane? He thought back—to tea the day before, and breakfast before that. He looked at the monkey's ear, lying on the sideboard. His father had made three wishes and nothing had happened.

Or had it?

"It worked!" he muttered. "The monkey's ear . . ."

"What are you talking about?" his father demanded.

"It worked, Dad! At least, it worked—sort of. But . . ." It took Bart a few moments to collect his thoughts. But he knew he was right. He had to be.

"The monkey's ear didn't give us anything," Brenda said.

"But it did, Mom." Bart reached out and took it. "We made three wishes and we got three things—only they weren't the right things. It's as if it didn't hear us properly. Maybe that's why it was so cheap."

"Twenty dollars isn't cheap," Brian sniffed.

"No, Dad. But if the monkey's ear had been working properly, it would have been a bargain."

"What are you going on about?"

Bart paused. "What was your first wish?" he asked.

"I wanted a ton of money."

"No." Bart shook his head. "Your first wish was a Rolls-Royce. And what happened? There was that funny Japanese man at the door and he gave you—"

"He gave us some horrible sushi," Brenda interrupted.

"Yes. But what are sushi? They're rolls of rice! Don't you see? The ear didn't hear you properly. You asked for a Rolls-Royce and it gave you some rolls of rice!"

"The second wish was a ton of money," Brenda said.

"That's right. And then you met that woman and she gave you a tin of honey. It was almost the same, but it got it wrong a second time. And then, last night . . ."

"I said I wanted my hair again," Brian remembered.

"Yes. And what did we get instead?" Brian and Brenda stared at Bart. "We got a hurricane!"

There was a long silence. All three of them were staring at the ear.

"It's a deaf monkey!" Brian shouted.

"Yes."

"Blooming heck!" He licked his lips. "But in that case, if only I'd spoken a little louder . . . I could have had anything I wanted!"

Brenda's eyes widened. "You've still got one wish left!" she exclaimed.

Bart snatched the ear. "But it's my monkey's ear!" he said. "You bought it for me and this time I want to make the wish. I can get a new bike. I can never have to go back to school. I can be a millionaire. I want to make the wish!"

"Forget it!" Brian's hand flew out and grabbed hold of the ear. "We've only got one more chance. I'm head of this family—"

"Dad—"

"No!"

Father and son were both fighting for the ear while Brenda looked on, still trying to make sense of it all.

"I want it, Dad!" Bart yelled.

"I wish you'd go to hell!"

The words were no sooner out of Brian's mouth than there was a flash and an explosion accompanied by a cloud of green smoke. When Brian and Brenda next opened their eyes, the monkey's ear was lying on the kitchen table. There was no sign of Bart.

Brenda was the first to recover. "You idiot!" she screeched. "You nincompoop! What did you say?"

"What did I say . . . ?" Brian remembered his words and his face went pale.

"You told him to go to hell!" She sat down, her mouth dropping open. "Our son! Our only boy! That was what you wished!"

"Wait a minute! Wait a minute!" Brian thought feverishly. "You heard what he said! The monkey's ear is broken. It doesn't hear properly."

"You told him to go to hell!"

Since then, Brian and Brenda Becker have looked for Bart on a hill and in a well. Recently, they moved to the city of Hull and they're almost certain that one day he'll turn up there.

But they haven't found him yet.

The
Hitchhiker

Why did my father have to stop? I told him not to. I knew it was a bad idea. Of course, he didn't listen to me. Parents never do. But it would never have happened if only he'd driven on.

We'd been out for the day, just the three of us, and what a great, really happy day it had been. My fifteenth birthday, and they had taken me to Southwold, a small town on the Suffolk coast. We'd gotten there just in time for lunch and had spent the afternoon walking on the beach, looking in the shops, and losing money in the crummy arcade down by the pier.

A lot of people would think that Southwold was a rubbish place to go, especially on your birthday. But they'd be wrong. The truth is that it's special. From the multicolored beach huts that have probably been there since Queen Victoria's time, to the cannons on the cliff that have certainly been there a whole lot longer. It's got a lighthouse and a brewery and a sloping village green that all look as if they've come out of an old-fashioned English novel. None of the shops seem to sell anything that anyone would actually want and there's one, on the High Street, that has these fantastic wooden toys. A whole circus that comes to life for twenty-five cents. And the talking head of Horatio Nelson who puts his telescope up to his missing eye and sings. You get real fish and chips in Southwold. Fish that were still swimming while you were driving to the restaurant. Sticky puddings with custard. I don't need to go on. The whole place is so old-fashioned and so English that it just makes you want to smile.

We started back at about five o'clock. There was a real Suffolk sunset that evening. The sky was pink and gray and dark blue and somehow there was almost too much of it. I sat in the back of the car and as the door slammed, I felt that strange, heavy feeling you get at the end of a really good day. I was sad that it was over. But I felt happy and tired, glad that it was over too.

It was only about an hour's drive and as we left Southwold it began to rain. There's nothing strange about that. The weather often changes rapidly in Suffolk. By the time we reached the highway, the rain was falling quite heavily, slanting down, gray needles in the breeze. And there, ahead of us on the road, was a man, walking quickly, his hands clenched to the sides of his jacket, pulling it around him. He didn't turn around as we approached but he must have heard us coming. Suddenly his hand shot out. One thumb jutted out; the universal symbol of the hitchhiker. He wanted a lift.

There were about fifteen seconds until we reached him. My father was the first to speak.

"I wonder where he's going."

"You're not going to stop," my mother said.

"Why not? It's a horrible evening. Look at the weather!"

And there you have my parents. My father is a dentist and maybe that's why he's always trying to be nice to people. He knows that nobody in their right mind really wants to see him. He's tall and disheveled, the sort of man who goes to work with his hair unbrushed and with socks that don't match. My mother works three days a week at a real estate agency. She's much tougher than him. When I was young, she was always the one who would send me to bed. He'd let me stay up all night if she wasn't there.

There's one more thing I have to tell you about them.

They both look quite a bit older than they actually are. There's a reason for this. My older brother, Eddy. He died suddenly when he was twelve years old. That was nine years ago and my parents have never really recovered. I miss him too. Of course, he bullied me sometimes like all big brothers do, but his death was a terrible thing. It hurt us all and we know that the pain will never go away.

Anyway, it was typical of my dad to want to stop and offer the man a lift and just as typical of my mom to want to drive on. In the backseat, I said, "Don't stop, Dad." But it was already too late. Just fifteen seconds has passed since we saw the hitchhiker and already we were slowing down. I'd told him not to stop. But I'd no sooner said it than we did.

The rain was coming down harder now and it was very dark, so I couldn't see very much of the man. He seemed quite large, towering over the car. He had long hair, hanging down over his eyes.

My father pressed the button that lowered the window. "Where are you going?" he asked.

"Ipswich."

Ipswich was about twenty miles away. My mother

didn't say anything. I could tell she was uncomfortable.

"You were heading there on foot?" my father asked.

"My car broke down."

"Well—we're heading that way. We can give you a lift."

"John . . ." My mother spoke my father's name quietly but already it was too late. The damage was done.

"Thanks," the man said. He opened the back door.

I suppose I'd better explain.

The A12 highway is a long, dark, anonymous road that often goes through empty countryside with no buildings in sight. It was like that where we were now. There were no streetlights. Pulled in on the hard shoulder, we must have been practically invisible to the other traffic rushing past. It was the one place in the world where you'd have to be crazy to pick up a stranger.

Because, you see, everyone knows about Fairfields. It's a big, ugly building not far from Woodbridge, surrounded by a wall that's fifty feet high with spikes along the top and metal gates that open electrically. The name is quite new. It used to be called the East Suffolk Maximum Security Prison for the Criminally Insane.

And right now we were only about ten miles away from it.

That's the point I'm trying to make. When you're ten miles away from a lunatic asylum, you don't stop in the dark to pick up someone you've never met. You have to say to yourself that maybe, just maybe, there could have been a breakout that night. Maybe one of the loonies has cut the throat of the guard at the gate and slipped out into the night. And so it doesn't matter if it's raining. It doesn't even matter if the local nuclear power station at Sizewell has just blown up and radioactive slush is coming down in buckets. You just don't stop.

The back door slammed shut. The man eased himself into the backseat, rainwater glistening on his jacket. The car drove forward again.

I looked at him, trying to make out his features in the half-light. He had a long face with a square chin and small, narrow eyes. His skin was pale, as if he hadn't been outdoors in a while. His hair was somewhere between brown and gray, hanging down in clumps. His fingers were unusually long. One hand was resting on his thigh and his fingers reached all the way to his knee.

"Have you been out for the day?" he asked.

"Yes." My father knew he had annoyed my mother and he was determined to be cheerful and chatty, to show that he wasn't ashamed of what he'd done. "We've been in Southwold. It's a beautiful place."

"Oh yes." He glanced at me and I saw that he had a scar running over his eye. It began on his forehead and ended on his cheek and it seemed to have pushed the eye a little to one side. It wasn't quite level with the other one.

"Do you know Southwold?" my father asked.

"No."

"So where are you coming from today?"

The man thought for a moment. "I broke down near Lowestoft," he said, and somehow I knew he was lying. For a start, Lowestoft was a long way away, right up in Norfolk. If he'd broken down there, how could he have managed to get all the way to Southwold? And why bother? It would have been easier to jump on a train and go straight to Ipswich. I opened my mouth to say something but the man looked at me again, more sharply this time. Maybe I was imagining it but he could have been warning me. Don't say anything. Don't ask any difficult questions.

"What's your name?" my mother asked. I don't know why she wanted to know.

"Rellik," he said. "Ian Rellik." He smiled slowly. "This your son in the back?"

"Yes. That's Jacob. He's fifteen today."

"His birthday?" The man uncurled his hand and held it out to me. "Happy birthday, Jacob."

"Thank you." I took the hand. It was like holding a dead fish. At the same time I glanced down and saw that his sleeve had pulled back, exposing his wrist. There was something glistening on his skin and it wasn't rainwater. It was dark red, trickling down all the way to the edge of his hand, rising over the fleshy part of his thumb.

Blood!

Whose blood? His own?

He pulled his hand away, hiding it behind him. He knew I had seen it. Maybe he wanted me to.

We drove on. A cloud must have burst because it was really lashing down. You could hear the rain thumping on the car roof and the windshield wipers were having to work hard to sweep it aside. I couldn't believe we'd been walking on the beach only a few hours before.

"Lucky we got in," my mother said, reading my mind.

"It's bad," my father said.

"It's hell," the man muttered. Hell. It was a strange choice of word. He shifted in his seat. "What do you do?" he asked.

"I'm a dentist."

"Really? I haven't seen a dentist . . . not for a long time." He ran his tongue over his teeth. The tongue was pink and wet. The teeth were yellow and uneven. I guessed he hadn't cleaned them in a while.

"You should go twice a year," my father said.

"You're right. I should."

There was a rumble of thunder and at that exact moment the man turned to me and mouthed two words. He didn't say them. He just mouthed them, making sure my parents couldn't see.

"You're dead."

I stared at him, completely shaken. At first I thought I must have misunderstood him. Maybe he had said something else and the words had gotten lost in the thunderclap. But then he nodded slowly, telling me that I wasn't wrong. That's what he'd said. And that's what he meant.

I felt every bone in my body turn to jelly. That thing about the asylum. When we'd stopped and picked up the hitchhiker, I hadn't *really* believed that he was a madman who'd just escaped. Often you get scared by things but you can still tell yourself that it's just your imagination, that you're being stupid. And after all, there are lots of stories about escaped lunatics and none of them are ever true. But now I wasn't so sure. Had I imagined it? Had he said something else? *You're dead.* I thought back, picturing the movement of his lips. He'd said it all right.

We were doing about forty miles per hour, punching through the rain. I turned away, trying to ignore the man on the seat beside me. Mr. Rellik. There was something strange about that name and without really thinking I found myself writing it on the window, using the tip of my finger.

RELLIK

The letters, formed out of the condensation inside the car, hung there for a moment. Then the two *l*s in the middle began to run. It reminded me of blood. The name sounded Hungarian or something. It made me think of someone in *Dracula*.

"Where do you want us to drop you?" my mother asked.

"Anywhere," Mr. Rellik said.

"Where do you live in Ipswich?"

There was a pause. "Blade Street," he said.

"Blade Street? I don't think I know it."

"It's near the center."

My mother knew every street in Ipswich. She lived there for ten years before she married my father. But she had never heard of Blade Street. And why had the hitchhiker paused before he answered her question? Had he been making it up?

The thunder rolled over us a second time.

"I'm going to kill you," Mr. Rellik said.

But he said it so quietly that only I heard and this time I knew for certain. He was mad. He had escaped from Fairfields. We had picked him up in the middle of nowhere and he was going to kill us all. I leaned forward, trying to catch my parents' eyes. And that was when I happened to look into the rearview mirror. That was when I saw the word that I had written on the window just a few moments before.

R E L L I K

But reflected in the mirror it said something else.

KILLER

What was I supposed to do? What would you do if you were in my situation? We were still doing forty miles an hour in the rain, following a long empty road with fields on one side, trees on the other, and thick darkness everywhere. We were trapped inside the car with a man who could have a knife on him or even a gun or something worse. My parents didn't know anything but for some reason the man had made himself known to me. So what were my choices?

I could scream.

He would lash out and stop me before I had even opened my mouth. I could imagine those long fingers closing on my throat. He would strangle me in the backseat and my parents would drive on without even knowing what had happened. Until it was their turn.

I could trick him.

I could say I was feeling carsick. I could make them stop the car and then, when we got out, I could somehow persuade my parents to run for it. But that was a bad idea too. We were safer while we were still moving. At least Mr. Rellik—or whatever his real name was— couldn't attack my father while he was driving. The car would go out of control. He couldn't reach my mother either. That would mean lunging diagonally across the car and somehow getting over the back of her seat. No, I was the only one in danger right now . . . but that would change the moment we stopped.

Could I talk to him? Reason with him? Hope against hope that I had imagined it all and that he didn't mean us any harm?

And then I remembered.

I was sitting behind my mother for a reason. When we had set out that morning, my father had told me to sit there because there was something wrong with the door on the other side. It was an old car, a Volkswagen station wagon, and the catch on one of the passenger doors had broken. My mother had said it was danger-ous and had told me to sit on the left-hand side and to be sure that I wore my seat belt. I was wearing it now. But Mr. Rellik wasn't.

I shifted around in my seat as if trying to get more comfortable. Mr. Rellik was instantly alert. I could see that if I was going to try something, I would have to move fast. He had told me who he was. He knew that I knew. He was almost expecting me to try something.

"We'll drop you off at the next exit," my father said.

"That'll be fine." But the hitchhiker had no intention of getting out at the next roundabout. His face darkened. The eye with the scar twitched. As I watched, his hand slid into his jacket and curled around something underneath the material. I didn't have to see it to know what it was. A knife. A moment later his hand reappeared and I caught the glint of silver. I knew exactly what was going to happen. He would attack me. My father would stop the car. What else could he do? Then it would be his turn. And then my mother's.

I yelled out. And then everything happened in a blur.

I had already gotten myself into position, curled up in the corner with my shoulders pressed into the side of the car to give me leverage. At the same time, my legs shot out. Mr. Rellik had made a bad mistake. With his hand underneath his jacket he couldn't defend himself. Both my feet slammed into him, one on his shoulder, one just above his waist. I had kicked him with all my strength and as my legs uncoiled he was thrown against the opposite door.

The catch gave way. Mr. Rellik didn't even have time to cry out. The door swung open and he was thrown out. Out into the night and the rain. My father must have speeded up without my noticing because we were doing almost sixty then and it seemed that the wind plucked Mr. Rellik away. He hit the road in a spinning, splattering somersault. And it was worse than that. Although I hadn't seen it, a tractor trailer had been coming the other way, doing about the same speed as us. Mr. Rellik fell under its front wheels. The truck made mincemeat of him.

My mother screamed. My father stopped the car.

The tractor trailer stopped.

Suddenly everything was silent apart from the rain hammering on the roof.

My father twisted around and stared at me. The side door was still hanging open. "What . . . ?" he began.

Quickly I explained. I told him everything. The name on the window. The lies Mr. Rellik had told. The things he had said to me. The blood on his hand. The knife. My mother was in total shock. Her face was white and she was crying quietly. My father waited until I had finished, then he reached out and laid a hand on my arm. "It's all right, Jacob," he said. "Wait here."

He got out of the car and walked up the road. I could see him out of the back window. The truck driver had stopped on the hard shoulder and the two of them met.

There was no sign of Mr. Rellik. He must have been spread out over a fair bit of the A12. It had been horrible, what had happened, but I wasn't afraid anymore. I had done what I had to do. I'd saved both my parents and myself. We should never have stopped.

My father walked back to the car. The rain had eased off a little but he was still soaking wet.

"He's going to call the police," my father said. "We're nearly there, so I said we'd go on. He's going to give our information to the police."

"Did you tell him what happened?" I asked.

"Yes." My father got back in behind the steering wheel. My mother was still crying. "He knows you did the right thing, Jacob. Don't worry. We're going to leave now."

We drove for another ten minutes and then, just past the first sign for Woodbridge, we turned off down a narrow lane. It twisted through woodland for about a mile and then we came to a high brick wall with spikes set along the top. We stopped in front of a pair of metal gates with an intercom system just in front. My father leaned out of the car window and said something. The gates clicked and swung open automatically.

I knew where we were. We had come to Fairfields.

The East Suffolk Maximum Security Hospital for the Criminally Insane.

My father had to tell them what had happened, of course. He'd agreed on that with the truck driver. This is where Mr. Rellik had come from and we had just killed him. In self-defense. They had to know.

I asked my father if that was why we had come here.

"Yes, Jacob," he said. "That's why we're here."

We drove toward a big Victorian house with towers and barred windows and bloodred bricks. I could see how the place had gotten its new name though. It was surrounded by attractive gardens, the lawns spreading out for some distance underneath the high-voltage searchlights. Before we had even stopped, the front door of the house opened and a bald, bearded man in a white coat came running out.

"Wait here," my father said again.

I waited with my mother while the two of them spoke but this time I managed to hear a little of what they said. My father did most of the talking.

"You were wrong, Dr. Fielding. You were wrong. We should never have taken him . . ."

"None of us could have known. He was doing so well."

"He was fine in Southwold. He was fine. I thought he was . . . normal. But then . . . this!"

"I don't know what to say to you, Dr. Fisher. I don't . . ."

"Never again, Dr. Fielding. For God's sake! Never again."

The two men came to the car. My father leaned in. "We're going in with Dr. Fielding," he said.

"All right," I said.

My mother didn't look up as I got out of the car. She didn't even say good-bye. That made me a little sad.

Dr. Fielding put a hand on my shoulder. "Let's go inside, Jacob," he said. "We have to talk about what happened."

"All right," I said.

Later on, they told me that the hitchhiker's name was Mr. Renwick and that I had misheard him. Apparently Mr. Renwick was a gardener who had been working outside Lowestoft. His car had broken down and he had managed to hitchhike as far as Southwold, which was where we'd picked him up. They told me that it was mud I had seen on his wrist, not blood. And that when they had scraped him off the tarmac he had been holding not a knife but a cigarette case.

That was what they told me, but I didn't believe any of it. After all, they also told me a lot of lies after my brother, Eddy, fell under that train. They even wanted me to believe that I'd pushed him! Nobody ever understood.

So here I am, back in my room, looking out of the barred window at the same old view. I had such a nice day in Southwold. I just hope I won't have to wait another nine years before they take me out again.

The
Sound
of Murder

I.

Her name was Kate Evans. She was thirteen years old, small and slim with long dark hair and a pale, rather serious face. She was in her last year at Brierly Hall, a prep school in Harrow-on-the-Hill, just north of London. Her best subjects were English, history, and geography but she was pretty good at anything so long as it didn't involve figures. She was popular with both the teachers and the other children. There was only one thing that made her different from everyone else at the school. Kate Evans was deaf.

It had been an accident of birth. Her mother had caught the measles while she was pregnant and the doctors had been worried even before Kate arrived in the world. They had known almost at once that something was wrong . . . or at least, not quite right. Kate wasn't completely deaf. She could hear some sound but speech in general was just a blur to her. The medical name for her condition was sensorineural deafness. Part of her ear, the bit called the cochlea, wasn't working properly. She could hear a telephone ring or a dog bark but she couldn't hear a whole lot else.

Kate had learned to lip-read but she didn't really need to. When she had started at Brierly Hall, she had been given a special hearing aid that fitted behind her ear and that had two settings. It could be used for day-to-day conversation. And it could also be plugged into a box, a little larger than a pack of cigarettes, which Kate carried in her top pocket. This was for use in class. Whoever was teaching the lesson carried a second box, this one attached to a radio transmitter. The teacher spoke. The sound was transmitted across the room. Kate heard. It was as simple as that.

It was so simple, in fact, that Kate never thought of herself as deaf or disabled or even particularly different. The hearing aid even had certain uses. During more boring lessons—math with Mr. Thompson, for example—she could surreptitiously turn down the volume so that she no longer had to listen to him. It was also possible—if she was asked something and couldn't think of the answer—to play for time by pretending that the device was broken. Most of the teachers were too delicate to pursue the matter any further and so she nearly always got off the hook. And sometimes the machine did malfunction, with unusual results. One summer she had picked up popular radio stations, which certainly livened up the day. Another time, it had been snatches of police radio communications. This had been alarming at first but the broadcasts became so interesting that soon everyone was pestering her to tell them what was going on in the fight against North London crime.

Brierly Hall wasn't a boarding school. Every afternoon Kate was picked up by the au pair, a German girl called Heidi, who spoke English that was so mangled that it was almost impossible to understand—with or without a hearing aid. Both Kate's parents worked. Her mother was a computer programmer. Her father had something to do with finance—bonds and equities and that sort of thing. She didn't have any brothers or sisters and she sometimes wondered if her parents had decided to stop having children when they had discovered that their first one wasn't perfect. She had never asked them. They were so busy, so wrapped up in their own worlds, that they never had a lot of time for her. They were kind, loving. But distant.

Kate didn't mind. She had plenty of friends. She was doing well at school. And at the time of her last year— the Christmas term—at Brierly Hall, she was definitely enjoying life.

But that was the term that the new French teacher, Mr. Spencer, arrived. And it was with the coming of Mr. Spencer that the whole nightmare began.

II.

To start with, he looked just like all the other teachers who had chosen to lock themselves away in the secluded world of Brierly Hall. He wasn't exactly young anymore but he wasn't particularly old either. He seemed to be stuck somewhere in between. He was wearing an old-fashioned sport jacket, corduroy trousers, white shirt, tie (striped, of course), and a V-neck sweater. All of his clothes looked well lived in. He had dark eyes, dark, curly hair, and a beard. Although he was a physically large man, there was something about him that made him look beaten down, defeated. His shoulders were hunched. His eyes blinked frequently. He didn't smile.

Kate saw him on the first day of the semester. She was walking down the corridor with her best friend, a boy named Martin White. He and Kate were just passing the staff room when the door opened and the new teacher came out and hurried past them on his way to class. He didn't speak to them but his arm briefly touched Kate's shoulder and it was then, at that moment of contact, that it happened.

Kate's hearing aid malfunctioned. There was a loud whistling in her ear; so loud that she actually recoiled, her hand stretching out and her face contorting. The sound cut right through her head. She could feel it even after it was gone.

"What is it?" Martin asked. He had seen Kate double up.

"Feedback." Kate took a deep breath. Fortunately, it seemed to be over. She tapped at her ear. "I've never had it so loud. Just my luck if my hearing aid's acting up on the first day of class." She looked back at the new teacher, who was just disappearing through a set of double doors. "Who's that?"

"I think it must be Mr. Spencer. Or Monsieur Spensaire, perhaps, I should say."

"The new French teacher."

"*Oui, oui!*" Martin sniffed. "He looks even more boring than the last one."

Their old French teacher, Mr. Silberman, had announced his retirement the term before—much to the
relief of almost everybody. He must have been at least
eighty years old and was one of the only teachers who
regularly fell asleep during his own lessons. Kate had
been hoping for a younger, sexier replacement. Her first
glimpse had left her distinctly disappointed.

And it was strange the way her hearing aid had re-
acted when he touched her. The piercing feedback. It
was almost as if . . .

No. She put the thought out of her mind. Mr.
Spencer hadn't caused the problem. It had simply happened when he walked past.

She met the new teacher for a second time that afternoon. French was the first lesson of the day. Mr.
Spencer had taken over Mr. Silberman's old classroom
and had already removed the posters showing the different varieties of French cheese, which at least proved
he had a bit of sense. But as he took their names,
handed out the new textbooks, and did all the things
that teachers always do on the first day of classes, he
seemed about as cheerful and lively as a French dictionary. He even forced them to sit in alphabetical order.
Mr. Silberman had never done that.

He was, of course, wearing the radio transmitter that allowed Kate to hear him. He had slipped the box into his top pocket and clipped the microphone to his tie. But throughout the lesson, the machine malfunctioned with a series of hisses, bleeps, and squawking noises that had Kate reeling. She was relieved when the final bell went off, even if it added to the headache she'd already gotten. It was about the only thing she heard properly.

She was the first to stand up and was already making her way to the door when Mr. Spencer spoke. There were just two words but this time she heard him quite clearly. She stopped dead in her tracks. She was certain the words were addressed to her.

"Rotten cow!"

Kate turned around. She was blushing—though whether with embarrassment or anger she wasn't sure. Mr. Spencer was standing at his desk clutching a pile of books. For the first time she noticed that the backs of his hands were covered in dark hair. "I'm sorry, sir?" she said.

He looked up. "What is it, Kate?" he asked. He knew her name. But of course, new teachers always remembered her name first.

"What did you say?" Kate asked. She was aware that she sounded angry. Everyone had stopped what they were doing. They were all looking at her.

"I didn't say anything," Mr. Spencer said. He smiled at her. "Did you hear everything all right during the lesson, Kate? I did mean to ask . . ."

"Yes . . ." Kate stammered, suddenly unsure of herself. Could she have misheard him? Or had the two words come from somewhere else—like the radio or the police reports? But no . . .

"Rotten cow."

She had heard him. It had been his voice.

"I'll see you tomorrow, then." Mr. Spencer was still smiling. The smile changed his face. He looked a whole lot more human.

Kate turned and left the class.

III.

The next day, the problems with the hearing aid were even worse. And it wasn't just the distortions. While Mr. Spencer took the class through a fairly simple comprehension test, all Kate heard was a barrage of swearwords. They came into her ear from nowhere. Nasty, jabbing words that she would never have dreamed of using herself. She remembered how she had picked up those radio stations the summer before and wondered if the same thing wasn't happening again. But these words weren't out of any radio station. Nobody would be allowed to say things like this on the air.

She did the best she could with the comprehension, but knew that she'd missed at least half of it and probably mistranslated the rest. She handed in her paper with a heavy heart, and as her fingertips approached those of Mr. Spencer, she was rewarded with another scream of static and interference. She wondered how she would get through the rest of the day.

And yet the strange thing was that, after French, the hearing aid worked perfectly. She had no problems in math or history and it was only in the corridor just before lunch that the receiver started acting up once again. Even as she felt the hiss rising up in her eardrums, Kate was turning around. And sure enough, there he was. Mr. Spencer was ambling into the staff room, his hands in his pockets, his shoulders hunched. She watched the door close. The hissing stopped.

That afternoon, after lunch, she told Martin what had happened. Martin was a good-looking thirteen-year-old with blue eyes and straw-colored hair that hung in his eyes. He was always number one in PE but even his best friends had to agree that he wasn't particularly bright. For a long minute he thought about what Kate had said. "Are you telling me," he said, "that there's something about Mr. Spencer that sets off your hearing aid? That he's . . . like . . . transmitting signals or something?"

"That's exactly what I'm saying," Kate replied. "But it's never happened to me before. I wouldn't have said it was possible!"

"I did once hear about this man who kept on hearing concerts," Martin said. "I mean, he got voices and operas and classical music in his head and it was driving him mad. He was going to commit suicide. But then they found he had a filling in his back tooth and it was picking up radio stations."

"What's that got to do with anything?" Kate asked.

Martin shrugged. "I was just trying to be helpful."

The afternoon seemed to stretch on forever. Kate didn't have any more French lessons and she didn't get any more interference, but even so, she found it hard to concentrate. It was like being on some sort of ghost train. As each minute ticked by, she was expecting something to jump out at her—a swearword, another electronic scream. By the end of the day her nerves were shattered and she decided she'd have to talk it over with her parents. She was beginning to feel almost nervous. She couldn't understand it but she was becoming afraid.

Heidi came for her at four o'clock. The German au pair was always smiling and friendly but sometimes Kate suspected that she didn't understand a single word. She drove a red Nissan and Kate was just about to get in when a single faint whine in her ear made her stop and turn around, already knowing what she would see.

And there he was. Mr. Spencer had just come out of the school with a pile of books under his arm. He was walking toward a waiting VW Golf, and as he reached it he must have stumbled, because suddenly all the books slipped from under his arm and fell to the ground. At once the door of the Golf opened and a woman got out. It had to be Mrs. Spencer; a thin, bony woman with hair between brown and gray tied tightly behind her head. Everything about her was tight. Her clothes—a cable-knit sweater and jeans. Her eyes. The way she moved.

She was saying something to her husband and he

seemed to be apologizing. They were too far away for Kate to be able to hear but she found herself doing something she had been told she should never do, something she knew was wrong. She lip-read the conversation.

"... so clumsy! Just get a move on, George. I haven't got all day."

"Yes, dear. Sorry, dear."

"You're a complete waste of time! A boring little man in a boring little job. Have you got them all?"

"I think so, dear."

Kate blinked and looked away, immediately guilty about eavesdropping. But even without sound, even from this distance, she had been able to detect the venom in the woman's voice. And once again she thought about the two words she had heard in the French lesson.

"Rotten cow . . ."

"Are you now coming, please, Katie?" Heidi called out to her in her singsong voice.

Kate watched Mr. and Mrs. Spencer drive away. Then she got in next to the au pair.

She wanted to talk to her parents that evening but when she got home, there was a note on the kitchen table. They'd gone out to dinner and wouldn't be home until late. She went to bed with her own thoughts and that same, nudging sense of fear.

IV.

Nothing more happened for about a week. The evenings got darker and the weather got worse. The interference continued but Kate got used to turning the transmitter off during French class. If she was reading or writing, she didn't need it, and she could lipread . . . even though it was next to impossible in French. It was when they had oral work that she was forced to turn the thing back on and put up with whatever came her way. And it was during one of those lessons that the voice came again.

They were reading a book, each taking a turn to read the words out loud in French and then to translate them. It was Kate's turn. She was standing with the book open in front of her.

"Bonne-Maman arrivait toujours en taxi et ne donnait jamais de pourboire au chauffeur," she read.

Mr. Spencer looked at her with his watery, dark eyes. *"I'm going to kill her,"* he said.

Kate faltered, then went on. *"Elle était petite . . ."*

"I'm going to kill her . . ."

". . . et paraissait rapetisser un peu plus chaque annee."

"Nobody will know."

"Elle avait des cheveux . . ." Kate was suddenly aware that everyone was looking at her. One or two of the other girls were giggling. She stopped, blushing without quite knowing why. There was a whine in her ear. She waited until it had died away.

"Didn't you hear me, Kate?" Mr. Spencer asked. He was staring at her, puzzled.

"I'm sorry, sir?" Kate sat down. The classroom was beginning to spin slowly around her and she wondered if she was going to faint.

"I asked you to translate."

"Oh. Right." Kate tried to concentrate on the book.

"I'm going to murder her!"

"Murder?" Kate repeated the word. At least, the word slipped out of her lips before she could stop it.

Something glimmered in the French teacher's eyes. "What did you say?" he demanded.

"Mother . . . I mean grandmother!" Kate gazed at the black-and-white pages of the book, trying to bury herself in them. "Grandma always came by taxi," she began. "And she never gave the driver . . . she never gave the driver . . ." She had stumbled on a word.

"Pourboire," Mr. Spencer said. *"I'm going to murder her tonight."*

Hands were going up around the class. He had asked them if they knew the word *pourboire.* That was what he had said. But that wasn't what Kate had heard.

"With a kitchen knife."

"Does it mean 'a drink,' sir?"

"No."

"A tip?"

"Yes. Well done, Nicholas. *I'm going to stab her with a kitchen knife. Nobody will know."*

Kate got to her feet. She had knocked her chair over behind her. "I'm sorry," she said. "I don't feel well."

She ran out of the room.

V.

The school nurse said it was flu. But the nurse always said everything was flu. There was a joke in the school that if you went to the nurse with both your legs chopped off and a spear in your neck, she'd give you a half an aspirin and tell you to come back the next day.

Fortunately, it was a Friday afternoon. The nurse told Kate to have plenty of rest over the weekend and to stay indoors. She didn't even give her the half aspirin.

Kate did two things that weekend.

The first was to visit her doctor and arrange for a new hearing aid to be sent to her. But somehow she knew she was wasting her time. The hearing aid worked in every class except French. It worked at home and it worked at the doctor's. Try as she might, Kate couldn't think of any reason why it should act up when she was close to Mr. Spencer. Could there be something in Martin's ridiculous story about the filling? Could Mr. Spencer have a false tooth or something that was interfering with the signal? But, no. Kate knew that she was dealing with something different, something that had no easy explanation. She kept on thinking about what she had heard. The words had been so vicious, and so deliberate. They echoed in her head, even when she was asleep. The worst thing was, she still wasn't sure where they had come from. They couldn't have come from Mr. Spencer himself. She had never actually seen them cross his lips.

And so, on Sunday, she tried to tell her mother what had happened. Tried and failed. It was a bad time of the

year for Caroline Evans. She had just set up a compli-
cated computer system for a chain of organic super-
markets. As always, there were teething problems and
the moment anything went wrong, she was the one
who got the blame. When Kate came into the sitting
room after breakfast, her mother was already in a bad
mood. The fax had been spitting out pages all morning.
Mangoes in Manchester and leeks that had failed to arrive in Leeds.

"Mum . . ."

Caroline Evans looked up from her laptop, a cigarette halfway to her lips. She always smoked when a
new system was coming online. The rest of the year she
spent trying to quit. "Yes, darling?"

"I need to talk to you about something that's happening at school."

"What is it?" Caroline was genuinely concerned.
That was the thing about her. She did worry about
Kate—when she had time.

"It's this teacher. And my hearing aid . . ." Kate
began, but then the telephone rang and it was the IT
manager from the supermarket, and suddenly the conversation was all bytes and modules and ten minutes
later Caroline was still arguing on the phone.

At last she hung up. "I'm sorry, darling," she said. "Now what was it about this teacher?"

"It doesn't matter," Kate said. She had decided. She would handle this on her own.

And on Monday, she went back to school with the same resolve. There was a simple solution to her problem. She would talk to Mr. Spencer himself! She would explain the problem to him and between them they would work out what was causing it.

But Mr. Spencer wasn't at school on Monday.

As soon as she arrived she knew something was wrong. The first class had been canceled and instead there was to be an assembly in the school auditorium. She saw one or two of the teachers looking shaken and upset. As she made her way across the school yard, Martin hurried up to her. "Have you heard?" he whispered. But before he could tell her, Miss Primrose, the music teacher, had stepped between them and Martin could say no more.

There were three hundred and twenty children at Brierly Hall and it was a tight squeeze inside the auditorium. They sat, shoulder to shoulder, while the staff took their places on the stage. Then the principal appeared. His name was Mr. Fellner and normally he was a lively, humorous man. It was said that he was the most popular principal that Brierly Hall had ever had. But today he was grim-faced and serious.

"I'm afraid I have some bad news for you," he said, and there was something about the tone of his voice that made everyone know that he was about to tell them the very worst news possible. "I would have preferred to tell your parents before I tell you, but unfortunately that won't be possible because it will be on the television news tonight and I would prefer you to hear it from me first." He paused. "As some of you may have already noticed, Mr. Spencer is not with us today. The reason for this is that something awful has happened. His wife has died.

"You may be wondering why this should be on the news. Well, I spoke to the police this morning and although it's a very shocking thing and I'm sure many of you will want to talk about this with your homeroom teachers after this assembly, it would appear that Mrs. Spencer has been murdered."

A whisper that quickly rose into an excited buzz zigzagged its way through the rows of children, but for Kate it was as if she had been snatched out of her seat and sent spinning into outer space. Murdered!

"I'm going to kill her!"

It wasn't possible. Murders happened in books and on television shows. You read about murders in the newspapers or heard about them on the news.

"I'm going to murder her!"

The voice had told her it was going to happen. It had warned her. And she had refused to listen.

"There is no need for any of you to be afraid," Mr. Fellner was saying. "Geraldine Spencer lived in Stanmore, which is quite a long way from here. As far as we know, from what the police have told us, she was attacked while she was out walking on Stanmore Common. She was attacked . . ."

"With a kitchen knife."

". . . with some sort of knife. Possibly it was somebody wanting to rob her. I will of course give you further information when I have it.

"But right now I think it would be appropriate if we put our hands together and prayed. Mr. Spencer has only been with the school for a short time but even so he is still part of the family, here at Brierly Hall. I spoke to him on the telephone briefly this morning and of course he's completely devastated. He'll be away for the next few weeks at least, possibly until the end of term, but I'm sure it would be of comfort for him to know that our thoughts are with him. Let's start with the Lord's Prayer . . ."

And the school prayed. But not Kate.

She was sick, frightened, confused. A whirl of images flashed through her mind. There was Mr. Spencer, walking down the corridor for the first time. There were his hands with the dark hair reaching almost to his fingers. And again, outside the school, dropping the books while the woman waited for him in his car. With a thrill, Kate realized that she had actually seen Mrs. Spencer, the wife who was now dead, killed with a knife while she was walking in the park. The two of them hadn't seemed very happy at the time. How could they have known that it was going to be one of their last days together?

How could they have known?

Could they have known?

Could one of them have known?

Kate fainted—and that was something else she thought happened only on TV shows. The room took one lurching spin around her and then jerked away as she collapsed off her chair and onto the floor. Later on, of course, the other children would tease her. Trust a girl to faint just because there'd been a murder. But of course, none of them understood.

Mr. Spencer had murdered his wife. And only Kate knew.

VI.

Strangely enough, it was Martin who first mentioned the word *telepathy*. Martin didn't have that many four-syllable words in his vocabulary.

He was talking to Kate the next day after they had all heard the big announcement. By this time, the murder had indeed been reported on the television news and had also appeared in all the newspapers. Most of them had carried photographs of Geraldine Spencer and there had been pictures of George Spencer too in the *Daily Mail* and the *Telegraph*. At school, of course, nobody had talked about anything else and it was getting harder and harder to distinguish facts from gossip, gossip from rumor, and rumor from fantastic lies.

But Kate knew this much.

Geraldine Spencer had been stabbed at four o'clock on Saturday afternoon while she was walking her dog, a poodle, on Stanmore Common. The police hadn't yet found the murder weapon. According to the senior detective who was leading the inquiry, this would be a vital clue if it ever turned up. There had been no witnesses. Geraldine Spencer had been forty-two years old and had been married to George Spencer for seventeen years. There were no children. Surprisingly, Mrs. Spencer was a wealthy woman. It turned out that her father had run a chain of hotels and she had inherited a lot of money a few years before. All this money would go to her husband.

George Spencer was the prime suspect in the murder. He had been interviewed by the police . . . once, or several times. It depended on whom you believed. But it seemed that he had an alibi. He had been at the movies that afternoon. Without the murder weapon, there was absolutely no evidence against him. He was now at home. Alex Burford, who was in Kate's class and who actually lived near Stanmore, said that his mother had seen Mr. Spencer at the funeral, sobbing uncontrollably and at one point even trying to throw himself into his wife's grave. But nearly everything Alex said was untrue and nobody believed him now.

Although Kate had been teased nonstop for fainting during the assembly, she had said nothing. At least, not the first day. But by the end of the second she'd had enough, and after the last lesson she'd taken Martin to one side and described everything that had happened—not because she thought he could help but because she simply had to get it off her chest.

At least Martin hadn't laughed at her. Nor had he refused to believe her. He had listened in silence, scratched his head, and then finally given his opinion.

"This voice you heard," he said. "If it wasn't the radio and it wasn't what he was saying, you don't think it could have been . . . sort of, what he was thinking? Like telepathy or something?"

"Telepathy?"

"I saw this show on television once. It was about that man who can bend spoons and stuff. Anyway, he did this trick where someone drew a picture on a sheet of paper and sealed it in an envelope. And then he drew the same picture. He said he could read the other person's mind. He actually did it! Because he was telepathic."

"But, Martin! I *can't* read people's minds!"

"No. I know. But maybe it has something to do with . . . I don't know. But the moment you met him you said your hearing aid went all screwy. So maybe for some reason you can't hear what he says but you can hear what he thinks."

"That's crazy . . ." Kate regretted the words the moment they were spoken. Martin looked glum and she realized she'd offended him. Martin knew he was thick. He'd often said as much. But he didn't like it when people treated him as if he *was* thick. She reached out and put a hand on his arm. "I mean, it sounds crazy. But . . . I don't know . . . !"

And the more she thought about it, the more she began to wonder if Martin hadn't somehow stumbled on the truth.

George Spencer didn't love his wife. That much Kate knew from the brief sight she had had of them together. The voice had said he was going to murder her, stab her with a kitchen knife. And that was what had happened. Martin was right. The only time the hearing aid acted up was when Mr. Spencer was near. So maybe, impossibly, it had transmitted . . .

. . . not what he was saying.

What he was thinking.

Kate lifted the receiver out of her top pocket and stared at it. The little silver box seemed so small, so ordinary. Although she depended on it every day of her life, she had never really given it much thought. It was just a machine.

Martin stood up suddenly. He had seen his mother draw up in her BMW convertible. Martin's parents were divorced, and as he often liked to tell Kate, his mum had gotten the house, the car, the money . . . everything, including him!

"You know," he muttered,"I hope for your sake you're not telepathic."

"What do you mean?" Kate asked.

"Well, if Mr. Spencer did bump off his wife, and you know what he's thinking, what are you going to do when he comes back?"

VII.

Mr. Spencer came back two weeks before the end of the term. The principal made another speech at assembly the day before he arrived.

"Mr. Spencer has asked to come back before the end of term because he wants his life to return to normal as soon as possible and I am sure that all of us here at Brierly Hall will do everything we can to help him. As I'm sure you all know, the police have been unable to find the wicked person who attacked and killed Geraldine Spencer. Mr. Spencer has of course been questioned about the death of his wife but it's important that you understand that this is entirely normal in an investigation of this sort and that there is no question that he was in any way involved. I must ask you, all of you, to be kind and to be sympathetic. Christmas is just a few weeks away. Let's look forward to that and put this whole dreadful business behind us."

And there he was, suddenly, almost as if he had never been away. Mr. Spencer was thinner and some people said there was a touch more gray in his hair. He walked more slowly and when he spoke there was a softness, even a sadness, in his voice that hadn't been there before. There was one other thing that was different about him. He had bought himself new clothes; a new jacket and black shiny shoes that squeaked a little when he walked.

For Kate, French was the first class of the day—and she was dreading it. As she streamed into the classroom with the other children, she saw Martin holding one hand up, two fingers crossed. Even now, she wasn't sure if he really had taken her seriously. Martin loved science fiction and Marvel comic books and Kate sometimes wondered if he knew where real life ended and fantasy began. Everyone took their seats. Mr. Spencer was standing at the blackboard, writing out the conditional tense of *aimer*. He turned around and spoke to them.

"I got away with it. I killed the old cow, and the police couldn't touch me!"

Sitting in the front row, Kate let out a stifled cry. The teacher's dark eyes were suddenly on her.

"What is it, Kate?"

"Nothing, sir."

"I've got her money. I'm rich! And I'm free of her." The hearing aid whined.

Kate writhed in her seat. Everyone was looking at her. Mr. Spencer too. She could see the puzzlement in his face. Worse, she could hear it.

"That girl again! What's wrong with her? Does she know something? No! That's not possible. But why is she looking at me like that?"

Kate forced herself to look away.

"She's looking away! It's almost as if she knows what I'm thinking! No. Don't be stupid. She doesn't know anything. The police don't know anything. The knife! They haven't found the knife. They'll never find the knife."

Kate couldn't bear it anymore. The hearing aid was screaming and buzzing in her ear. She opened her textbook and buried herself in it, hoping that if she concentrated enough on the words, she could make the voice go away.

And it worked. Her head was still filled with interference but somewhere, in the distance, she could hear Mr. Spencer walking across the room—*squeak, squeak, squeak.* The sound of his new shoes was one thing that transmitted perfectly. Now he was talking to the rest of the class. "The conditional tense is formed by taking the infinitive, *aimer,* and adding . . ."

Somehow she made it to the end of the lesson although it was the longest fifty minutes of her life. At last the bell went off, followed by the usual shuffling of books and slamming of desks.

"I will see you tomorrow," Mr. Spencer called out over the din. Then . . . "Kate! Can I have a word with you, please?"

Kate stopped dead in her tracks. She glanced despairingly at Martin, who shrugged helplessly, already on his way out. For a moment she was tempted to run. But that was ridiculous. Where would she go? She forced herself not to panic. There was nothing Mr.

Spencer could do. Not here, in school, in the middle of the day. She turned around slowly and looked at the teacher, who was sitting by his desk. The hearing aid crackled. She walked over to him. Suddenly there were only two of them in the room.

"Is something the matter?" Mr. Spencer asked.

"What do you know? How do you know? I killed Dina! Killed my wife! Stabbed her with a knife."

"Nothing's the matter, sir," Kate said. She had to concentrate. Listen to the first voice. Ignore the second.

"You were behaving very strangely in my class."

"They can't find the knife. I've got the knife."

"My hearing aid . . . it's . . . it's not working," Kate said. She was begging him to stop. She didn't want to know.

"It's in the spare locker."

"You should get it seen to," Mr. Spencer said.

"Yes, sir."

"In the spare locker. In the spare locker. Nobody will look there. Nobody knows."

Mr. Spencer was staring at her now, as if he were trying to see inside her head. Kate forced herself to look ordinary, to pretend that nothing was happening. He was suspicious. She knew it. She had to make him trust her.

"I was very sorry, sir," she stammered. "I mean, we were all very sorry about what happened to Dina. I'm sure the police will find who did it. You must be very sad."

"I am very sad," Mr. Spencer said. But then he frowned. "Why did you call her Dina?" he asked.

The hearing aid was howling.

"I thought that was her name," Kate said.

"Her name was Geraldine. I used to call her Dina, though. But I'll tell you something very strange, Kate. I was the only person who called her that. And nobody else knew. It was a private name."

"I thought . . ."

"What did you think, Kate? How did you know that name?"

"I just thought it was her name, sir."

Mr. Spencer's eyes went blank and for the first time the noise in Kate's head stopped. He stood up and, despite herself, Kate took a step back. She was afraid of him. And he knew it. It was obvious.

"Make sure you get your hearing aid seen to, Kate,"

Mr. Spencer said. "We don't want you missing any French."

"Yes, sir."

"All right. You can go."

Relieved, she gathered up her things and walked over to the door, but just as she was about to leave, he called out to her.

"Stop, Kate. There's something I want to say."

"Yes, sir?" She stopped and turned around.

And knew that he had tricked her.

Mr. Spencer hadn't said anything at all. He had thought it. As crazy as his suspicions had been, he had decided to put them to the test. And now he knew.

Kate opened her mouth to speak but she could see the sudden flare of cruelty in those dark eyes and knew that Geraldine Spencer would have seen exactly the same before the knife sliced into her.

She ran through the door and down the corridor, never once stopping to look behind.

VIII.

What could she do?

She could go to Mr. Fellner. But she knew that the principal would never believe her. The main difference between adults and children isn't that adults are older, bigger, smarter, or more experienced. It's that they don't believe. Adults always have to find explanations for everything and Kate knew that if she went to Mr. Fellner he would think she was either hysterical or crazy but he certainly wouldn't believe her.

She could go to her parents. But that wasn't easy. Her father was at some bank in Zurich for three days. Her mother had gone to visit a new client in Edinburgh and wouldn't be home until the weekend. That left Heidi but it would be a day's work just to get the au pair to understand what she was saying, and even then Kate doubted there would be anything she could do.

Could she telephone the police? No. The police were adults too. At best they would treat the telephone call as some cruel sort of hoax. The fact was that, apart from Martin, there was probably no one in the world who would believe her story of . . . telepathy or whatever it was. She still wasn't sure that she believed it herself.

"The trouble is, you've got no proof," Martin said. During lunch she had told him what had happened and once again he had surprised her. He hadn't questioned a word of what she had said. And once again he was right.

"Proof?"

"It's your word against his. And if you go to the police talking about telepathy and that sort of thing, they'll think you're raving mad."

"I'm not the mad one!" Kate remembered the look in Mr. Spencer's eyes and shivered.

"What about the knife?"

"What about it?" Kate didn't even want to think about it.

"You know where it is!"

It was in the locker. That was what Mr. Spencer had said—or thought.

Brierly Hall had been around for about a hundred and fifty years. Even in Victorian times it had been a school. Of course, most of it had been rebuilt more recently than that. The more successful the school had become, the more money it had attracted, and in the eighties and nineties they'd built the auditorium, the music wing, three new classrooms, and a heated swimming pool. But the core of the school was old. The central building (A Block) belonged to another century, with thick, tile-covered walls, bare wooden floors, arched windows, and—in the basement—a series of dusty rooms and passageways containing hot-water tanks, heating systems, and generators. The dining hall and the principal's office were in A Block. So was the staff room. And on the other side of the staff room there was a row of wooden lockers, one for every teacher in the school.

"It's in the spare locker."

"I bet it's got his fingerprints on it," Martin said. "And bits of his wife's blood . . ."

"Shut up, Martin!" Kate didn't want to hear this.

But Martin went on, excited. "If you got the knife, they'd have to believe you. It wouldn't even matter how you found it. Didn't you read what the police said? They said it was a vital clue."

"Yes! But how am I supposed to get it?" Kate asked miserably. "The lockers are next to the staff room and we're not allowed anywhere near them."

"You could sneak in . . ."

"With everyone there?"

"You could do it after school."

"When?"

"Today! I'll help you. We could do it together."

"But if Mr. Spencer knows that I know about the knife . . ."

"He won't know!" Martin said. "I mean, you only

know because you heard him thinking about it. But how could he know that he was thinking about it just then? If you get the knife, then you've got the proof. And if you've got the proof, you can go to the police . . ."

"I'm not sure." Kate sighed. "What happens if someone sees us? And it'll be dark . . ."

"It'll only take us two minutes." Martin smiled and Kate saw that to him this was just some crazy adventure, something to boast about afterward. It was different for her. She had been inside Mr. Spencer's head. She knew what was there.

"You promise you'll stay with me?" Kate said.

"I promise!"

"OK." There were games that afternoon and naturally the two of them were on different teams. "I'll meet you over by the toilets. At a quarter to four."

"I'll be there."

IX.

He wasn't there, of course. It should have been easy. But everything went wrong.

Later that day, Kate found herself watching the last of the children pour out of the school and into the waiting cars. After lunch, she had telephoned Heidi and told her that she was going to be late. Heidi had agreed to come at four-thirty. *"Halb funf."* Kate had translated it to be sure. She looked at her watch. It was already ten to four. But there was no sign of Martin.

There was a movement close by and she saw another of the boys, Sam Twivey, hurrying past, late as usual. She called out to him. "Sam?"

The other boy saw her and stopped.

"Have you seen Martin?"

"Didn't you hear? He got hurt playing football."

"What?"

"Someone kicked him in the . . . you-know-where. He got carried off. His mom came for him and he went home."

The boy looked away into the gloom. "My dad's here. I've got to go . . ."

So she was on her own.

The sensible thing, of course, would have been to have gone. To have left the school and gone home. It was dark and there were a few wisps of fog in the air, hanging across the road, a screen that cut her off from the world outside Brierly Hall. As far as she could tell, all the teachers had left. She was completely on her own. Heidi wouldn't be here for another twenty-five minutes. It was cold. She would be better off waiting inside . . . that was what she told herself. But even as she turned around and walked back into A Block, she knew what she was going to do. She had to find the knife.

She simply couldn't take any more. Waiting for French class, wondering what she was going to hear. She wanted the whole thing to be over with, and with or without Martin, she was going to do it now. Find the knife. Take it to the police. Tell them her story. Whether they believed her or not, they would have the evidence in front of them. They would have to act.

It was strange, walking through the school on her own. Normally the corridors would be full of movement and color, children hurtling from class to class, doors swinging open and shut. Empty, everything was different. The ceilings felt higher. The corridors felt longer. The photographs of teachers and old boys on the walls were suddenly ghostlike and Kate shivered. Many of these pictures had been taken decades ago. Many of the black-and-white faces watching her as she tiptoed back toward the staff room would indeed belong to the dead.

She reached a set of swinging doors. The emptiness

had made them bigger and heavier and she felt she was using all her strength to open them. It was as if they didn't want her to pass through. Something moved. She stopped and twisted around, expecting to see someone behind her, but there was nobody in the corridor. Just shadows creeping in on her from all sides.

This was stupid. This was a mistake. But it was too late. She was almost there. She might as well get it over with.

She opened the door of the staff room. Children were never allowed in here, not at any time, and Kate felt a twinge of guilt as she crossed the threshold and went in. The room was so shabby and untidy. Half the armchairs were worn out (a bit like some of the people who sat in them, she thought). She could smell cigarette smoke even though the principal was always lecturing them about the dangers of smoking. It was like going backstage during a magic show. Or peeking into the kitchen of a classy restaurant. This was a side of the school that Kate wasn't meant to see.

She went through as quickly as she could. The passage with the lockers was on the other side. It connected the staff room with another exit that was only used during fire drills. That was how Kate knew where the lockers were. She wished now that she had thought to bring a flashlight. There were only two windows and they were high up. The fog, pale and white, nuzzled against the glass. Little light came in.

Eighteen lockers, gnarled and wooden, stood shoulder to shoulder along one wall. Fourteen of them were in use. Each of these had a rectangle of white cardboard with a name written in black letters: ELLIS, THOMPSON, STANDRING, PRIESTMAN . . . Padlocks of different shapes and sizes, some with keys, some with combinations, fastened the doors. The four lockers at the very end of the corridor were unmarked. One of them had a broken hinge and a door hanging off at an angle. Spare lockers. This was what Mr. Spencer had been thinking about. This was where he had hidden the knife.

The first locker was empty. The second, the one with the broken door, contained a pile of moldy books. Kate opened the third locker and jerked back as a spider, brown and hairy, scurried out and across the floor. That just left one locker, the farthest one away. She reached out for the door and pulled it open. There was a bundle of what looked like old clothes thrown into the corner. Was there something wrapped inside? She reached in.

Her hearing aid exploded into life inside her ear.

A hand touched her shoulder.

"Are you looking for this?" Mr. Spencer said.

Kate jerked around and fell back against the wall, shock and disbelief coursing through her. The French teacher was hovering over her, his eyes glistening in the dim evening light, his lips drawn back. There was a kitchen knife in his hand.

"I wondered if you'd come," he whispered. "I couldn't be sure. In the classroom. But somehow I knew you'd found out. You knew about the knife! How did you do it, Kate? Can you read my mind?"

"I have to kill her . . ."

"Do you know what I'm thinking now?"

Kate tried to speak but the words wouldn't come. She couldn't move. Sheer terror had swept away all her strength. She forced herself to take a breath. "You killed your wife . . ."

Mr. Spencer nodded. He was sweating. She could see globs of perspiration on his forehead. A trickle of sweat snaked down the side of his face. When he spoke, his voice was low, the words tumbling out one after another. "Yes. I killed her. You're just a child. You don't understand. That woman! Always nagging me. I was never good enough for her. She never left me alone. Seventeen years of it! No children. No love. She enjoyed being cruel to me. But I couldn't divorce her. It was her house. Her money. She'd have taken everything. And every day, she went on and on and on at me. I hated her. And in the end I couldn't bear it anymore . . ."

"I have to kill her. She mustn't tell . . ."

Kate could hear what he was thinking. The words were as clear as the ones he was speaking. She had to distract him. Play for time. Keep him talking. Someone would come . . .

"Why did you hide the knife here?" she asked.

"I had to put it somewhere! The murder weapon. They're clever . . . the police. They'd know it was mine. I couldn't dump it. It would be found. So I hid it. Not in my locker. They looked there. I knew they would." He smiled. Saliva was flecking his lips, hanging in the tangle of his beard. "But in the old locker. Under those clothes. Nobody thought of that."

"Except you. Did you read my mind? Are you reading my mind now?"

"You can't do anything to me," Kate began.

"Yes, I can."

"I told lots of people about you. My mom and dad . . ."

"She's lying."

"If you hurt me, people will know . . ."

And then Kate saw it. Not words this time. Pictures. The horrible pictures that were inside Mr. Spencer's head. The knife stabbing forward. Going into her. He was going to kill her because he had decided he had no choice. She would disappear and maybe he would get away with it. What did it matter anyway? He was already a murderer. One more death would make no difference.

She saw his thoughts. She saw him draw back the knife a second before he actually did it. And that was what saved her. She screamed and threw herself forward, into him. He was caught off balance. Half a second later and the knife would have been swinging toward her, but she had been that half second ahead of him. Somehow Kate managed to scramble to her feet and then she was off, back down the corridor and into the staff room, knowing that Mr. Spencer was only inches behind.

"Come back! Kill her! Little brat! Die!"

The words shuddered through her hearing aid and

into her skull. Static howled and hissed. Blind with panic, Kate stumbled through the empty staff room, crashing into a table and almost losing her balance. Her hand flailed out and caught hold of an upright lamp, standing near the door. She jerked and pulled it down behind her. The lamp hit Mr. Spencer, the wire tangling around his feet. She heard him cry out and fall. And then she had reached the door. She slammed it behind her, wishing it had a key that she could turn. Without stopping to breathe, she headed off down the corridor, hurtling into the darkness of the deserted school.

She had gone the wrong way. She felt the wind on the back of her neck as the door crashed open behind her and knew that she should have headed back toward the exit and out into the street. Ahead of her was the dining room, the secretary's office, stairs going up to classrooms and down to the basement. Which way now? She threw open the door of the dining room. Long rows of empty tables stretched down with the hatchways into the kitchen beyond them. No. Not that way. She'd be trapped. She left the door open, thinking she could fool Mr. Spencer into thinking she'd gone in. Instead she took the stairs. Up or down? Down was faster. But that was a mistake too. The stairs led to the basement. Another dead end.

"Where is she? Where is she? Where is she?"

She could only just hear what he was thinking. He had slowed down. He must still be in the upstairs corridor.

"In here . . . ?"

Kate froze. Mr. Spencer was outside the dining room. He was looking in through the empty door. And maybe because the school was empty, maybe because there were no distractions, it wasn't just his thoughts that were being transmitted to her. She could also see with his eyes.

"Listen? Nothing! Is she in here? No. She wouldn't go in here. But she can't be far. Find her. Kill her. Cut her throat and bury her. No one will know."

Kate took a couple of steps forward.

She could see nothing. Nothing at all. She had only been in the basement once before . . . she had gone down there as a dare. She remembered a long, low-ceilinged room with archways leading off it, a bit like a wine cellar. There were machines. She could feel them humming now. A bank of electric generators on one side and a tangle of wires and pipes. It was very warm in the basement. There were heating systems too. She wanted to turn the light on but knew that she couldn't. That would bring him to her. And there was no way out.

Somewhere, above her, she heard a floorboard creak. No. She couldn't have heard it. But Mr. Spencer had. She was hearing with his ears! He had reached the stairs.

"Where is she? Did she go up? Upstairs . . ."

Another creak. He had taken the stairs. He was climbing up. Kate swayed in the darkness, almost faint with relief. But then he stopped.

"No! I'd have heard her! No carpet on the stairs. If she'd gone up, I'd have heard her. She must have gone down."

She heard him turn. Heard him come down.

Kate was petrified. In science class she'd once seen a bug, millions of years old, caught in a piece of amber. That was how she felt now. the inky darkness was crushing her. She couldn't breathe.

Squeak. Squeak. Squeak. The French teacher, wearing his new shoes, moved slowly down the stairs. Kate backed away. Her left hand touched a wall and there was a clink as her watch came into contact with something, metal against metal. The sound was tiny. But he'd heard it.

"She's here. Where's the light? I can't find the light. Wait . . ."

He found a switch outside in the corridor and turned it on. Yellow light spilled in through a doorway, only reaching halfway into the room. Kate squeezed herself backward. She was between two bulky machines. Thick cables pressed against her back. The air smelled of hot metal. She tried to make herself as small as she could. What was Mr. Spencer doing? Kate closed her eyes and concentrated.

Think!

And suddenly she was seeing what he was seeing. It was as if she were inside his head, looking through his eyes. She could see the knife that he was holding in his hand, the long, evil blade slicing through the air as he carried it ahead of him. She could see the narrow basement with the cables snaking along the walls. She could see a patch of dark shadow between two of the generators and knew, with sheer terror, that this was where she was hiding and that he was looking straight at her.

But did he know she was there? She could only see the pictures. She couldn't hear any words.

He began to walk toward her and for Kate it was as if she were watching herself on television. There was nothing she could do. She was about to be killed but at the same time she was the killer, watching with his eyes. She couldn't scream. She couldn't run. She could only wait.

He stopped in front of her. But she knew he hadn't seen her because she couldn't see herself. He was hesitating, uncertain. If she was going to do anything, she would have to do it now.

Kate screamed and lashed out with her foot, kicking Mr. Spencer with all her strength.

Mr. Spencer swung with the knife. And now Kate felt the movement. She felt the signal from the brain to the hand. She knew what he was going to do at the very second he decided to do it.

She dived down. The knife missed her.

And then there was a brilliant flash. A scream. Sparks exploded all around her and the link between her and the French teacher was ripped apart. The knife had gone over Kate's head and into one of the cables behind her. If she had been reading Mr. Spencer's mind at that moment, she would have known what it was like to be electrocuted. The teacher was still standing.

Electricity crackled and flared. A smell of burning filled the air. Then there was a bang as the generator short-circuited and he toppled to one side.

Sobbing, Kate dragged herself to her feet and, half-blind, with smoke in her eyes and the smell in her nostrils and a scream still trapped in her throat, she staggered out of the room.

Her hearing aid had been knocked out of her ear. Automatically, she pressed it back in again. It was silent. She could hear nothing. It was finally over.

X.

Nobody ever found out what happened that night.

Heidi was the only person who saw Kate when she staggered out, pale and trembling, from the empty school. Of course she was worried. Kate didn't say a word as the two of them drove home. She sat hunched up in the backseat of the Nissan, her arms crossed and her hands clutching her shoulders. Looking in the rearview mirror, Heidi could see that she was crying. When they got home, the German au pair wanted to call a doctor but she let Kate dissuade her. After all, her English was so poor. And she had already decided to return to Heidelberg. She didn't want any trouble.

Kate dealt with it her own way. She didn't sleep that night, or for many nights to come. But she had decided not to tell anyone about her involvement in Mr. Spencer's death. There were too many difficult questions. All her life she had battled against the idea of being thought different. If the truth came out, she knew people would treat her like a freak. She didn't even tell Martin what had happened. When he asked, a few days later, she told him that when he had failed to show up outside the school, she had left too.

Nobody ever found out.

Brierly Hall was closed for three days after Mr. Spencer's rigid, blackened body was discovered by the school janitor in the generator room. In that time, Kate was able to recover. And the police were able to begin their investigations—even if this was one mystery they soon decided they were never going to solve.

They must have realized that Mr. Spencer had, after all, killed his wife. How else could they explain the fact that the murder weapon had at last been found—still gripped in the dead man's hand? But they never managed to explain what he had been doing in the basement—or why he had plunged that same knife into the main power cable in what looked like a bizarre form of suicide.

The police examined everything. They asked questions. They examined everything again. And eventually they went away. Nobody at the school ever heard anything more. Presumably the case was shuffled away into some filing cabinet marked UNSOLVED.

Meanwhile, Mr. Spencer was buried at St. Mary's Church, Harrow-on-the-Hill. At the last minute, it was decided that the school should send a small deputation. Two teachers and three children would attend the funeral, as a sign of respect. Mr. Fellner, the principal, asked for volunteers at morning assembly, and to her own surprise, Kate found herself raising her hand. She didn't want to go. She wanted to forget all about him. But at the same time, it seemed somehow right that she should be there. A final curtain. A chance to say good-bye forever.

And that was how she found herself on a brilliant winter's day, standing in a cemetery with Martin at her side and Mr. Fellner wrapped in a thick black coat just behind her. The sun was shining but there was a deep chill in the air and the ground was icy hard. Martin was shivering, stamping his feet and wondering why on earth he was there. There were only a handful of mourners clustered around the open grave. Kate noticed the detective among them. The last time she had seen his face, it had been on TV.

A bell began to toll and four men in dark suits appeared, walking out of the church with the coffin stretched out on their shoulders. Kate looked away, wishing more than ever that she hadn't come. A rosy-faced vicar led the way, his prayer book clutched against his chest. A blackbird dropped out of the sky and perched on a gravestone as if interested in what was taking place.

The coffin drew closer. Dark brown oak with brass handles.

"Ashes to ashes . . ." the vicar began.

Kate's hearing aid crackled.

And then the voice.

"I'll come back. I'll get you one day . . ."

And Kate began to scream.

Burned

July 10

Three weeks in Barbados. A fancy hotel on the beach. Surfing, sailing, and waterskiing. All expenses paid. It sounds like the star prize on a TV game show and I suppose I ought to be over the moon. Or over the Caribbean anyway. But here's the bad news. I'm going with Uncle Nigel and Aunt Sara.

Mom told me this morning. The new baby is due in the middle of August and she's not going anywhere. There's no question of Dad going anywhere without her. He's gone completely baby mad. If he spends any more time in Baby Gap they'll probably give him a job there. The point is, if I don't go with Nigel and Sara, I'm not going to get a summer vacation and Mom thinks it would be easier for everyone if I was out of the way. This is what comes of having another baby thirteen years after the last one. The last one, of course, was me.

A Note on Sara Howard

She's quite a bit older than Mom and looks it. Forty-something? She's fighting a battle with old age and I'm afraid she's not on the winning side. Gray hair, glasses, a slightly pinched face. She never smiles very much, although Mom says she was a hoot when she was young. She has small, dark eyes that give nothing away. Dad says she's sly. It's certainly true that you can never tell what she's thinking.

She has no children of her own and Mom said she was happy to take me with her to Barbados but I know this is not true. I overhead them talking last night.

SARA: I'm sorry, Susan. I can't take him. The thing is, I have plans.
MOM: But Tim won't get a vacation if you don't help out, Sara. He'll be as good as gold and we'll pay his way . . .
SARA: It's not a question of money . . .
MOM: You said you wanted to help.
SARA: I know. But . . .

And so on. I wondered why she was being so difficult. Maybe she just wanted to be on her own with Uncle Nigel.

A Note on Nigel Howard

I don't like him. That's the truth. First of all, he's such an awkward, ugly man that I feel embarrassed just being with him. He's tall, thin, and bald. He has a round, pale face, no chin, but a very long neck. He reminds me of a diseased ostrich. All his clothes came from Marks & Spencer and none of them fit. He's the headmaster of a small private school in Wimbledon and he never lets you forget it. All in all, he has the same effect on me as five fingernails scratching down a blackboard. I wonder why Sara married him?

August 12

Stayed last night in N&S's house in West London. A Victorian terrace with rising fog. Cases packed and in the hall. We're waiting for the taxi that hasn't arrived. My uncle and aunt had quite an argument about it. He blamed her for not calling the firm that he always uses.

NIGEL: Speedway is much more reliable. Why didn't you call Speedway?
SARA: Because you're always telling me they're too expensive.

NIGEL: For God's sake, woman! How much do you think it's going to cost us if we miss the plane?

Then they argued about the packing. It turns out that Uncle Nigel is absolutely determined to get a suntan. I wouldn't have said this was possible as he has pale, rather clammy skin that looks as if it's never even seen the sun. Dad once told me that his nickname at the school where he teaches is Porridge . . . which is, I'm afraid, more or less his color. Anyway, Nigel wanted to be certain that Sara had packed his suntan oil and in the end she was forced to open the case and show him.

He had six bottles of the stuff! He had those bottles that come locked together with different sun-protection factors. The higher the factor number, the greater the protection. He had oil to go on first thing in the morning and more oil for last thing at night. He had water-resistant oil, hypoallergenic oil and UVA-protective oil. But he still wasn't satisfied. "Have you opened this?" he asked, taking out one of the bottles. "Of course I haven't opened it, dear," Sara said. She put the bottle back in the case and closed it up again.

The taxi has just arrived. Uncle Nigel was so angry about how late it was that he smashed a vase in the hall. It was the vase Mom gave to Aunt Sara for her birthday. She's sweeping up the pieces now.

August 15
Things are looking up.

Barbados is a really ace place. Palm trees everywhere and sea so blue it's dazzling. When you go swimming you see fishes that come in every shape and color and the night is filled with steel drums and the smell of rum. The beaches go on forever and it's boiling hot, at least ninety. Our hotel is on the west side of the island, near Sandy Lane Bay. It's small and modern but right on the beach and friendly and there are other boys of my age staying here so I'm not going to be on my own.

Anyway, N&S have more or less forgotten me, which suits me fine. Sara has spent the last two days by the pool, under a big sun umbrella, reading the latest Stephen King. Nigel doesn't like Stephen King. He gave us a long lecture over dinner about how horror stories are unhealthy and pander to people's basest instincts . . . whatever that means. Apparently he banned Goosebumps from his school.

He's bagged a sun lounger out on the beach and he spent the whole day out there, lying on his back in his baggy Marks & Spencer swimming trunks. He made Sara rub Factor 16 all over him and I could tell she didn't much enjoy it. Without his clothes on, Nigel manages to be scrawny and plump at the same time. He has no muscles at all and his little potbelly hangs over the waistband of his trunks. He has a thin coating of ginger hair. I suppose he must have been ginger before he went bald. I watched Sara sliding her hands over his chest and shoulders, spreading the oil, and I could see the look on her face. It was as if she was trying not to be sick.

While she read and he sunbathed, I went out with Cassian, who's thirteen and who's here with his family for two weeks. They come from Crouch End, which isn't too far from where I live. We went swimming and snorkeling. Then we played tennis on the hotel court. Cassian's going to ask his mom and dad if we can hire a Jet Ski tomorrow but he says they'll probably only pay for a pedalo.

Dinner at the hotel. Uncle Nigel complained about the service and Sara asked him to keep his voice down because everyone was listening. I thought they were going to argue again but fortunately he was in a good mood. He was wearing a white polo shirt, showing off his arms. He says that he's got a good foundation for his tan. I've noticed that whenever he passes a mirror he stops and looks at himself in it. He's obviously pleased, although if you ask me, he's looking rather red.

He says that tomorrow he's going to move down to Factor 9.

August 16
Uncle Nigel has burned himself.

He didn't say as much but it's pretty obvious. We had lunch in a café on the beach and I could see that his skin was an angry red around his neck and in the fleshy part of his legs. He also winced slightly when he sat down, so his back is probably bad too. Sara said she'd go into Bridgetown and buy some calamine lotion for him but he told her that he was perfectly all right and didn't need it.

But he did say he'd move back to using Factor 16.

It's very strange, this business of the tan. I don't quite understand what Uncle Nigel is trying to prove. Sara told me (while he was in the toilet) that it's the same every year. Whenever he goes on vacation he smothers himself in oil and lies rigidly out in the open sun but he never has much success. I suppose his obsession must have something to do with his age. A lot of parents are the same. They get into their forties and off they go to the gym three times a week, pushing and pedaling and punishing themselves as they try to put a bit of shape back into their sagging bodies. Uncle Nigel's body is beyond hope as far as muscles are concerned. But at least he can give himself a bit of color. He wants to go back to school bronzed and healthy. Perhaps for one semester they'll stop calling him Porridge.

They didn't let me hire a Jet Ski even though it's my own money. Mom and Dad gave me a hundred dollars to spend. So Cassian and I went for a walk and then played football with some local kids we met. Before we left, I saw Nigel, stretched out in his usual place. He was reading *A Tale of Two Cities* by Charles Dickens but the oil and sweat were dripping off his fingers and blotching the pages. He also had the sun in his eyes and was having to squint horribly to read the words. But he won't wear sunglasses. He doesn't want them to spoil his tan.

Got back to the hotel at six o'clock. Uncle Nigel was taking a shower by the pool. I could see that he'd fallen asleep in the sun. He was very red. At the same time, he must have left the Dickens novel leaning against him when he dropped off because there was a great rectangle on his stomach—the same size as a paperback book—which was as white as ever. The sun lounger had also made a wickerwork pattern on his back.

I waved to him and asked him how he was. He said he had a headache. He also had a heat blister on one cheek.

August 17

Cassian's parents took me out for the day. We drove in an open-top jeep through the center of the island. Lots of sugarcane and old plantation houses that make you think of pirates and slaves. We visited a cave. We had to wear plastic hats for protection and a trolley took us deep down into the ground, through amazing caverns with petrified waterfalls, stalagmites, and stalactites. I can never remember which is which. Cassian's dad is a writer. His mom is some sort of TV producer. The two of them didn't argue, which was a change.

I was sort of dreading getting back to the hotel, wondering about N&S. No surprises there. He was still out on his sun lounger and Sara was sitting next to him, reminding him to turn over every half hour . . . like a chicken on a spit. She told me that he had decided he would be all right with Factor 9 again but I wouldn't have agreed. His shoulders were badly burned and there were two more blisters on his nose.

She rubbed in some more oil for him. I was surprised at how horrible it smelled. It's yellow and it oozes out of the bottle, rippling between her fingers as she rubs it in. Disgusting.

I've been out in the sun a lot myself but I'm being careful. I wear a T-shirt with wide sleeves and a Bart Simpson baseball cap. I've got my own suntan lotion too. If you ask me, Uncle Nigel is out of his mind. Hasn't he heard of skin cancer?

August 19

He's got a tan! It's not exactly a Mr. Universe shade of bronze but he's definitely brown from head to toe. There are one or two areas where the skin is still a bit red, under his arms and on the very top of his head, but he says they'll soon blend in with the rest of him. He was in a really good mood this afternoon and even said that perhaps I can go on a Jet Ski after all.

It rained for the first time this afternoon. The rain out

here is strange. One moment it's blazing sunlight and the next it's just bucketing down and everyone has to run for cover. But it's not like English rain. The water is softer. It's like standing in a warm shower. And it's over as quickly as it started, as if someone threw a switch.

Sara took me on the bus to Bridgetown, leaving Nigel on the beach (Factor 4). We walked around the port, which was a jumble of sailing boats and huge, fat cruisers. She looked into chartering a boat for the day but when she found out the price she soon forgot that idea. Nigel would never agree to pay, she said, and at the same time she sort of sighed. So I asked her something I'd always wondered. "Why did you marry Uncle Nigel?" I asked. "Oh," she said. "He was very different when he was young. And so was I. I thought we'd be happy together."

We went to a bar down on the dock. Sara bought me an ice cream. For herself she ordered a large rum punch even though it was only half past three in the afternoon. She made me promise not to tell Uncle Nigel.

August 21
Bad news. Uncle Nigel has completely peeled. So now he's back to square one.

August 22

Uncle Nigel spent the entire day (eight hours) on the beach but it looks as if his new skin is refusing to tan. He has moved down to sun protection Factor 2.

He and Sara had an unpleasant argument yesterday . . . the day he lost his tan. Apparently, when they woke up, the sheets were covered with bits of brown. At first Sara thought it was mold or something that had flaked off the ceiling. But it was actually dead skin. She said it made her feel sick and Nigel just blew up at her. You could hear their voices down the corridor.

I saw Nigel stripping down on the beach. There was a bright pink strip going from his neck to his belly as if someone had been trying to unwrap him in a hurry. This was where the old skin had fallen away. But new skin had already grown to take its place. As for the rest of his tanned skin, it was obvious that he was going to lose that too. It was already muddy and unhealthy. He couldn't move without a bit flaking off. He was doing what he could to save it. I noticed that he'd brought down a big bottle of After Sun and he was rubbing that in as if he thought it would somehow stick him back together again. I didn't think it would work.

I went out again with Cassian and also with his older brother, Nick. I told them about Uncle Nigel and they both thought it was very funny. Nick told me that in Victorian times nobody wanted to have a suntan. It was considered socially inferior. This is something he learned at school.

When I got back to the hotel, Uncle Nigel was still lying there with Aunt Sara just a few yards away, sitting with her Stephen King under an umbrella. The book must have been amusing her because there was a definite smile on her face.

As for my uncle, I think the whole situation is getting out of control. His new skin isn't tanning. But it is burning. It's already turned a virulent shade of crimson. Unlike me, he hasn't been wearing a hat and a large heat bubble has formed in the middle of his head. It's like one of those white blobs you see in cartoons when Jerry hits Tom with a hammer. All the other hotel guests have begun to avoid him. You can see, when they walk down to the sea. They make a circle so they don't have to get too close.

I notice, incidentally, that he's still reading *A Tale of Two Cities*. But we've been here now for almost two weeks and he's still only on page twelve.

August 25

Cassian and Nick left today and the hotel feels empty without them. Another family arrived . . . three girls! To be honest, I'm beginning to look forward to going home. No news from Mom. She still hasn't had the baby. I miss her. And I'm really worried about Uncle Nigel.

All his old skin has gone now. It's either fallen off or it's been taken over by the new skin, which is a sort of mottled mauve and has a life of its own. His whole body is covered in boils like tiny volcanoes. These actually burst in the hot sun . . . I swear I'm not making it up. They burst and yellow pus oozes out. You can actually see it. Every ten minutes he seems to have another boil somewhere on his skin. There are also lots more sores on his face. They run down the side of his cheeks and onto his neck. If he had a chin I'm sure that would be covered in sores too.

And he's still trying to get a tan! This afternoon I'd had enough. I don't often talk to Uncle Nigel. For some reason I always seem to irritate him. But I did try telling him that he looked, frankly, horrible, and that I was really worried about him. I should have saved my breath! He almost chewed my head off, using the sort of language you wouldn't expect to hear coming from a headmaster. So then I tried to tell Aunt Sara what I thought.

ME: Aunt Sara, aren't you going to do something?
SARA: What do you mean?
ME: Uncle Nigel! He looks awful . . .
SARA: *(with a sigh)* What can I do, Tim? I'm afraid your uncle has never listened to me. Not ever. And he's determined to get this tan.
ME: But he's killing himself.
SARA: I think you're exaggerating, dear. He'll be fine.

But he isn't fine. Dinner tonight was the most embarrassing night of my life.

We went to a fancy restaurant. It should have been beautiful. The tables were outdoors, spread over two terraces. We sat with paper lanterns hanging over us and the silver waves almost lapping at our feet. Nigel walked very stiffly, like a robot. You could tell that his clothes were rubbing against his damaged skin and to him they must have felt like sandpaper.

He didn't make much sense over dinner. He ranted on about a boy called Charlie Meyer who obviously went to his school and who, equally obviously, was no favorite of his. He was still using a lot of four-letter words and I could see the other diners glancing around. One of the waiters came to see what the matter was and suddenly Uncle Nigel was violently sick! All over himself!

We left at once. Uncle Nigel groaned as we bundled him into a taxi. I could feel his skin under his shirt. It was damp and slimy. Aunt Sara didn't say anything until we got back to the hotel. Then . . . "You can order from room service, Tim. And you'll have to put yourself to bed."

"What about Uncle Nigel?"

"I'll look after him!"

August 27

Uncle Nigel is no longer able to talk. Even if he could construct a sentence anyone could understand, he would be unable to say it, since he has now managed to burn his lips so badly that they've turned black and shriveled up. What was left of his hair has fallen out and his new skin has shrunk and torn so that you can actually see areas of his skull. I think he has also gone blind in one eye.

The hotel manager, Mr. Jenson, has banned him from the beach as the other guests had finally complained. Mr. Jenson had a meeting with my aunt and me. He said that in his opinion my uncle shouldn't be sunbathing anymore.

JENSON: Forgive me, Mrs. Howard. But I think this is a very unhealthy situation . . .
SARA: I have tried to stop him, Mr. Jenson. This morning I even locked him in the bathroom. But he managed to force open the window and climb down the drainpipe.
JENSON: Perhaps we should call for a doctor?
SARA: I'm sure that's not necessary . . .

She said she'd been trying to stop him but I'm not sure that's true. She was still rubbing oil into him every morning and evening. I'd seen her. But I didn't say anything.

I am beginning to feel very uneasy about all this.

August 28
Yesterday evening, Ungle Nigel ran away.

He had another argument with Aunt Sara. I heard

vague, muffled shouts and then the slamming of the door. When I looked out of the window—the sun was just beginning to set—I saw him race out of the hotel, staggering toward the beach. He could hardly stand up straight. He was wearing shorts and nothing else and he was completely unrecognizable. He had no skin at all. His eyes bulged out of his skull and his lips had shrunk back to reveal not just his teeth but his gums. Every step he took, he moaned. At one point he staggered and fell back against the hotel wall. One of the guests saw him and actually screamed.

This morning he was gone. But he had left a bloody imprint of himself on the wall.

August 30

I can't help but feel that Aunt Sara is completely different. There has been no news of Ungle Nigel and he hasn't been seen for two days but she hasn't been worried. She has been drinking a lot of rum. Last night she got drunk and ended up dancing with one of the waiters.

I can't wait to get home. I spoke to Mom this morning. It seems I have a baby sister. They're going to call her Lucy.

Mom asked me about the trip. I told her about the island and about the family I met but I decided not to say anything about Ungle Nigel.

August 31
Ungle Nigel is dead!

Some fishermen found him yesterday, lying flat on the beach. At first they thought he must have been eaten up and spit out by sharks. His whole body was a mass of oozing sores, gashes, and poisoned flesh. He no longer had any eyes. What had happened was that he had fallen asleep again in the sun. And this time he hadn't woken up.

The only way they were able to recognize him was by his Marks & Spencer shorts.

Aunt Sara didn't even sound surprised when they told her. She just said, "Oh."

And I thought I saw her smile.

September 2
Back in England. Thank goodness.

Mom and Dad were supposed to meet me at Heathrow Airport but as it turned out there was one last, nasty surprise waiting for me when we finally landed. It turned out that my new sister, Lucy, had caught some sort of virus. It wasn't anything very serious—just one of the things that newborn babies often get—but she'd had to go back to the hospital for the night and Mom and Dad were with her. Sara's name was called out over the intercom and we lugged our cases over to the information desk, where we were given the news. I was going to have to stay at her house—just for the night. Mom and Dad would come and pick me up in the morning.

So it was back to Fulham and the Victorian terrace. I have to say that I walked in with a certain feeling of dread. It was Sara's house now, of course. But it had once been Nigel's and I could still feel him in there. It wasn't just his ghost. In a way it was worse than that. The drab wallpaper and the shelves stuffed with fat, serious books. The old-fashioned furniture, the heavy curtains blotting out the light, the damp smell. It was as if his spirit was everywhere. He was dead. But while we were in the house, his memory lived on.

Aunt Sara must have felt it too. Before she'd even unpacked, she called a real estate agent and told him that she wanted to put the house on the market immediately. She said she planned to emigrate to Florida.

We had supper together—Chinese takeout—but neither of us ate very much and we hardly talked at all. She wanted to be alone. I could tell. In a funny way, she seemed almost suspicious of me. I noticed her glancing at me once or twice as if she was worried about something. It was as if she was waiting for me to blame her for Nigel's death. But it hadn't been her fault. She hadn't done anything wrong.

Had she?

I went to bed early that night. In the spare room. But I couldn't sleep.

I found myself thinking about everything that had happened. Over and over again the pieces went through my mind until a picture began to form. I rolled over and tried to think of something else. But I couldn't. Because what I was seeing now, what I should have seen all along, was so horribly obvious.

"I have plans . . ."

That's what Sara had told my mom before we left for vacation. She hadn't wanted me to come from the very start. It was almost as if she had known what was going to happen and hadn't wanted me to be there, as a witness. She hadn't made Uncle Nigel lie in the sun, but now that I thought about it, she had never actually discouraged him either. And his death hadn't upset her at all. She'd been drinking rum and dancing with the waiters before they'd even discovered the corpse.

No! It was crazy! After all, she *had* packed all those bottles, the different suntan lotions. She'd even rubbed them in for him. As I lay in the darkness, I remembered the yellow ooze spilling out of the bottle, rippling through her fingers as she massaged his back. Once again I smelled it—thick and greasy—and at the same time I remembered something Nigel had said just before we'd left. He'd been examining one of the bottles and he'd said:

"Have you opened this?"

Maybe that was what made me get up. I couldn't sleep anyway, so I got up and went downstairs. I don't know why I tiptoed but I did. And there was Aunt Sara, standing in the kitchen, humming to herself.

She was surrounded by bottles. I recognized them at once. Factor 15, Factor 9, and Factor 4. The water-resistant oil, the hypoallergenic oil, and all the other oil. The Before Sun and the After Sun protection. She was emptying them, one at a time, into a large green tin. And no matter what it said on the labels, it was the same gold-colored oil that poured into the tin and I guessed that this was where the oil had really come from in the first place.

QUIKCOOK VEGETABLE OIL—FOR
FASTER FRYING

Big red letters on the side of the tin. My aunt continued emptying the bottles, getting rid of the evidence. I crept back to bed and counted the hours until my parents finally came.

Flight
715

There are some nightmares so horrible that even when you wake up they won't quite go away. You lie in bed with the gray light of the morning beating at the window and even though you're in your own bed, in your own room, you still wonder. Because the creatures of your dreams, the ghosts and the monsters are still with you, hiding in the shadows, just out of sight. And maybe you lie there for five minutes, for ten minutes, thinking about it, wondering. But finally you convince yourself—you have to. It was only a dream.

Judith Fletcher had just such a dream on the last day of her vacation in Canada and even as her parents slept on in their room and her younger sister, Maggie, snored noisily in the bed next to her, she lay there and remembered.

This was her dream.

She was at a funeral. There was something wrong with the cemetery. It was far too big and the grass simply didn't look like grass. It was as flat as cardboard and that strange color that you only see in dreams; a green-silver-gray that had no name. There was a church bell ringing and, in the distance, a clock showing three minutes past six. Judith didn't walk into the cemetery. She was carried, lifted by unseen hands. It was only as she floated toward a single grave, a black rectangle that seemed to have been cut out rather than dug, that she felt the first wave of terror. This wasn't any funeral. This was hers.

She tried to wake up but sleep had become a prison. She tried to scream but only the faintest whisper escaped her lips.

And then she saw the mourners. There were about three hundred of them, standing around the grave, none of them speaking. Even though she was asleep, it struck her as curious that none of them had dressed for the funeral. They were wearing their everyday clothes, watching her with empty, blank faces. Most of them were carrying suitcases. Some had duty-free bags.

There was a fat woman with big eyes and a shock of curling hair. A little boy holding a teddy bear that was missing an arm. A sullen-faced husband and wife, holding hands, not talking to each other. A black man in a leather jacket, biting his fingernails. Later on, she would remember every one of them as if she had known them all her life, even though she was certain she had never seen them before.

And then there was the vicar. At least, Judith assumed he was the vicar as he seemed to be in charge. But at the same time she was aware that the man wasn't wearing church clothes; indeed, he seemed to be dressed in some sort of uniform. He was a thin man with long, fair hair. His nose had been broken at some time and there was a thin scar running down his cheek. He was standing alone, nearest the grave, and as Judith arrived he said four words.

"Flight Seven One Five."

The invisible hands lowered Judith into the grave. Darkness rushed in on her. And that was when the nightmare became unbearable, when she struggled with all her being to break free. She couldn't breathe. She had never known such utter blackness. It seemed to be not just outside her but inside too, at the back of her eyes, in her throat, reaching to the pit of her stomach. She was falling into it, endlessly falling. The tiny rectangle of light that had been the entrance to the grave was now a mile away. At the same time she was aware of two distinct sounds; first a huge explosion, then the scream of ambulances that grew louder and louder until she couldn't take any more.

She woke up.

She wasn't dead. She was alive and lying in a rented apartment in Vancouver. Her name was Judith Fletcher and she was thirteen years old. Her father, an architect, had been appointed to work on a new hotel complex in the city and he had taken the opportunity to bring the whole family over to travel around Canada. That was where they had been for the past three weeks. And today they were due to fly back to London.

On Flight 715.

Judith got up, went into the bathroom, and splashed cold water over her head. She looked into the mirror. Two blue eyes set in a round, freckled face, with fair hair hanging long on each side, looked back. In the bedroom, she heard Maggie wake up and call out for her. That was Maggie through and through. The only time her eight-year-old sister ever stopped talking was when she was asleep. But Judith ignored her. She had to think.

She knew it had just been a dream, a horrible dream. But at the same time she was certain that it was something more. It had all been so real. She had dreamed before, but never in such detail. And no dream had stayed with her the way that this one had. She could still remember everything. And even as the water trickled down her cheeks and dripped off her chin, she realized that this dream had one other difference too. She knew what it meant.

It couldn't have been simpler. She was going to die. At three minutes past six . . . that was the time she had seen on the clock. She even knew how she was going to die. The vicar-who-wasn't-a-vicar had told her.

Flight 715.

The plane was going to crash.

Judith wasn't superstitious. She didn't believe in ghosts, witches, UFOs, telepathy . . . or any of the other things that the boys at school were always talking about. She had watched one or two episodes of *The X-Files* but the stories hadn't interested her simply because she couldn't take them seriously. Just because something couldn't be explained, that didn't make it supernatural. There was no such thing as the supernatural. That was what she had always thought.

Until now.

Now she remembered—there was a word for what she had experienced. Clairvoyance. There were people who dreamed things that were going to happen, things that did happen. They were called clairvoyants. And they weren't all weirdos either. Judith's history teacher had once said that Joan of Arc was a clairvoyant. So was the American president Abraham Lincoln, who had actually dreamed of his own assassination a week before it happened! A writer—Mark Twain—had dreamed of the death of his brother. There was even some guy who had described the sinking of the *Titanic* in every detail . . . fourteen years before it had happened.

The dream had changed everything. Because she knew in her heart that it hadn't simply been a dream. It had been something altogether more frightening. A warning. It didn't matter what she believed or what she didn't believe. She couldn't ignore what she had seen.

She left the bathroom and went back into her bedroom to get dressed. Sweatshirt, jeans, sneakers, and baseball cap. Her parents were also awake and had quickly fallen into the chaos of last-minute packing.

"Where are the tickets?" she heard her dad call out from the other room.

"By the bed." That was her mom. Sandra Fletcher worked as a hospital administrator. She had taken unpaid leave in order to make the trip.

And in a few hours' time, the four of them would be boarding a plane, Flight 715 to London, and they would all die. At three minutes past six (the plane was due to land at a quarter past six in the morning) something would go horribly wrong and . . .

"Do you want some breakfast, girls?"

Mark Fletcher had poked his head through the door, breaking off Judith's thoughts. He was a fit, athletic man in his early forties, just a few streaks of gray in his hair.

"I'm starving!" Maggie was standing on her bed. Now she began to jump up and down, her pigtails flying. She's excited about the flight, Judith thought.

The flight . . .

She said nothing while Sandra served up their last Canadian breakfast: waffles and crisped-up bacon with maple syrup. There were cases everywhere. The family had taken so much luggage with them that they had almost been charged extra at Heathrow and since then they'd added more than a few pounds of souvenirs, clothes, and—ever since the girls had found they were half price in Canada—Rollerblades and CDs. Her mother pushed a plate in front of her but she ignored it. She had been frightened by what had happened. But she was almost as frightened at the thought of what she now had to do.

"What's the matter, Judith?" Mark Fletcher had noticed the look on his daughter's face.

"I'm not going home." And there it was. She'd done it, said it. As easy as that.

Mark laughed. "Thinking about school, are you?"

"Vacations have to end sometime, Judith," her mother said.

"No." Judith's face was almost expressionless. "I'm not going on the plane."

Her parents exchanged a look, a little puzzled now.

"What do you mean?" her father asked.

"She's scared!" Maggie giggled and dipped her finger into the maple syrup, drawing a circle on her plate.

"The plane's going to crash," Judith said. "I'm not going on it. None of us are."

Sandra had been holding a mug of coffee. She put it down. "What are you talking about, darling?" she said.

She sounded so reasonable but Judith knew she wouldn't be that way for long. "You've never been scared of flying."

"I'm not scared. I mean, I'm not scared of flying. But I'm not going on that flight. Seven One Five . . ."

Mark smiled, still trying not to take his daughter too seriously. "We can't change the tickets," he said. "You know that."

"We can buy new ones."

"Do you have any idea how much that would cost?"

"There's no question of buying new tickets!" Sandra exclaimed. "What is all this, Judith? Why are you being so silly?"

"I'm not being silly . . ." She had to tell them, even though she knew what they would say. "I had a dream."

"A dream!" Her mother relaxed. Judith saw she was relieved. A dream was something she could handle. It was something she understood. "We all have bad dreams," she said.

"It's only natural." Mark took over from his wife. "It's a long flight. Uncomfortable . . ."

"Airline food!"

"Yuck!" That was Maggie's contribution.

"Nobody enjoys flying," Mark went on. "But just because you have a bad dream about something doesn't mean anything's going to happen."

Judith felt a sudden sadness. She had never known her parents to be so predictable. "It wasn't an ordinary dream," she said. "It was different. I was in a cemetery—"

"We don't really need to hear about it," Sandra interrupted. She was a little bit angry now and somehow that was predictable too. "For heaven's sake! You're thirteen years old now, Judith. You know what dreams are!"

"You'll have forgotten it before we get to the airport," Mark said.

"I'm not going to the airport."

Mark and Sandra looked at each other again, suddenly helpless. Judith knew what they must be thinking. She had never behaved this way before. But she had never felt this way either. Even now, sitting with her breakfast in front of her and suitcases everywhere—everything so normal—she felt as if she were only half there. The other half was still trapped in the dream. And she knew. That was the worst of it. She knew with cold certainty that she was right, but that there was nothing she could do or say that would persuade them. Judith had never been more alone.

Her father tried another approach. Humor her. Reason with her. And if that doesn't work, get angry with her. *Practical Parenting for Difficult Daughters.* Chapter Three.

"This is ridiculous, Judith. Nothing's going to happen to the plane."

"You're just upsetting Maggie."

"Anyway, there's no point arguing about it. We're leaving on Flight 715 at midday. If you're really so childish that you're going to let a dream upset you, that's your problem."

"But what if I'm right, Dad?" Judith knew it was hopeless but she had to try one last time. "What if it wasn't a dream? What if it was . . . something more?"

"You don't believe that nonsense. You've never believed it."

"You've been watching too much television."

"You know, Judith, this is so stupid . . ."

And it was that last line, the scorn and the superiority in her father's voice, that convinced her. She had known what she was going to do, almost from the moment she had left the bathroom, but she had been unsure whether she would have the strength to do it. Now she acted without thinking. Suddenly she stood up. Then, before anyone could stop her, she pushed away from the table, jumped over one of the suitcases, and ran out of the room, slamming the door behind her.

"Judith . . . ?" her father called out. But even if he had guessed what Judith was planning, it was already too late.

Judith ran across the hall, her heart thudding so hard it made her ears ring. Without stopping, she reached the front door. It wasn't locked. Her hand was trembling as she turned the handle and opened it. And then she was out in the warm sunshine, running across the lawn and onto the pavement.

The sidewalk. That's what they call it in Canada.

It was a crazy thought. But it was all crazy. She was crazy. That was what her parents would think. Before they murdered her.

She would worry about that later. The apartment was on Robson Street in one of the busiest parts of Vancouver. In less than a minute Judith had been swallowed up by the crowd of morning commuters. Even if her parents had realized what she had done and followed her out, they would never find her.

She had been around the city only the day before and knew where she was going. She made her way down to the waterfront and found a snack bar with a view across the lake to the Burrard Inlet, with mountains and pine trees behind. She had ten dollars in her pocket. Enough for a few drinks. Enough to allow her to stay as long as she needed.

Judith Fletcher eased herself into a plastic chair, pulled her baseball cap down over her eyes—hiding herself from the world—and prepared to wait until the flight had left.

Her parents, of course, were furious when she slunk back to the apartment just before midday. She had never seen them so angry. Their anger almost made them ugly, twisting their faces, burning in their eyes.

"How could you, Judith? We've been looking everywhere for you!"

"We've been worried sick about you. A young girl out in the city on her own!"

"Do you know how much this is going to cost us?"

"Were you out of your mind?"

"When we get back to England, you are going to pay for this, young lady. I don't know how . . . But you're going to pay!"

Her father had never smacked her. Not once in her entire life. This time, Judith knew he had come close. Perhaps if she had been a boy it would have been easier. A quick whack with a slipper and the tension would have been released. Instead, her parents' anger slowly wore itself out and the rest of the day was spent in a silence as flat and as unforgiving as the cemetery of her dream. Mark Fletcher made a telephone call and managed to persuade the airline to take them—at no extra charge—on a flight the following day. That at least helped. The bags remained packed. Mark worked. Sandra went for a walk, bought a takeout lunch for them all (Judith didn't eat), and killed time.

The afternoon crept slowly on. Maggie watched television, then went out for a walk with her father. Sandra wrote a letter. Judith spent most of the time sitting by herself. She was ignored by everyone. Her parents were sullen. Maggie seemed completely baffled . . . as if her big sister had been taken over by someone else.

And all the time Judith thought about Flight 715. Where was it now? Crossing the Arctic Circle? Dipping south over the Atlantic? The strange thing was, even now she had no doubts. The plane was due to land at ten o'clock Canadian time and she still knew with a horrid, cold certainty that at that moment her parents would understand. The plane would crash. The dream had told her as much. She thought of the passengers. All of them would die. She could almost see the fireball of flame, hear the ambulances tearing across the runway as she had heard them that morning in bed. Now she was guilty. Shouldn't she have warned them too? Couldn't she have stopped the plane from taking off? No. She forced the thoughts out of her mind. She couldn't have done more than she had done. The rest was out of her control.

But at ten-fifteen her parents would understand. And then they would forgive her. Everything would be all right.

At five past ten her father got up and left the room. Maggie was already in bed but Mark and Sandra hadn't said a word to their other daughter and she knew that they had allowed her to stay up on purpose, that they wanted her to be with them now. Mark made the call from the hallway. Again, he didn't say what he was doing but Judith knew he was calling England.

She heard her father's voice, a low murmur on the other side of the door. Sandra was reading a paperback novel she had bought for the journey home. She flicked a page. There was a rattle, the sound of the telephone receiver being replaced. Mark Fletcher came back into the room.

He stood in the doorway. Judith waited for him to speak. And at last the words came.

"Flight 715 landed at Heathrow fifteen minutes ago. It was ahead of schedule. Now I'm going to bed."

Judith never knew.

Nor did her parents.

None of them ever found out.

Because they weren't at Heathrow, they didn't see the passengers come off the plane. There were about three hundred of them. Apart from the Fletchers' own empty seats, it had been a full flight.

The first person off the flight was a fat woman with large eyes and a shock of yellow hair. Then a young boy holding a teddy bear that was missing an arm. His parents were right behind him; a sullen-faced husband and wife, holding hands, not talking to each other. They were followed by a black man in a leather jacket. He was biting his fingernails. And so it went on . . .

The last person off the plane was the pilot. He was a thin man with long, untidy hair. Years ago he had been injured in a motorbike accident. There was a scar on his cheek and he had broken his nose. As he left the plane, he was looking tired and sick. His face was pale. He had been sweating. His shirt was still damp, sticking to his chest.

There were three officials waiting for him. "Are you all right?" one of them asked.

The pilot shook his head and said nothing.

But an hour later he told his story. The officials sat opposite him across a long table, taking notes.

"It was the plumbing system," he said. "It must have sprung a leak. God knows how many gallons of water there were swilling around down there. And then, of course, with the altitude, it froze. Ice is heavier than water . . . I don't need to tell you that. And it was heavy! I knew something was wrong . . . the way the plane was handling. But it was only when the flight attendant told me they couldn't flush the toilets in economy . . ."

He smiled but there was no humor in his face.

"Anyway, by then it was too late. There was nothing I could do. As you know, I radioed ahead. Got all the emergency vehicles waiting. I could just about fly but I wasn't sure I could land. Not with all that weight. It was a full flight." The pilot had opened a can of Coke. He drank it all in one gulp. "To tell you the truth," he went on, "if there had been one extra ham sandwich on that plane, I don't think we'd have made it."

"You were lucky," one of the officials said.

"You're right. I heard that there was a no-show at the last minute. A family of four and a ton of luggage."

"Why weren't they on the plane?" the official asked.

The two other officials shook their heads. "I've no idea," the pilot said. "But I'm glad they weren't. Because I'm telling you, I'm not exaggerating. If they'd been on that flight and we'd had that extra weight on board . . ." He crumpled up the can and looked at it for a moment, lying in the palm of his hand. "None of us would be here now," he said. "They saved us."

He threw the can into a wastepaper basket and quietly left the room.

Howard's End

Howard Blake didn't even see the bus that ran him over. Nor did he feel it. One minute he was running across Oxford Street with a stack of CDs in his hand and the clang of the alarm bell ringing in his ears and the next . . . nothing. That was the trouble with shoplifting of course. When you were caught, you just had to run and you couldn't stop at the edge of the street for such niceties as looking left and right. You just had to go for it. Howard had gone for it but unfortunately he hadn't made it. The bus had hit him halfway across the street. And here he was. Fifteen years old and already dead.

He opened his eyes.

"Blimey!" he croaked. "This isn't happening."

He closed them again, counted to ten, then slowly opened them, one at a time. There could be no doubt about it. Unless this was some sort of hallucination, he was no longer in London. He was . . .

"Oh blimey!" he whispered again.

He was still wearing the same black leather jacket, T-shirt, and jeans but he was sitting on a billowing white substance that looked suspiciously like a cloud. No. He couldn't pretend. It *was* a cloud. The air was warm and smelled of flowers and he could hear music, soft notes being plucked out on the strings of what he knew must be harps. About fifty feet away from him there was a pair of gates, solid gold, encrusted with dazzling white pearls. Light was pouring through the bars, making it hard to see what was on the other side. And there was something strange about the light. Although it looked very much like sunshine, the sky was actually dark. When Howard looked up he could see thousands of stars, set against a backdrop of the deepest, darkest blue. It seemed to be both night and day at the same time.

Howard was not alone. There was a line stretching back as far as he could see . . . stretching so far that even the people in the middle were no bigger than pinpricks. Looking at the ones who were closer to him, he saw that there were men and women from just about every country in the world and dressed in an extraordinary variety of clothes, from three-piece suits to saris, kimonos, and even Eskimo furs. A great many of them were old but there were also teenagers and even young children among them. They were waiting quietly, as if they had always expected to end up here and were cheerfully resigned now that they'd arrived.

But arrived where?

The answer, of course, was obvious. Howard had been to church only once in his life and that was to steal the silver candlesticks on the altar, but even he got the general idea. The line, the clouds, the harps, the pearly gates . . . it took him right back to Cross Street Comprehensive and religious education classes with Doris Witherspoon. So the old bat had been right after all! There *was* such a thing as heaven. The thought almost made him giggle. "Our Father who art in heaven . . ." How did the rest of the prayer go? He'd forgotten. But the point was, he'd always assumed that heaven and hell were just places they made up to scare you into being good. It was remarkable to discover that it was actually true.

He stood up, his feet sinking gently into the cloud, which shifted to take his weight. Howard was not particularly bright. He'd only been to school half a dozen times that year and had fully intended to stop altogether as soon as he turned sixteen, but now his brain began to grind into motion. He was in a line of people outside the gates of heaven. All the people were presumably dead. So it had to follow that he must be dead too. But how had it happened? He couldn't remember being murdered or anything like that. Had he been ill? It was true he'd smoked at least ten cigarettes a day for as long as he could remember, and his mother was always warning him he'd get cancer—but surely he'd have noticed if it had actually happened.

He thought back. That morning he'd woken up in his house in the development where he lived just out-side Watford. He'd eaten his breakfast, kicked the dog, sworn at his mother, and gone to school. Of course he hadn't actually arrived at the school. He'd missed so many days that the social workers had been around looking for him, but as usual he'd given them the slip. He'd gone into town. That's right. Cheated on the sub-way, buying a child's fare, then gone to the West End. He'd eaten a second breakfast in a greasy spoon, then gone to a little pool hall behind Goodge Street . . . the sort of place that didn't ask too many questions when he went in, and certainly not about his age. He'd thought of going to the new James Bond film but he had an hour to kill before it started, so he'd decided to do a little shoplifting instead. There were plenty of big stores on Oxford Street. The bigger the store, the easier the snatch. He'd slipped a couple of CDs under his jacket and was just picking out some more when he'd noticed the store detective closing in on him. So he'd run. And . . .

What had happened? Now that he thought about it, he had seen a blur of red out of the corner of his eye. There'd been a rush of wind and something had nudged his shoulder, very gently. And that was it. That was the last thing he remembered.

However he looked at it, there could only be one answer. He had been killed! No doubt about it! And . . .

The next thoughts came very quickly, all in a jumble.

Heaven exists. So hell exists. You don't want to go to hell. You want to go to heaven. But there's no way you're going to heaven, mate. Not with your record. Not unless you manage something pretty spectacular. You're going to have to pull the wool over their eyes good and proper and the sooner you get started . . .

Howard pushed his way into the line, stepping between a small Chinese man with the ivory hilt of a knife
protruding from his chest, and an old woman who was
still wearing her hospital identity bracelet.

"What are you doing?" the woman demanded.

"Get lost, Grandma," Howard replied. Even though
all the cigarettes had stunted his growth, Howard was
still thickset and muscular. He had a pale face, greasy
hair and dark, ugly eyes, which—along with his black
leather jacket and the silver studs in his ears, left cheek,
nose, and lip—made him look dangerous. He wasn't
the sort of person you argued with, even if you could
see that he was no longer alive. True to form, the old
lady fell silent.

The line shuffled forward. Now Howard could make
out a figure sitting on a sort of high stool beside the
gates. It was an ancient man with long white hair and
a tumbling beard. Dress him in red, Howard thought,
and you'd have a heavenly version of Santa Claus. But
in fact his robes were white. He was holding a large
book, a sort of ledger, and there was a bunch of keys
tied around his waist. The man turned briefly and
Howard was astonished to see two huge wings sprouting out of his back, the brilliant white feathers tapering

down behind him. There were two younger men with him and Howard realized with a shiver that he knew who—or at least what—they were. The keepers of the keys. The guardians at the gates of heaven. He threw his mind back, trying desperately to remember what Miss Witherspoon had said. What was the man with the keys called? Bob? Patrick? Percy? No—it was Peter! Saint Peter! That was it! That was the guy he had to persuade to let him in.

It took another hour but at last he reached the gates. By now, Howard had composed himself. He could see heaven in front of him. But he could imagine hell. He knew which he preferred.

"Name?" Saint Peter (it had to be him) asked.

"Howard," Howard replied. "Howard Blake, sir." He was pleased with the *sir*. He had to show respect. Butter the old fool up.

"How old are you, Howard?"

"I'm fifteen, sir." Howard tried to sound very young and innocent. He wished now that he had thought to remove all the silver pins from his face.

One of the younger angels leaned forward and whispered to Saint Peter. The old angel nodded. "You were killed on Oxford Street, this afternoon," he said.

"Yes, sir. I can't imagine what my old mom will say. It'll break her heart, I'm sure . . ."

"Why weren't you in school?"

Howard swallowed. If he told them he was playing hooky, he'd be done for. He had to think of something. "Well, sir . . ." he gurgled. "It was my mom's birthday. So I asked the teacher if I could take the afternoon to cop something for her . . . I mean, buy something for her. I wanted to buy her something nice. So I popped into town."

"Were you always kind to your mother, child?"

Howard remembered all the names he had called her that morning. He thought of the money he had stolen from her handbag. Sometimes he'd stolen the entire handbag too. "I tried to be a good boy," he said.

"And did you work hard at school?"

"Oh yes. School is very important. Religious education was always my favorite class. And I worked as hard as I could, sir."

"You look like a strong boy. I hope you never bullied anyone."

Images flashed in front of Howard's eyes. Glen Roven with a black eye. Robin Addison, crying, with a bleeding nose. Blake Ewing with a twisted arm, shouting while Howard stole his lunch money. "Oh, never, sir," he replied. "I hate bullies."

"Hatred is a sin, child."

"Is it? Well, I quite like bullies, really. I just don't like what they do!"

Howard was sweating, but the angel seemed content. He made a few notes in his book. He was using a feather pen, Howard noticed. He wondered if the angel had made it out of his own wing.

Saint Peter peered at him closely and for a moment Howard was forced to look away. The angel's eyes seemed to look right into him and even through him. He wondered how many thousands—how many millions of people those eyes had examined.

"Do you repent of your sins?" Saint Peter asked.

"Sins? I never sinned!" Howard felt his hand curling into a fist and quickly unclenched it. He somehow didn't think it would be a good idea to punch Saint Peter in the nose. "Well, maybe I forgot to feed the dog once or twice," he said. "And I didn't do my math homework one evening last June. I repent about that. But that's it, sir. There ain't nothing more."

There was a soft clunk and Howard noticed that one of the CDs he had been stealing had fallen out of his leather jacket. He glanced at it, blushing. "Hey! Look at that!" he said. "I wonder how that got there?" He picked it up and handed it to Saint Peter. "Would you like it, sir? It's Heavy Vomit. They're my favorite group."

Saint Peter took the CD, glanced at it briefly, then handed it to one of his aides. He smiled. "All right, my child," he said. "You may go through the gates."

"I may?" Howard was amazed.

"Enter!"

"Thanks a bunch, sir. God bless you and all the rest of it!"

He had done it! He could hardly believe it. He had smiled and simpered and called Saint Peter "sir" and the old geezer had actually bought it. And his reward was going to be heaven! Howard straightened his shoulders. Ahead of him, the gates opened. There was a swirl of music as a thousand harps came together in a billowing, flowing crescendo. The music seemed to scoop him up in its arms and carry him forward. At the same time he heard singing, like a heavenly choir. No! It *was* a heavenly choir, ten thousand voices, invisible and eternal, singing out in celestial stereo. The light danced in his eyes, washing through him. He walked on, noticing that his black leather jacket and jeans had fallen away to be replaced by his very own white robe and sandals. He passed through the gates and saw them swing gently shut behind him. There was a *click* and then it was over. The gates had closed. He was in!

The next few days passed very happily for Howard.

He floated along through a landscape of perfect white clouds where the sun never set, where it never rained, and where it was never too hot or too cold. Harp music and the soft chanting of hallelujahs filled the great silence. There wasn't any food or water but that didn't matter because he was never hungry or thirsty. It occurred to him that although there must have been millions and millions of people in heaven, the place was so vast that he didn't see many of them. He did pass a few people who waved at him and smiled pleasantly, but he ignored them. He was glad to be there with the other angels but that didn't mean he actually had to talk to them.

It was heaven. Sheer heaven.

The days became weeks and the weeks months. The harps continued to play soft, tinkling music that followed Howard everywhere. The truth was, he was getting a little bit fed up with the harps. Didn't they have drums or electric guitars in heaven? He was also a little sorry that heaven didn't have more color. White clouds and blue sky were all very well but after a while it was just a bit . . . repetitive.

He set out now to meet other people, deciding that, after all, he would probably enjoy the place more if he wasn't on his own. Certainly the angels were very friendly. Everybody smiled at him. They always seemed happy to see him. But at the same time they didn't have a whole lot to say beyond "Good morning!" and "How are you?" and (at least a hundred times a day) "God bless you!"

Despite the fact that everything was unquestionably perfect, Howard was getting bored and after he had been there for . . . well, it could have been a year or it could have been ten—it was hard to tell when nothing at all was really happening—he decided that he would purposefully pick a fight, just to see what happened.

He waited until he had found an angel smaller than himself (old habits die hard) and stumped over to him.

"You're very ugly!" he exclaimed.

"I'm sorry?" The angel had been sitting on a cloud doing nothing in particular. But then, of course, there was nothing particular to do.

"Your face makes me sick," Howard said.

"I do apologize," the angel replied. "I'll leave at once."

"Are you chicken?" Howard cried.

"Am I a chicken?"

"You're scared!"

"Yes. You're absolutely right."

The angel tried to leave and that was when Howard hit him, once, hard. The angel jerked back, surprised. Howard's fist had caught him square on the chin but there was no blood, no bruising. There wasn't even any pain. It took the angel a moment or two to realize what had happened. Then he gazed sadly at Howard. "I forgive you," he said.

"I don't want to be forgiven!" Howard exclaimed. "I want to have a fight."

"God bless you!" the angel said, and drifted away.

Another thousand years passed.

The harps were still playing. The clouds were still a perfect, whiter-than-white white. The sky was still blue. The weather hadn't changed, not even a little drizzle for just a minute or two. The choirs sang and the angels wandered along, smiling dreamily and blessing one another.

Howard was tearing his hair out. He had torn it out several times, in fact, but it always grew again. He kicked at a cloud and bit his lip as his foot passed right through it. He hadn't been ill, not once in all the time he had been here. He would have quite liked it really. A cough or a cold. Even a bout of malaria. Anything for a change. Nor had he found anyone to talk to. The other angels were all so . . . boring! Recently—about a hundred and twenty years ago—he had started talking to himself but he had already discovered that he also bored himself—and anyway he hated the sound of his own voice. He had been in a few more fights but they had all ended as disappointingly as the first and he had finally decided there was no point.

And then, quite by chance one day (he had no idea which day, and as there was no night he wasn't even sure if it *was* a day) he realized that he had somehow made his way back to where it had all begun. There were the pearly gates, and standing with his two helpers, there was Saint Peter, still dealing with the line that stretched to the horizon and beyond. With the first spurt of hope and excitement he had felt in centuries, Howard hurried forward, the sandals flapping on his feet, his white robes billowing around him.

"Excuse me!" he cried, interrupting Saint Peter as he talked to a man with a kilt but no legs. "Excuse me, sir!"

"Yes?" Saint Peter turned to him and smiled through the bars of the gate.

"You probably don't remember me. But my name is Howard . . . Howard, um . . ." Howard realized that he had forgotten his own surname. "I came here quite a long time ago."

"I remember perfectly well," Saint Peter said.

"Well. I have to tell you something!" Suddenly Howard was angry. He'd had enough. More than enough. "Everything I said when I came here was a lie. I didn't go to school and when I did go to school I bullied everyone, including the teachers. I kicked the cat— or maybe it was a dog. I hated my mom and she hated me. I lied and I cheated and I stole and I know I said I was sorry for what I'd done but I was lying then too because I'm not. I'm glad I did it. I enjoyed doing it."

"What are you trying to say?" Saint Peter asked.

"What I'm saying, you horrible old man, is that I don't like it here!" Howard was almost shouting now. "In fact I hate it here and I've decided I don't want to stay!"

"I'm afraid you have no choice," Saint Peter replied. "That decision is no longer yours."

"But you don't understand, you bearded twit!" Howard took a deep breath. "I'm all wrong for heaven. I shouldn't be in heaven. You should never have let me in."

The angel didn't speak. Howard stared at him. His face had changed. The beard had slipped, like something you buy at a novelty store. Underneath, the chin was pointed and seemed to be covered in what looked suspiciously like scales. And now that he looked more closely, Howard noticed that there was something poking through the old man's hair. Horns?

"Wait . . ." he began.

Saint Peter—or whoever, whatever he really was—began to laugh. Two red flames flickered in his eyes and his lips had drawn back to reveal teeth that were viciously sharp.

"My dear Howard," he said. "What on earth made you think you'd gone to heaven?"

The
Elevator

"Let's go over this again," the detective lieutenant said.

Charles Falcon was a small, unhappy-looking man with graying hair and tired blue eyes. He was wearing a dark suit with a striped tie hanging halfway down his chest. His clothes were, like him, crumpled. He had been a policeman for thirty years and as far as he was concerned that was about twenty years too long. He had lost count of the number of murders he had investigated. The stabbings and shootings, the batterings and stranglings. And that was in addition to the armed robberies, burglaries, kidnappings, and assaults. He was glad it was almost over. Two more months. Then retirement back to Norfolk. A little house in Hunstanton, a dog, long walks along the beach, and no more death.

Two more months and then this had to come along.

He was sitting at his desk in New Scotland Yard. There was a second man opposite him, thirty years his junior, neat and enthusiastic. His name was Jack Beagle, and he was a detective of lower rank than Charles. He had his notebook open in front of him.

"Where do you want to start?" Beagle asked.

"From the top," Falcon said. "Let's start with the family."

Beagle flipped through the pages in his book. "All right," he said. "Arthur and Mary Smith live in Steyning. It's a small village near the South Downs. They own the fruit shop there. They have one son, Eric, age eleven. As a Christmas present, they decided to bring him to London. Christmas shopping, lunch at a pizzeria, then the afternoon performance of *The Phantom of the Opera*. They had seats in the orchestra. A23 to—"

"All right! Get on with it!" Falcon interrupted. That was the trouble with Beagle. Too many details. Give him half a chance and he'd be describing what sort of ice creams they'd had during the intermission.

Beagle flicked a page. "After the show, they went to Covent Garden. There's a place in the new piazza that sells gadgets. Eric wanted a South Park clock. Insisted on it. So although they were tired, they went. They got to the station at a quarter to five. That was when he vanished."

"Eric Smith," Falcon muttered. He closed his eyes and sighed.

Covent Garden is one of London's oldest and deepest subway stations. There are only two platforms—the Piccadilly Line runs east and west. There are also no escalators. Four elevators connect the top and the bottom. There's a steep, twisting staircase but not many people use it, as it has one hundred and ninety-nine steps.

"It was very busy," Beagle went on. "After all, it was only three weeks to Christmas and the station was full of people shopping and all the rest of it. There was quite a crowd waiting for the elevators and that was when it happened. This boy, Eric . . . I'm afraid he doesn't sound like a very nice kid. A bit spoiled and disobedient—"

"You're not saying his parents did him in?" Falcon cut in gloomily. He'd investigated just such a case about ten years before.

"Oh no, sir. He's their only son and they dote on him. That's why I mentioned the seats. They were the most expensive in the theater."

"Go on."

"They were waiting for the elevators and there were people all around them. Hundreds of people. The

Smiths were at the back of the line. And then what happened was, two elevators arrived at exactly the same time, one next to the other. The line moved forward and Arthur, Mary, and young Eric just managed to squeeze into the elevator on the left. But then, for some reason, Eric decided he'd get into the elevator on the right. He dodged out of one and into the other. His parents called out to him, but it was already too late. The elevator doors closed. Both at the same time. And that was that."

"So he was in one elevator and they were in the other."

"Yes, sir. They weren't very happy about it. They'd told Eric to stay close to them but, like I say, he doesn't sound like the sort of boy who does what he's told. Even so, they weren't particularly worried. After all, it only takes about a minute to get to the top and both elevators would arrive at exactly the same time."

"Which they did."

"Yes, sir. They arrived at the top and the doors opened at exactly the same second. The crowd poured out. And here's the rub! There was no sign of Eric. The boy had disappeared."

"They were certain he'd gotten into the elevator."

"We have a witness—a Mrs. Nerricott—who saw him run out of one elevator and into the other."

"Did Mrs. Nerricott get into the elevator with him?"

"No, sir. There wasn't room. But she definitely saw the door close with the boy inside."

"All right." Falcon reached into his pocket and took out a chocolate bar. It was his last one. He ate it himself. "So Eric was in one elevator and his parents were in another. Could he have slipped out ahead of them at the top?"

"No. They'd have seen. And anyway, there's the security tape."

"Let's take another look at it!"

There were closed-circuit television cameras at Covent Garden, just as there are at every London station. The time-coded tape had been sent over to New Scotland Yard and for the tenth time Falcon ran it on his monitor. The film was black-and-white, a little muddy, but still clear enough. He could see everything.

There were Arthur and Mary Smith, both of them weighed down with a load of bags and packages. Arthur was short and bald, in his late forties. Mary was a slightly mousy woman with permed hair, wearing a thick coat. Eric was standing next to them. He wasn't holding anything. He was plump, with jug ears and freckles. His hair was spiky and (Falcon knew from color photographs sent to his office) ginger-colored. He was wearing combat pants and a down vest with a scarf around his neck but no jacket.

The film showed exactly what happened. That was the hell of it. The whole thing had been recorded.

At 16:44:05, the two elevators arrived simultaneously at the bottom. The crowd surged forward. Falcon saw Arthur and Mary Smith get into the car on the left with their son. And there, on the screen, was Eric, suddenly running into the car on the right, squeezing in behind the crowd. He saw Arthur turn and realize what the boy had done. He saw Arthur call out, although of course there was no sound. Both elevator doors were already closing. It was all exactly as Beagle had described.

Cut now to the top floor. There was no camera inside the elevators.

The time on the tape was 16:45:03. Fifty-eight seconds had passed. Both elevator doors opened. The elevators at Covent Garden actually have two sets of doors—one in the front and one in the back. You enter the elevator from one side but you exit through the other. Arthur and Mary were the last to come out. There were people everywhere, bustling forward through the automatic turnstiles. The camera mounted over the exit picked up every one of them and Falcon leaned forward, examining the faces carefully.

There were old people and young people. Well-dressed people and scruffy ones. A big man with a beard and a wart on his nose fed his ticket into the machine. A teenager carrying a football followed right behind him. Then there was a woman chewing gum, another woman walking with her arms crossed. There was a man blowing his nose into a handkerchief, a second man already lighting a cigar. A Chinese woman with a swollen cheek and an old lady bent over double, supporting herself on a thick walking stick. A constant stream of humanity flowing out of the elevator and away from the station.

But there was no sign of Eric. It was an impossible magic trick. Arthur and Mary were there, on the screen, searching everywhere, beginning to panic. A few minutes later they would call the police. But it was already too late. The boy had gone.

Falcon flicked a button and the picture froze. "So what do you think?" he asked.

"I don't know, sir." Falcon had never heard his junior officer sound so defeated. "I just can't work it out at all. I mean, we can actually see it. That's what beats me. It happened exactly how Mr. and Mrs. Smith described it!"

"Where are the parents?"

"They're waiting downstairs."

Arthur and Mary were sitting in a room that smelled of new paint and old disinfectant. Her eyes were red from crying. Her husband had one hand resting on her arm, trying to comfort her, but he looked as lost as she did.

"We don't often come up to London," he said. "But Eric insisted. He wanted to go to Hamleys and see this musical."

"We should have run after him," Mary stammered. Fresh tears brimmed at her eyes. "But it was very difficult."

"We had all his presents," Arthur explained. "Eric had chosen a new train set, and the walkie-talkies, the keyboard . . ."

". . . the Rollerblades . . ."

". . . and the modeling kit. We had so many bags we could hardly move."

"My little angel!" Mary wailed.

"He wasn't a complete angel," Arthur said gently. "I mean, we'd told him to stay close to us but he wouldn't listen. And the truth is, he'd been in a bad mood all day. He was very upset when we wouldn't buy him that remote-control helicopter."

"But it was two hundred dollars!"

"He was also sick after that third ice cream at the theater. Maybe that was why he decided to run out of the elevator like that." Arthur Smith shook his head. "We did tell him to stay close."

"Just find him for us," Mary said. She took out a handkerchief and dabbed at her eyes. "He's got to be somewhere!"

Late that night, the two detectives returned to the Covent Garden station. The subway had already closed down but the station was busy. There were police officers everywhere, searching through the ticket office and moving slowly, step-by-step, up and down the stairs. There were more policemen below, some with dogs sniffing along the platforms and even following the tracks into the tunnel itself. Both the elevators were being examined by forensic scientists in white coats and plastic gloves. The ticket machine had been opened and all the tickets—thousands of them—retrieved. There was just a chance that the police might find a fingerprint on one of them. Maybe it would lead them to a maniac, a murderer . . . but even that wouldn't explain how the eleven-year-old boy with at least thirty complete strangers packed in tight all around him had managed to evaporate into thin air.

Falcon peered into the elevator that had carried Eric up. It was an ugly metal box with a heavy sliding door at each end. There was a small window in the side but the glass was too dirty to see through and anyway it was impossible to climb out. There was something almost Victorian about it all. The whole station was grimy and old-fashioned. The passageways, lined with off-white tiles, curved into the distance. The floor was black concrete. With no trains coming and no passengers to add color and movement, the place was somehow eerie and unnerving. The cold night air whispered over Falcon's neck and he shivered.

He turned to Beagle. "Have you spoken to anyone who got into the elevator with the boy?" he asked.

"No, sir." Beagle shook his head. "By the time the parents realized the boy had gone, it was too late. They'd all passed through the turnstiles and out into the street. We've put up a sign outside asking for people to come forward . . ."

"Yes. I saw it."

". . . but so far, no luck."

There was a movement behind them and one of the forensic men appeared clutching a plastic evidence bag. There were three dirty swabs inside. "Excuse me, sir . . ." he began.

"Yes?"

"We've found traces of blood on the floor of the elevator." He handed Falcon the bag. "Type O. And it's fresh."

"The boy's?"

"Impossible to say at this stage, sir. But I'd think it's likely."

"And that's all?"

"One button. Off a shirt. Could be his, could be anyone's. We're going to try and match it up."

"Thank you . . ."

Falcon took the elevator back up to the surface. He felt almost suffocated, standing inside the metal box. There was a lurch as the car began to rise and then nothing but the creak of the ancient cables pulling him slowly up. What had happened to Eric Smith when he had taken the elevator at a quarter to five that afternoon? He couldn't have climbed onto the roof or anything like that. He couldn't have left it at all until the doors opened. But he had definitely gotten in and he definitely hadn't gotten out.

It was enough to drive a detective crazy!

There was a team of policemen on the top floor, examining a great pile of tickets taken out of the machines. One of them looked up as Falcon emerged from the elevator. What was his name? Williams or Willard or something . . .

"What have you got?" Falcon demanded.

"Nothing very much, sir. Except one thing . . ."

"Go on."

"When the used tickets are sucked into the machine, they fall into a compartment, sir. They're emptied regularly throughout the day, but nobody touched the machines after the boy disappeared, so at least we've been able to work out more or less where people were coming from at around about a quarter to five this afternoon."

"And . . . ?"

"Well, it's quite strange really. There were about

forty tickets from the same station . . . Burnt Oak. It struck me as odd . . ."

"Why?"

"Well, sir. Burnt Oak isn't a very important station, tucked away at the end of the Northern Line. And it just seemed strange that so many people should have made the same journey—Burnt Oak to Covent Garden—at exactly the same time."

"All right, Williams," Falcon said. "Have the tickets sent to my office."

"Yes, sir." The policeman scowled. "My name's Willard, sir . . ."

Later that night, Falcon lay in bed in the small apartment he rented in a backstreet in Victoria. He was only half-asleep. He was trying to dream about Norfolk. He could just picture himself out on the beach, watching the sunset with his dog. What sort of dog would he buy? An Alsatian perhaps? No—that would remind him too much of the police.

But try as he might, he couldn't dream what he wanted to dream. The scene kept changing. There was Eric Smith, standing on the sand in his combat pants, surrounded by people carrying packages and shopping bags. Something rose out of the sea. It was the elevator. The doors slid open and Eric walked into it. But now the elevator had changed. It had become some sort of metallic monster and the doors had been replaced by jagged teeth that sliced down. Eric screamed. The waves rolled in. And Falcon woke up with a start, surprised and relieved to see that it was seven o'clock, the start of another day.

Beagle was waiting for him at the office. "We've had a breakthrough," he said.

"Oh yes?" Falcon had bought himself a bacon-on-a-roll on the way in. It was still in the bag, beginning to get cold.

"One of the men on the screen," Beagle said. He was pleased with himself and Falcon guessed that he had probably been working all night. "One of the men in the elevator with the boy. I thought I knew him from somewhere and I was right."

He took out a photograph and slid it onto the desk in front of Falcon. A big man with a beard and a wart on his nose. Falcon remembered him from the security pictures. "Who is he?" he asked.

"He's a professor at the University of London. Also a writer. His name is Abraham Orlov."

"Doesn't sound English!"

"I believe he was born in the Ukraine."

Falcon studied the photograph. "You said you knew him," he muttered. "Has he got a criminal record?"

"No, sir. But I was at London University and although I never met him personally, he stuck in my mind. Do you remember that plane crash about eight years ago?"

Falcon shook his head.

"A small plane went down in the Arctic Circle. There were seventy people on board—mainly academics, geologists . . . that sort of thing. They'd been studying the ozone layer up in Greenland. It was assumed that they were all killed but in fact more than half of them survived. Stuck on the ice for almost five months."

"Yes. . . ." Falcon did remember something now. The story had made every newspaper at the time. There was something about it that made him feel uneasy. What was it?

"Orlov was one of them," Beagle went on. "He wrote a book about it afterward. *The Will to Survive*. That was the title. I never read it myself. Anyway, at least it means we've found one person who was in the elevator with Eric Smith. I thought you might want to speak to him."

"Do you have an address?"

Half an hour later, Falcon and Beagle were sitting in a small room on Gower Street, close to the Tottenham Court Road subway station. The room was so cluttered with books that it was almost impossible to move. There were books on shelves, on every seat, and in great stacks on the carpet. A pair of tattered curtains hung over a window that looked out onto a bare brick wall. Very little light found its way into the room.

Abraham Orlov was a big man; bigger even than the camera had made him appear. He was wearing a red vest, stretched over a great barrel of a chest, and his shoulders were so broad that his head seemed almost lost, balanced on a sprawling cushion of a beard that totally concealed his neck. His hands and wrists were also hairy and he had thick, bushy eyebrows. He wore thin gold glasses and smoked a pipe that had filled the room with a cloud of blue-gray smoke.

"Yes, indeed, Lieutenant," he was saying. He had a loud, hollow voice and an Eastern European accent. "I was most certainly in London last night."

"May I ask what you were doing?" Falcon said.

"My dear sir! You may ask what you like! I have nothing to hide!" He smiled and Falcon felt a shiver of disgust. The man had repulsive teeth. They were yellow and uneven and somehow looked too sharp for a human being. He had seen more attractive teeth than that in a dog. "Last night was an important anniversary. I met some very dear friends at our club and then we traveled into town together to see a concert."

"It was your birthday, sir?"

"No, no. You haven't read my book, Lieutenant?" The eyes twinkled behind the glasses. "It was exactly eight years since my rescue——our rescue—from the Arctic ice cap. Everyone thought we were dead but then they found we were living. You can imagine, my dear sir, that we survivors became very close, trapped in the wreckage of our plane for so many months. When we were returned to civilization, we decided to form a club. We purchased our own small clubhouse, tucked away in the north of this delightful city. Nothing elaborate! It's just somewhere private where we can talk in comfort. And we often meet there . . . socially."

"This clubhouse wouldn't happen to be in Burnt Oak, would it, sir?" Beagle asked.

"As a matter of fact it is! Just off the Edgware Road.

We all met there at about three o'clock in the afternoon and then traveled into town together."

"How many of you were there?"

"There are fifty-one members in the club including myself. Not everyone could make it last night but thirty-five of us set out together. On the Northern Line from Burnt Oak station." He nodded at Beagle. "Change at King's Cross . . ."

"Fifty-one members," Falcon said. He remembered what Beagle had told him that morning. "But I understood there were seventy people on the plane."

"Alas, nineteen of them failed to survive," Orlov said. He twisted his face into an expression of pain. "You must know the story, Detective Lieutenant. I made no secret of it. In fact I wrote a book about it. Nineteen people were killed in the crash. The rest of us were trapped. We had water . . . we could use melted ice. But we had no food. I'm afraid that the will to survive forced us to make a painful decision."

"Yes, sir?" Falcon said, but he already knew what was coming. Now he remembered the newspaper reports from eight years before.

"We were forced to cannibalize the corpses. For five months we ate nothing but human flesh." For a brief moment Orlov's tongue appeared, protruding out of his lips above his beard. Then it was sucked back into his mouth. "It was painful and, of course, disgusting. To cut strips of flesh and lay them out on the wreckage of the aircraft's wings . . . to dry in the sun. To be forced, day after day, to swallow our unfortunate companions. I don't need to describe it to you. If you want to know more, you should read my book. But it was a simple choice. We could eat or we could die. We chose to live."

"If I may get back to what happened yesterday," Falcon said. Suddenly he wanted to get out of this office, away from the smoke, out into the winter sunlight. "I wonder if you noticed an eleven-year-old boy get into the elevator with you at Covent Garden station?"

"I did indeed, Lieutenant. A rather fat little boy with ginger hair. Wearing baggy trousers and a scarf . . ."

"That was him."

"He pushed his way in just before the elevator doors closed. Then he forced his way to the front of the elevator. He was the first to leave. I was a little worried about him, as he seemed too young to be out on his own. But before I could do anything, he was out of my sight. I saw him go through the turnstile and into the street. But then he was gone."

"You saw him exit onto the street?" Beagle asked.

"Absolutely."

"But forgive me, sir." Beagle was confused. "The security cameras at the station show you leaving the elevator. But there was no sign of the boy."

Orlov frowned and sucked his pipe. Smoke trickled over his lips and into his beard. "Could it be, perhaps, that the camera was malfunctioning?" he said at last. "Because, I assure you, I saw him leave. With my own eyes."

"It is possible," Falcon agreed. He stood up. "Thank you very much, Mr. Orlov. I'm sorry to have taken up your time."

"Anything I can do to help!" Orlov waved a pudgy hand like a king dismissing a courtier.

Falcon paused at the door. "One last question, sir? Did you go to the concert? You and your friends?"

"Indeed so. Mozart and Brahms. At St. Christopher's Church in Covent Garden. It was a delightful evening."

"And I suppose you went on to dinner afterward."

Orlov hesitated, the pipe halfway to his lips. "No. As a matter of fact we didn't. We weren't hungry."

The two policemen left.

Falcon said nothing until they got back to New Scotland Yard. Sitting next to him in the car, Beagle had become more and more frustrated and when they reached the office he finally broke out. "He was lying! The boy never left the elevator. And the camera's fine. It's already been checked."

"I know, Jack," Falcon said.

The video camera with the security tape was still there and he turned it back on, but he knew what to expect. He was feeling sick. Just two months until he retired, nine months until he left London forever. And this had to come along.

Eric Smith had come to London with his parents and just for a laugh he had disobeyed them and slipped into an elevator on his own at Covent Garden subway station. Normally nothing would have happened. Normally he would have found himself surrounded by strangers and he would have arrived at the top at the same time as his mom and dad. They would have told him off and he would have sulked and that would have been the end of it. But this hadn't been a normal day. This had been a one-in-a-million chance.

Eric had gone into an elevator with thirty-five

cannibals, going out for their anniversary dinner. When the doors had closed, he had found himself alone with them for fifty-eight seconds.

Orlov had been lying, of course. He had said that his experience in the Arctic Circle had been painful and disgusting. But Falcon had seen the truth. He had seen it in the flash in those eyes behind the gold-framed spectacles and that little tongue, so pink and moist as it passed over his lips. Perhaps they'd hated it at first, the survivors in that plane. Having to survive for five months, eating human flesh.

But suppose they had come to enjoy it? Suppose they had come to like the taste? They had nineteen bodies. Thirty-eight roast shoulders. Thirty-eight roast legs. One hundred and ninety stewed knuckles. Day after day, they would have sat there, feasting.

But then, after they were rescued, how would they have coped? No more human flesh! Oh yes, they could meet in their little clubhouse and talk about it, relive all those happy meals. But they could only dream of the succulent, pink meat. And all the time they would be hungry, so hungry . . .

. . . until a small, plump boy walked right into the middle of them and a door closed and they suddenly realized they couldn't resist it anymore and as one they had fallen on him with teeth and nails . . .

Falcon didn't like to think about it. At least it would have been over for Eric very quickly.

He forced himself to look at the screen. There was Orlov, walking out of the elevator. Orlov and his friends. Was it really gum that the woman was chewing? Was the man with the handkerchief blowing his nose or wiping his mouth? That Chinese woman! Was her cheek swollen or was it just that her mouth was full? The old woman with the walking stick! Looking more closely, Falcon could see that the handle was shaped very much like a child's foot. And as for the teenager with the football, he wondered now if it actually was a football at all . . .

He turned off the machine.

"Are you all right, sir?" Beagle asked.

"No." Falcon sat staring at the blank screen. Two questions were going through his mind. How was he going to tell the parents what he knew? And (no wonder Orlov had been so calm) how was he ever going to prove it?

The Phone Goes Dead

This is how Linda James dies.

She's walking across Hyde Park in the middle of London when she notices that the weather has changed. The sky is an ugly color. Not the blackness of nightfall but the heavy, pulsating mauve of an approaching storm. The clouds are boiling and seconds later there is a brilliant flash as a fork of lightning shimmers the entire length of the Thames.

It has been said that there are two things that you shouldn't do in a storm. The first is to make a telephone call. The second is to take shelter under a tree. Linda James does both of these things. As the rain begins to fall, she runs under the outstretched branches of a huge oak tree, then fishes in her handbag and takes out a cell phone.

She dials a number.

"Steve," she says. "I'm in Hyde Park."

That's all she says. There's another flash of lightning and this time Linda is hit dead-on. Seventy-five thousand volts of electricity zap through her, transmitted through the cell phone into her brain. Her body jerks and the phone is thrown about fifty feet away from her. This is the last physical action Linda James ever makes, and it goes without saying, she is dead before the phone even hits the ground.

We will never find out anything more about Linda. Was she married or single? Why was she crossing Hyde Park at six o'clock on a Wednesday evening and does it matter that, wherever she was going, she never arrived? Who was Steve? Did he ever find out that Linda was actually killed at the very moment she was speaking to him? None of these questions will ever be answered.

But the cell phone. That's another story.

The phone is a Zodiac 555. Already old-fashioned. Manufactured somewhere in Eastern Europe. It is found in the long grass the day after the body has been removed and by a long, circuitous route, it ends up in a secondhand store somewhere near the coast in the south of England. Despite everything, the phone seems to be working. Linda's SIM card—the little piece of circuitry that makes it work—is removed. The phone is reprogrammed and another SIM card put inside. Eventually, it goes back on sale.

And a few weeks later, a man called Mark Adams goes in and buys it. He wants a cell phone for his son.

David Adams holds the cell phone. "Thanks, Dad," he says. But he's not sure about it. A lot of his friends have got cell phones, it's true. Half of them don't even make any calls. They just think it's cool, having their own phone—and the smaller and more expensive the model, the smarter they think they are. But the Zodiac 555 is clunky and out of date. It's gray. You can't snap on one of those multicolored fronts. And Zodiac? It's not one of the trendier brand names. David has never heard of it.

And then there's the question of why his father has bought it in the first place. David is sixteen now and he's beginning to spend more time away from home, sleeping over with friends, parties on Saturday evening, surfing at first light on Sunday. He lives in Ventnor, a run-down seaside town on the Isle of Wight. He's lived his whole life on the island and maybe that's why he feels cramped, why he wants his own space.

He's talking about college on the mainland. Mark and Jane Adams run a hotel. They only have one son and they're afraid of losing him. They want to keep him near them, even when they can't see him. And that's why they've bought the cell phone. David can imagine the next Saturday evening, when he's out with his friends at the Spyglass, the trill of Bach's Toccata and Fugue (which is what the phone plays when it rings) in his back pocket and his father or his mother checking up on him. "You're only drinking lemonade, aren't you, David? You won't be home too late?"

But even so, it's his own phone. He can always turn it off. And now that he's started going out with Jill Hughes, who lives in the neighboring village of Bonchurch and who goes to the same school as him, it could be useful.

Which is why he says, "Thanks, Dad."

"That's OK, David. But just remember. I'll pay the line rental for you, but the calls are down to you. It's ten cents a minute off-peak, so just be careful you don't talk too much."

"Sure."

They're a close family. For half the year there are just the three of them shuffling around in the twenty-three rooms of the Priory Hotel, which stands on a hill, over-looking the beach at Ventnor. Mark and Jane Adams bought it ten years ago, when David was six. They got fed up with London and one day they just moved. Perhaps it was a mistake. The summer season on the Isle of Wight is a short one these days. Package vacations are so cheap that most families can afford to go to France or Spain, where they're more sure of good weather. It gets busy around June but this is only March and the place is quiet. As usual, it's hard to make ends meet. David helps his dad with the decorating and small maintenance jobs. Jane Adams has a part-time job with a yacht club in Cowes. The three of them get along. Mark still says he prefers Ventnor to London.

David isn't so sure. There are too many old people on the Isle of Wight. Everything feels run-down and neglected. People say that the whole place is fifty years behind the rest of England and he can believe it. Sometimes he looks at the waves, rolling into the shore, and he dreams of other countries—even other worlds—and wishes that his life could change.

It's about to.

• • •

The cell phone rings at half past four one afternoon when David is on his way home from school. Bach's great organ piece reduced to a series of irritating electronic bleeps. Only about six people have his number. Jill, of course. His parents. A few other friends at school. But when David manages to find the phone in his backpack, dig it out, and press the button, it is none of them on the line.

"Hello?" It's an old man.

"Yes?" David is sure that it's a wrong number.

"I want you to do something for me." The old man has one of those slightly quavering, do-what-you're-told voices. "I want you to go and see my wife at Number Seventeen, Primrose Hill."

"I'm sorry . . ." David begins.

"I want you to tell her that the ring is under the fridge. She'll understand."

"Who is this speaking?" David asks.

"This is Eric. You know my wife. Mary Saunders. She lives at Number Seventeen and I want you to tell her—"

"I know," David interrupts. "Why can't you tell her?"

"I can't reach her!" The old man sounds annoyed

now. As if he's stating the obvious. "Will you tell her it's under the fridge? It's under the fridge. She'll understand what you mean."

"Well . . ."

"Thank you very much."

The phone goes dead. David hasn't even asked how Eric Saunders got his telephone number or why he should have dialed it to ask him (why him?) to do this favor. But the fact is that David does vaguely know Mary Saunders. Ventnor being the sort of place it is, everyone more or less knows everyone, but there's more to it than that. Mary Saunders used to work at the hotel. She worked in the kitchen but she retired about a year ago to look after her husband, who had cancer or something. David remembers her; a small, plump, busy woman with a loud laugh. Always cheerful—at least, until she heard the news about her husband's illness. She used to bake cakes and she'd always be there with a cup of tea and a slice of something when David got back from school. She was all right. And Primrose Hill is only a few minutes' walk from where David is now, from where he took the call.

It's strange, Eric calling him this way, but David decides that after all it's not too much to ask. He hasn't even stopped walking. His footsteps carry him to Primrose Hill.

Number Seventeen is part of a long row of almost identical houses, tall and narrow, standing shoulder to shoulder on a steeply rising lane. Ventnor Down looms over them and they have no sea view. In fact most of the houses have no view at all. Lace curtains have been pulled over the windows to stop people from looking in. As if anyone would want to.

Feeling slightly foolish, David rings the bell. Even as he hears the chimes, he changes his mind and wishes he hadn't come, wonders why Eric Saunders chose him and why he even listened. But it's too late. The door opens and there is Mary Saunders—just as he remembers her and yet not quite the same. She is older and thinner. She looks defeated and somehow David knows that she doesn't laugh so much anymore. Even so, she's pleased to see him.

"David!" she exclaims. It's taken a moment or two to remember who he is and she's puzzled that he's come. "This is a nice surprise! How are you?"

"I'm fine, thanks, Mrs. Saunders."

There's an awkward pause. David is embarrassed. She has been caught off guard.

"Do you want to come in?" she asks at last.

"No. No, thanks. I was just passing on my way home from school."

"How are your parents? How's the hotel?"

"They're fine. Everything's fine." David decides to get this over with as quickly as possible. "I just got a phone call," he says. "I was asked to give you a message."

"Oh yes?"

"It was Eric. He said to tell you that the ring is under the fridge . . ."

But already Mary's face has changed. She's looking at David as if he's just spat in her face. "What . . . ?" she mutters.

"He said it was under the fridge and that you'd understand."

"What are you talking about? Is this some sort of joke?"

"No. It was him . . ."

"How can you be so cruel? How can you . . . ?" She blinks rapidly and David sees, with a sort of sick feeling, that she's about to cry. "I don't know!" she mutters, and then she slams the door. Just like that. Slams it in his face.

David stands on the doorstep, bewildered. But not for long. He should never have come here and now he's glad to go. One of the net curtains in the house next door twitches. A neighbor has heard the slamming door and looks out to see what's going on. But there's nobody there. Just a boy in a school uniform, hurrying down the hill . . .

That night, at dinner, David mentions—casually—that he saw Mary Saunders. He doesn't tell his parents about the phone call. He doesn't mention the door shutting in his face.

"Ah, Mary!" His mother was always fond of the cook. "I haven't seen her for a while. Not since the funeral."

"Who died?" David asks. But he remembers Mary's face when he spoke to her. He already knows.

"Her husband. You remember Eric," she says to Mark.

"He did some work in the garden." Mark remembers now.

"Yes. Very sad. He had lung cancer. It wasn't surprising really. He was smoking a pack a day." David's mother turns to him. "You saw her today? How was she?"

"She was fine . . ." David says, and he can't stop himself from blushing. Someone played a joke on him. A stupid, malicious joke. Who was it? Who had his number and knew about Eric Saunders? Who telephoned him and imitated the old man's voice? Could it have been Jonathan Channon? Jonathan is his best friend at school and he's always had a mischievous side. But David can still hear the old man's voice and knows that it *was* an old man. Not a boy pretending to be a man. He knows it wasn't a joke.

And a few days later, David meets Mary Saunders again. He's walking down the High Street and he's just reached the old pile that used to be the Rex Cinema and suddenly she's there in front of him. He'd avoid her if he could but it's too late.

"Hello, Mrs. Saunders," he says. He's ashamed. He can't keep it out of his voice.

But now she's looking at him very strangely. She seems to be struggling with herself. There are tears in her eyes again but this time she's not unhappy. She's fighting with all sorts of emotions and it takes her a few seconds to find her voice, to find the words to say, "You came to see me."

"I'm sorry," David stammers. "I didn't know . . ."

She raises a hand, trying to explain. "My Eric died just six weeks ago. It was a long illness. I nursed him to the end."

"Yes. My mom told me. I didn't mean . . ."

"We both had wedding rings. We were married thirty-seven years ago and we each had a wedding ring. Just silver. Nothing very expensive. My ring was inscribed with his name. And his had mine, on the inside. And after he died, I looked for his ring, and I couldn't find it. It really upset me, that did. Because he'd never taken that ring off. Not once in thirty-seven years. And it was meant to be buried with him. That was what he'd always wanted."

She stops. Takes out a tissue and dabs her eye.

"I don't know how you knew. What you told me . . . I don't want to know how you found out. But after you left me, I looked under the fridge. And the ring was there. He was so thin by the end, it must have fallen off his finger and rolled there. Anyway, David, I wanted you to know. I found the ring and the vicar's arranged for it to be put in the grave with my Eric. It means a lot to me. I'm glad you told me what you did. I'm glad . . ."

And she hurries on, up the hill. David watches her

go, knowing that she isn't angry with him anymore. But now she's something else. She's scared.

That afternoon, the telephone rings again.

"You don't know me," says the voice, and this time it's a woman, brisk, matter-of-fact. "But I met someone and they gave me your number. They said you might be able to pass a message on."

"Oh yes?" David can't keep the dread out of his voice.

"My name is Samantha Davies. I'd be very grateful if you could talk to my mother. Her name is Marion and she lives at Number Eleven, St. Edward's Square, Newport. Could you let her know that I think it's quite wrong of her to blame Henry for what happened and that I'd be much happier if the two of them were talking again."

Once again, the phone goes dead.

This time David doesn't just walk into it. This time, he makes inquiries. And he discovers that there is a Marion Davies who lives at Number Eleven, St. Edward's Square, in Newport, which is the largest town on the Isle of Wight. Mrs. Davies is a retired piano teacher. Last year, her eldest daughter, Samantha, was killed in a car accident. Her boyfriend, Henry, was driving.

David doesn't pass on the message. He doesn't want to get involved with someone he has never met. Anyway, how could he possibly explain to Mrs. Davies what he has heard on the phone?

The phone . . .

It begins to ring more often. With more and more messages.

"The name's Protheroe. Derek Protheroe. I got your number from Samantha Davies. I wonder if you could get in touch with my daughter in Portsmouth. She's seeing this young man and he's lying to her. He's a crook. I'm very worried about her. Could you tell her her father says . . ."

"It's my mom. She's missing me so much. I just want her to know that I'm not in pain anymore. I'm happy. I just wish that she could forget about me and get on with her life . . ."

"Do you think you could tell my wife that the bloody lawyer's made a mess of the whole thing. I added a codicil to the will. I don't suppose you know what that means but she'll understand. It's very important because . . ."

"Miss Fitzgerald. She lives in Eastbourne. This is her sister . . ."

On and on. After a few weeks, the phone is ringing six or seven times a day. Brothers and sisters. Husbands and wives. Sons and daughters. All wanting to get in touch.

And David doesn't tell anyone.

He wants to tell Jill, walking home with her from school. But she'd freak out. She'd think he was crazy. And he's afraid of losing her, his first real love. He wants to tell Jonathan Channon, his best friend. But Jonathan would only laugh. He'd think it was all a huge joke even though it doesn't amuse David at all. And above all he wants to tell his parents. But they're so busy, struggling to get the hotel ready for the next season. They've got plumbing problems, wiring problems, staff problems, and—as always—money problems. He doesn't want to burden them with this.

But he knows. He is in communication with the dead. For some reason that he cannot even begin to understand, the Zodiac 555 has a direct line to wherever it is that lies beyond the grave. Do cell phones have lines? It doesn't matter. The fact is that a tiny gate has somehow opened up between this world and the next.

That gate is the cell phone. And as word has gotten around, more and more of the dead have been lining up to use it. To get their messages across.

"Tell my uncle . . ."

"Can you speak to my wife . . . ?"

"They have to know . . ."

Bach's Toccata and Fugue. Every time David hears the sound, it sends a shiver through his entire body. He can't bear it anymore. In the end he turns the telephone off and buries it at the bottom of a drawer in his bedroom, underneath his old socks. But even then he sometimes imagines he can still hear it.

Diddley-dah.

Diddley-dah-dah . . .

He has nightmares about it. He sees ghosts and skeletons, decomposing corpses. They are lining up outside his room. They want to talk to him. They wonder why he doesn't reply.

Mark and Jane Adams get worried about their son. They notice that he's not sleeping well. He comes down to breakfast with a pale face and rings around his eyes. One of his teachers has told them that his work at school has begun to slip. They're worried that he might have broken up with Jill. Could he be into drugs? Like every parent, they're quick to think the worst without actually getting anywhere near the truth.

They take him out to dinner. A little restaurant on Smuggler's Cove where fresh crabs and lobsters are dragged out of the sea, over the sand, and onto the table. An intimate evening. Just the three of them.

They don't ask him any direct questions. That's the last thing you do with a teenager. Instead, they gently probe, trying to find out what's on his mind. David doesn't tell them anything. But toward the end of the meal, when the atmosphere is a little more relaxed, Mark Adams suddenly says, "What happened to that cell phone we gave you?"

David flinches. Neither of his parents notices.

"You haven't used it in a while," Mark says.

"I don't really need it," David says.

"I thought it would be useful."

"Well, I see everyone anyway. I'm sorry. I don't much like using it."

Mark smiles. He doesn't want to make a big deal out of it. "It's a bit of a waste of money," he says. "I'm paying the monthly rental."

"Where is the phone?" his mother asks. She wonders if he's lost it.

"In my bedroom."

"Well, if you don't want it, I might as well cancel the rental."

"Yeah. Sure." David sounds relieved. And he is.

That evening he gives the telephone back to his father and sleeps well for the first time in a week. No Bach. No dreams. It's finally over.

One week later.

Mark Adams is sitting in his office. It's a cozy, cluttered room at the top of the hotel, tucked into the eaves. There's a small window. He can see the sea sparkling in the sunlight. Outside, an engineer is working on the telephone lines. The hotel has been cut off for two hours. Mark has spent the morning working on the accounts. There are bills from builders and decorators. The new microwave in the kitchen. As always, they've spent much more money than they've actually made. Not for the first time, Mark wonders if they might have to sell.

He glances down and notices the cell phone sitting

on a pile of papers. He flicks it on. The battery is fully charged. He makes a mental note to himself. He ought to cancel the line rental. That's a waste of money.

And then there's a movement at the door and suddenly Jane is there. She's run all the way upstairs and she pauses in the doorway, panting. She's a short woman, a little overweight. Her dark hair hangs over her eyes.

"What is it?" Mark asks. He's alarmed. When you've been married as long as he has you can sense when something is wrong. He senses it now.

"I saw it on the television," Jane says.

"What?"

"David . . ."

David is away from home. There's a school skiing trip to France. He left this morning with Kate Evans, Jonathan Channon, everyone in his class. They flew to Lyon. A bus met them at the airport. It took them on the two-hour drive to the resort at Courcheval.

Or should have.

"There's been an accident," Jane explains. She's close to tears. Not because she knows something. But because she doesn't. "It was on the news. A bus full of schoolchildren. English schoolchildren. It was involved in a crash with a delivery van. It drove off the road. They said there were a lot of fatalities."

"Is it David's bus?"

"They didn't say."

Mark struggles to make sense. "There'll be a hundred buses at Lyon airport," he says. "It's spring break, for heaven's sake. There are schools all over the country sending kids to France."

"But David arrived this morning. That's when it happened."

"Have you called the school?"

"I tried. The phones aren't working."

Mark glances through the window, at the engineer working outside. Then he remembers the cell phone. "We can use this," he says.

He picks it up.

The phone rings in his hand.

Bach's Toccata and Fugue.

Mark is surprised. He fumbles for the button and presses it.

It's David.

"Hi, Dad," he says. "It's me."

Twist
Cottage

I never knew my mother. She died in a car accident the year after I was born and I was brought up, all on my own, by my dad. I had no brothers and no sisters. There were just the two of us, living in a house in Bath, which is down in the southwest, in Avon. My dad worked as a history professor at Bristol University and for ten years we had nannies or housekeepers living with us, looking after me. But by the time I was thirteen and going to a local school, we found we didn't really need anyone anymore, so there were just the two of us. And we were happy.

My dad's name is Andrew Taylor. He never talked about my mother but I think he must have loved her a lot because he didn't remarry and (although he doesn't like me to know it) he kept a photograph of her in his wallet and never went anywhere without it. He was a big, shaggy man with glasses and untidy brown hair that had just started to go gray. His clothes always looked old, even when they were brand-new, and they never fitted him very well. He was forty-five. He went to the movies a lot. He listened to classical music. And, like me, he was a big soccer fan.

The two of us always got along well, maybe because we always had our own space. We only had a small house in Bath—it was on one of the backstreets behind the antiques market—but we both had our own rooms. Dad had a small study on the ground floor, and when I was ten, he converted the attic into a play area for me. It was a little cramped with a slanting roof and only one small window but it was fine for me; somewhere private where I could go. In fact, we didn't see much of each other during the week. He was at the university and I was at school. But on weekends we went to the movies together, did the shopping, watched TV, or kicked a soccer ball around . . . all the things that every father does with every son. Only there was no mother to share it.

We were happy. But everything changed with the coming of Louise. I suppose it had to happen in the end. My dad might be middle-aged but he was still fit and reasonably good-looking. I knew he went out with women now and then. But until Louise, none of them had ever stayed.

She was a few years younger than him. She was a mature student at Bristol University. She was studying art but she had taken history as an elective and that was how they met. The first time I met her, she'd come over to the house to pick up a book and I have to say I could see what my dad saw in her. She was a very beautiful woman, tall and slim, with dark hair, brown eyes, and a very slight French accent (her mother lived in Paris). She was fashionably dressed in a silk dress that showed off her figure perfectly. The one thing that was strange, though, was that, for a student, she didn't seem particularly interested in either history or art. When my dad talked about some gallery he'd been to she was soon yawning (although she was careful to hide it behind a handkerchief) and whenever he asked her about her work she quickly changed the subject to something else. Even so, she stayed for tea and insisted on doing the dishes. My dad didn't say anything after she'd gone but I could see that he was taken by her. He stood in the doorway for a long time, watching her leave.

I began to see more and more of Louise. Suddenly there were three of us going to the movies, not two.

Three of us having lunch together during the weekend. And inevitably, there she was one morning when I came down to breakfast. I was old enough not to be shocked or upset that she'd stayed the night. But it was still a shock. I was happy for him but secretly sad for myself. And . . . well, for some reason, she worried me too.

My dad and I spoke about her only once. "Tell me something, Ben," he said, one day. We were out walking, following the canal path as it wove through Bath Valley. It was something we often liked to do. "What do you think of Louise?"

"I don't know," I said. In a way she was perfect but maybe that was what worried me. She was almost too good to be true.

"You know, there's never been anyone since your mother died," he said. He stopped and looked up at the sky. It was a lovely day. The sun was shining brilliantly. "But sometimes I wonder if I ought to be on my own. After all, you're almost fourteen. Any day now you'll be leaving home. What would you say if Louise and I were to—"

"Dad, I just want you to be happy," I interrupted.

The conversation made me feel uncomfortable. And what else could I say?

"Yes." He smiled at me. "Thank you, Ben. You're a good boy. You'd have made your mother proud . . ."

And so they got married at Bath Registry Office. I was the best man and I made a speech at the lunch afterward, tied a plastic dog poo to the car and threw confetti at them as they drove away. They had a week's honeymoon in Majorca and even that should have rung a slight alarm bell because my dad had told me that he'd really wanted to visit some of the historical towns in the South of France. But Louise had her own way and they must have had a good time because when they got back they were happy and relaxed, with deep suntans and a load of presents for me.

I suppose the marriage was a success for about three months but it all went wrong very quickly after that.

Although she agreed to come with us when we visited the new Tate Gallery in Millbank, Louise suddenly gave up her art classes. She said it bored her, and anyway, she wanted to spend more time looking after my dad. This sounded all right at the time and she may even have meant what she said. But the house got messier and messier. It was true that Dad and I had never been exactly tidy. Mrs. Jones, our old cleaning lady, was always complaining about us. But we never left dirty mugs in the bedroom, tangled hair in the sink, or crumpled clothes on the stairs. Louise did and when Mrs. Jones complained one Tuesday morning, there was a nasty argument and the next thing I knew was that Mrs. Jones had quit. Louise didn't do any more cooking after that. All the food she ever prepared seemed to have come out of cans or out of the freezer and as my dad was a bit of a health freak, mealtimes were always a disappointment.

Of course, neither of us had expected Louise to cook and clean for us. That wasn't the idea. My dad was really sorry she'd decided to give up her classes at the university. The trouble was that she didn't seem to want to fit in and the slightest argument always ended with her flying into a rage, with slamming doors and tears. At heart she was a bit of a spoiled child. She always had to have her own way. Shortly after she moved in, she suddenly insisted that Dad let her have my attic room because she wanted somewhere to paint. Dad came to me very reluctantly and asked me if I'd mind and I didn't argue because I knew it would lead to another fight and I didn't want him to be unhappy. So that was how I lost my room.

Dad was unhappy, though, and as the first year shuddered slowly by, I could see that he was getting worse and worse. He lost weight. The last traces of brown faded out of his hair. He never laughed anymore. Louise had told him that his clothes were old-fashioned and made him look middle-aged and one day she had given the whole lot to a charity shop. Now my dad wore jeans and T-shirts that didn't suit him and actually made him look older than he had looked before. He wasn't allowed to play classical music anymore either. Louise preferred jazz and most of the time the house was filled with the wail of trumpets and clarinets, fighting with the constant drone of the television, which she never seemed to turn off. And although she had loaded a few canvases and paints into my old room, she never actually produced anything.

My dad never complained about her. I suppose this was part of his character. If I'd been married to her, I'd have probably walked out by now, but he seemed to accept everything meekly. However, one afternoon toward the end of the summer, we found ourselves retracing our steps along the canal, and perhaps remembering our conversation from the year before, he turned to me and suddenly said, "I'm afraid Louise isn't a very good mother to you."

I shrugged. I didn't know what to say.

"Perhaps it would have been better if I'd stayed single." He sighed and fell silent. "Louise has asked me to sell the house," he suddenly blurted out.

"Why?"

"She says it's poky. She says she doesn't like living in the town. She wants me to move more into the countryside."

"You're not going to, are you, Dad?"

"I don't know. I'm thinking about it . . ."

He sounded so sad. And it should have been obvious to him, really. The marriage wasn't working, so why not divorce her? I almost said as much but perhaps it was as well that I didn't. For things came to a head that very night and I realized just how poisonous Louise could be.

The two of them argued quite often. At least, Louise did. Generally, my dad preferred to suffer in silence. But that night my dad got his bank statement. It seemed that Louise had bought herself a whole load of designer clothes and stuff like that. She'd spent over a thousand dollars. He didn't shout at her but he did criticize her. And suddenly she was screaming at him. I heard the whole thing from my bedroom. It was impossible not to.

"I know you don't love me," she cried in a whiny, petulant voice. "You and Ben have been against me from the day I arrived."

"I really don't think things are working out," my dad said quietly.

"You want me to go? Is that it? You want a divorce?"

"Perhaps we might both be happier . . ."

"Oh no, Andrew. If you want to divorce me, it's going to cost you. I want half of everything you have. And I'm entitled to it! You'll have to move out of this house—and that's just for a start. I'll tell the social workers how you've always left Ben on his own when he gets back from school. That's not allowed. So they'll take him away and you'll never see him again."

"Louise . . ."

"I'll tell the university how cruel you've been to me. I'll tell them you battered me and you'll lose your job. I'll take your money. I'll take your son. I'll take everything! You wait and see!"

"Please, Louise . . . there's no need for this."

After that, things quieted down. Louise knew she had my dad around her little finger and every day she found new ways to be cruel to him. I think she only asked him to move to upset him. She knew how happy we'd always been in that little house.

As always she had her way. About three months after the argument, my dad said he'd found somewhere.

The somewhere was a little house called Twist Cottage.

If Louise wanted to move into the countryside, she couldn't have chosen a better house than Twist Cottage, although it wasn't actually her who had chosen it. Dad found it. He came home one day with the details and we went to see it that same afternoon.

Twist Cottage was buried in the middle of a forest not far from the aqueduct where the Avon Canal and the River Avon cross paths. It's a strange part of the world. There are small towns scattered all over the place but walk a few yards into the woods and you seem to tumble into the middle of nowhere. Twist Cottage was as isolated as a cottage could be. It seemed to be imprisoned by the trees that surrounded it, as if they were afraid of its being found. And yet it was a very pretty little building, straight out of a jigsaw puzzle, with a thatched roof, black beams, and windows made of diamond-shaped pieces of glass. The cottage was as twisted as its name suggested. My dad said it was very old, Elizabethan or earlier, and time had worn all the edges into curves. It had a big garden with a pond in the middle. The grass was already long.

"We'll need a lawn mower," Louise said.

"Yes," my father agreed.

"And I'm not doing the mowing!"

Now, I don't know a lot about house prices but I do know that Avon is an expensive place to live, mainly because of all the Londoners who've bought second homes there. But the strange thing was that my dad bought Twist Cottage for only a hundred thousand dollars, which isn't very much at all. Not in Avon. I wondered about that at the time. I also noticed that the real estate agent—a Mr. Willoughby—seemed particularly happy to have sold it. He had an office in Bath and the day he sold Twist Cottage, he gave everybody the day off.

As it happened, one of my best friends at school was

a boy named John Graham and his older sister, Carol, was Mr. Willoughby's secretary. I was around at their house the week after the sale had been arranged and she told me about the day off. In fact, she told me a lot more.

"You're not really moving into Twist Cottage, are you?" she demanded. She was nineteen years old, with frizzy hair and glasses. She had a slightly turned-up nose, which suited her attitude about life. "Poor you!"

"What are you talking about?" I asked.

"Mr. Willoughby never thought we'd sell it."

"Is there something wrong with it?"

"You could say that." Carol had been painting her nails with scarlet polish. She closed the bottle and came over to me. "It's haunted," she said.

"Haunted?"

"Mr. Willoughby says it's *very* haunted. He says it's the most haunted house he's ever known."

John and I both burst out laughing.

"It's true!"

"Do you believe in ghosts?" John asked his sister.

"I don't believe in ghosts," I said.

"Well, there's something wrong with the house,"

Carol insisted. "Why else do you think your dad got it so cheap?"

She probably wouldn't have bothered talking to us, but she had nothing to do while her nails dried. So that was how I found out the recent history of Twist Cottage. And it wasn't very nice.

Over the last few years, six different couples had moved into the place and something horrible had happened to every one of them. A lady called Mrs. Webster was the first.

"She drowned in the bath," Carol said. "Nobody knew how it happened. It wasn't as if she was old or anything like that. When they found her, she was all bloated. She'd completely swollen up inside!"

That was the first time Willoughby sold the house. It was bought by a second couple, a Mr. and Mrs. Johnson from London. Just four weeks later, one of them had fallen out of the window and gotten impaled on the garden fence.

The next victim was a Dr. Stainer. Carol knew all the names. She was enjoying telling us her story, sitting in the living room of her house as the sun set and long shadows reached across the room. "This time it was a tile falling off the roof," she said. "Dr. Stainer's skull was fractured and death was instantaneous.

"After that, the house was empty for about six months. Word had got around, you see. All these deaths. But eventually Mr. Willoughby sold it again. I forget who bought it this time. But I do know that whoever it was had a heart attack just two weeks later and the house had to be sold for a fifth time.

"It was bought by a Professor Bell. The professor lasted just one month before falling down the stairs."

"Also killed?" John demanded.

"Yes. With a broken neck—and the house went back on the market once again. Poor Mr. Willoughby never thought he'd get rid of it. He didn't even want to handle it. But of course he was making money every time it was sold, even though the price was dropping and dropping. Who would want to live in a house where so many people had died?"

"Was my dad the next one to buy it?" I asked.

"No. There was one more owner before your dad. An Australian. Electrocuted while adjusting the thermostat on the deep freeze."

There was a long silence. Either Carol had been talking for longer than I thought or the sun had set more rapidly than usual because it was suddenly quite dark.

"You're not really moving in there, are you, Ben?" John asked.

"I don't know," I replied. All of a sudden I wasn't feeling too good. "Is this all true, Carol? Or are you just trying to scare me?"

"You can ask Mr. Willoughby," Carol said. "In fact, you can ask anyone. Everyone knows about Twist Cottage. And everyone knows you'd be crazy to live there!"

That night I asked my dad if he knew what he was getting himself into. Louise was already asleep. She'd started drinking recently and had gotten through half a bottle of malt whiskey before dragging herself upstairs and throwing herself into bed. Dad and I talked in whispers but we didn't need to. She was sound asleep. You could probably hear her snoring on the other side of Bath.

"Is it true, Dad?" I asked. "Is Twist Cottage haunted?"

He looked at me curiously. For a moment I thought I saw a flicker of anger in his eyes. "Who have you been talking to, Ben?" he demanded.

"I was at John's house."

"John? Oh . . . his sister." My dad paused. He was looking very tired these days. And old. It made me feel sad. "You don't believe in ghosts, do you?" he asked.

"No. Not really."

"Nor do I. For heaven's sake, Ben, this is the twenty-first century!"

"But Carol said that six people died there in just two years. There was an Australian, a Professor Bell, a doctor—"

"It's too late now!" my dad interrupted. He never raised his voice as a rule but this time he was almost shouting. "We're moving there!" He forced himself to calm down. "Louise likes the house and she'll only be disappointed if I change my mind." He reached out and tousled my hair like he used to, when I was younger, before Louise came. "You don't have anything to worry about, Ben, I promise you," he said. "You'll be happy there. We all will."

And so we moved in. I'd tried to forget what Carol had told me, but I have to admit I was still feeling a bit uneasy and things weren't helped by two accidents that happened the very day we arrived. First of all the driver of the moving van tripped and broke an ankle. I suppose it could have happened anywhere and it wasn't as if a ghost had suddenly popped up and gone "boo" or something like that, but still it made me think. And then, at the end of the day, a carpenter who had been called in to mend a broken window frame slipped with a saw and nearly cut off a finger. There was a lot of blood. It formed something that looked almost like a question mark on the windowpane. But what was the question?

Why have we come here?

Or—*What's going to happen next?*

In fact, nothing happened for a while. The next weeks were mainly spent unpacking boxes. There were piles everywhere—books, plates, clothes, CDs—and no matter how many boxes we unpacked there always seemed to be more waiting to be done. A new dishwasher was delivered and also a lawn mower big enough to deal with the garden, a great beast of a thing that Dad had found secondhand and that only just fit into the shed. Louise didn't help with anything. I couldn't help noticing that recently she had become very plump. Perhaps it was all the drinking. She liked to sleep in the afternoon and shouted at us if we woke her up.

Of course, I was out most afternoons. My dad had bought me a new bike, partly to cheer me up, but mainly because I now needed it to get to school. There was a bus I could catch into Bath from the nearby town of Bradford-on-Avon but that was still a ten-minute bike ride away. In fact, I preferred to bike that whole way, following the canal towpath where dad and I had often walked. It was a beautiful ride when the weather was good and this was the summer semester—warm and sunny. I'd leave the bus until the weather got cold.

Twist Cottage had three bedrooms. Mine was at the back of the house, with views into the woods. Well, all the rooms looked into the woods, as we were completely surrounded. It was a small room with uneven white walls that bulged slightly inward, and a curiously ugly wooden beam that ran along the ceiling just above the window. Once my bed was in and my soccer-team posters were on the wall, I suppose it was cozy enough, but in a way it was creepy too. All those trees cast shadows. There were shadows everywhere and when the wind blew and the branches waved the whole room was filled with flickering, dancing shapes.

And there was something else. Maybe I was just imagining it, but the cottage always felt colder than it had any right to be. Even in the middle of the summer there was a sort of dampness in the air. I could feel it creeping over my shoulders when I got out of the bath. It was always there, slithering around the back of my neck. When I got into bed I would bury myself completely under the quilt but even then it would still find a way to twist itself around my ankles and tickle my toes.

Dad was right, though. Louise did seem happier in Twist Cottage. She wasn't doing anything very much anymore. All her art stuff seemed to have gotten lost in the move and she spent most of the day in bed. She was getting fatter and fatter. I often used to see her sitting with a magazine and a box of chocolates with the TV on and the curtains closed. My poor dad had to do everything for her; the shopping, the cooking, the laundry . . . as well as his job at the university. But at least she didn't shout at him so much anymore. She was like a queen, happy so long as she was being served.

And then the incident happened that very nearly removed Louise from our life forever. I was there and I saw what happened. Otherwise I would never have believed it.

It was a Saturday, another warm day at the end of

August. Dad was in Bristol. I was at home mending a tire on my bike. Louise hadn't gotten up until about eleven o'clock and after her usual three bowls of corn-flakes and five slices of toast, she had decided to step out into the garden. This was in itself a rare event, but like I said, it was a lovely day.

Anyway, I saw her waddle down to the fishpond. She had a tub of fish food in her hand. Maybe her own enormous breakfast had reminded her that the fish hadn't actually been fed since we moved in. She stopped at the side of the water and tipped some of the flakes into her hand.

"Here! Fishy fishies!" she called out. She still had a little-girl voice.

Something moved in the grass behind her. She didn't see it, but I did. At first I thought it was a snake. A long green snake with some sort of orange head. But there are no huge green snakes in Avon. I looked again. That was when I saw what it was, and like I said, if some-body had described it to me I wouldn't have believed them, but I was there and I saw it with my own eyes.

It was the garden hose. Moving on its own.

I was sitting there with a bicycle chain in one hand and oil all the way up to my elbows. I watched the hose slither and twist through the long grass while Louise stood at the edge of the water, scattering a fistful of food across the surface. I opened my mouth to call out but no words came.

And then the hose looped itself around her ankles and tightened. Louise yelled out, losing her balance. Her hand jerked back, sending fish food flying in an arc behind her. She toppled forward and there was a tremendous splash as she hit the water. It must have surprised the fish.

The fish pond was deep and covered in slimy green algae. Despite the weather, the water was freezing. I have no doubt at all that if I hadn't been there, Louise would have died. It took me a few seconds to recover from the surprise but of course I dropped the bike chain and ran down to help her. No. That's not completely true. I didn't go right away. I hesitated. And a horrible thought flashed through my mind.

Leave her to drown. Why not? She's ruined Dad's life. She's made us sell our old house. She's cruel and she's lazy and she's always complaining. We'll be better off without her.

That's what I thought. But an instant later I was on my feet and running. I wouldn't have been able to live with myself if I'd done anything else. I got to the edge of the pond and reached out for her. I caught hold of her dress and pulled her toward me. She was filthy and sobbing, her yellow hair matted with dark green weeds. I managed to get her out onto the grass and she sat there, a great lump, water streaming down her body. And did she thank me?

"I suppose you think that's funny!" she moaned.

"No," I said.

"Yes you do! I can see it!" She wiped a hand across her face. "I hate you. You're a spiteful, horrible boy." And with that she stomped off into the house.

The hose lay where it was.

That evening, I told my dad what had happened. Louise had gone back to bed after the accident (if that's the right word). She'd also locked the bedroom door so he couldn't have gone in if he'd wanted to. I told him first that she'd fallen into the pond and I described how I'd saved her. Then I told him about the hose. But even as I explained what I'd seen, I saw his face change. I'd expected him to be incredulous, not to believe me. But it was more than that. He was angry.

"The hose moved," he said, repeating what I'd said. The three words came out slowly, heavily.

"I saw it, Dad."

"Was it the wind?"

"No. There was no wind. It's exactly like I saw. It sort of . . . came alive."

"Ben, do you really expect me to believe that? Are you saying it was magic or something? Fairies? I mean, for heaven's sake, you're fourteen years old. Hoses don't come alive and move on their own . . ."

"I'm only telling you what I saw."

"You're telling me what you thought you saw. If I didn't know you better I'd say you'd been sniffing glue or something."

"Dad—I saved her life!"

"Yes. Well done."

He walked out of the house and I didn't see him again that evening. It was only later, when I was lying in bed, that I realized what had really upset him. It wasn't a pleasant thought but I couldn't escape it.

Maybe he would have been happier if I had done what I was tempted to do. Maybe he would have preferred it if I'd left Louise to drown.

My story is almost over . . . and this is where I have to admit that I actually missed the climax. That happened about a week later and I was away for the weekend.

Perhaps it's just as well, because what happened was really horrible.

Louise got minced.

She had been lying in the garden sunbathing and somehow the lawn mower, the one I've mentioned, turned itself on. It rumbled out of the shed and across the lawn and toward her. She was lying on a towel, listening to music through headphones. That's why she didn't hear it coming. I can imagine her last moments. A shadow must have fallen across her eyes. She would have looked up just in time to see this great, metallic monster plunging onto her, the engine roaring, the blades spinning, diesel smoke belching out thick and black. When the police arrived, Louise was a mess. Parts of her had hit the wall fifty feet away.

Whenever a wife is killed in unusual circumstances—and circumstances couldn't have been more unusual than these—the police always suspect the husband. Fortunately, my dad was in the clear. At the time Louise had died, he had been lecturing to two hundred students. As for me, I was in London, so obviously I had nothing to do with it either. There was an inquest, a month after the death, and we all had to go to court and listen to police reports and witness statements. The lawn mower had been taken apart and examined and there was a report about that. But in the end, there could only be one verdict. Accidental death. And that was the end of that.

Except it wasn't.

We never went back to Twist Cottage. I was glad about that. I thought of all the deaths that had taken place there over the years . . . and now Louise! It could have been me or my dad next.

We rented a place in Bath and my dad took time off from the university to sort everything out. I wasn't sure what would happen to us, where we would live and stuff like that. But now it turned out that we were actually very rich. It seemed an incredible coincidence but just before we had moved into Twist Cottage, Dad had taken out an insurance policy on Louise's life. If she died as a result of an accident or an illness, my dad would receive three quarters of a million dollars! Of course, the insurance company was suspicious. They always are. But the police had investigated. There had been an inquest. There was nothing they could do except pay.

And so we were able to buy a new house in Bath, just around the corner from the one we had sold. We tried to put Louise behind us. Everything began to go back to the way it had been before.

And then, one day, I happened to find myself at Bristol University. I'd arranged to meet Dad when he finished work. We were going to the movies together—just like the old days. Only he'd gotten held up in a tutorial or something and I found myself kicking my heels in the little square box that he called his study.

There was a desk with a photograph of me (but not one of Louise, I noticed) and a scattering of papers. There were a couple of chairs and a sofa. Two of the walls were lined with shelves and there were books everywhere. I think there must have been a thousand books in the room. They were even piled up on the floor, half covering the window.

I figured I'd read something while I was waiting but of course they were all history books. Then I noticed a Marvel comic on one of the shelves and I reached up for that but somehow my fingers caught one of the books that had been lying flat, out of sight. It slid out and toppled into my arms. I found myself looking at the cover. It was called *Haunted Houses from the Elizabethan Age*.

I was curious. It was almost as if my dad had hidden the book right up on the highest shelf, as if he didn't want it to be seen. I carried it over to the desk and opened it. And there it was, on the first page, among the chapter headings.

Twist Cottage

I sat down and this is what I read.

One of the most famous witches of the sixteenth century was Joan Barringer, who lived in a cottage in the woods near Avoncliffe. Unlike many of the witches, who were usually elderly spinsters, Joan Barringer was married. Her husband, James Barringer, was a blacksmith. Sometime around the year 1584, in the twenty-seventh year of the reign of Queen Elizabeth, James Barringer began an affair with a local girl, Rose Edlyn, daughter of Richard Edlyn, a wealthy landowner.

It seems that somehow Joan Barringer found out about the affair. Her revenge was swift and terrible. She placed a curse on the unfortunate girl and in the weeks that followed, Rose Edlyn became ill. She lost weight. She lost her hair. She

went blind. Finally, she died. The recently discovered letters written by Richard Edlyn show
what happened next.

James Barringer was persuaded to testify
against his wife. She was summoned to court on
a charge of witchcraft and sentenced to death.
The method of execution was to be burning at the
stake. However, before the sentence could be carried out, she managed to escape from prison and
returned to her cottage in Avoncliffe. The house
was surrounded. The local villagers were determined that the evil woman should pay the price
for what she had done.

And it was then that Joan Barringer made her
appearance. Standing at an upstairs window,
with a rope draped around her neck, she
screamed out a final curse. Any woman who ever
entered Twist Cottage would die. She blamed
women for what had happened to her. Rose
Edlyn had been beautiful and had stolen her husband from her. She had been ugly and would
die unloved.

Then she jumped. The rope was tied to a beam.
It broke her neck and she ended up dangling in

front of the villagers, her head wrenched to one side. The last letter written by Richard Edlyn reads:

". . . and so we did discover that wretched, evil crone, a sight most horrible to behold. Her eyes were swolne and bloodie. Her fanges were drawne. And so she hung by her twysted neck beside that horrid, twysted house."

This is how Twist Cottage got its name.

So Dad had known about the history of Twist Cottage before we moved in. That was my first thought. But there was more to it than that. I remembered how angry he had become when I had asked him if it was haunted.

For heaven's sake, Ben, this is the twenty-first century . . .

That's what he'd said. But he'd known.

He'd known that the house had been cursed—and that the curse only worked on women! Could it possibly be true? I used the telephone in his office and called Carol, the girl who had warned me about Twist Cottage in the first place. Six people had died there, she had told me. And now she confirmed what I already knew. Mrs. Webster had drowned in the bath. Mrs. Johnson had fallen out of a window. Dr. Stainer had fractured her skull and Professor Bell had fallen down the stairs. Both of them had been women. Another woman had had a heart attack and an Australian woman had electrocuted herself.

I thought back to the day we had moved in. The driver who had broken an ankle and the carpenter who had slipped with a saw. Both of them had been women too.

My head was spinning. I didn't want to think about it. But there could be no avoiding the truth. Louise had ruined my dad's life and had refused to give him a divorce. All along he must have wanted to kill her but he couldn't do it himself. So he had moved her into Twist Cottage—knowing that, since we were both male, he and I would be safe—and had waited for the ghost of Joan Barringer to do the job for him.

It was incredible!

I put the book back on the shelf and left the room. I never, ever asked him about it. In fact, we never mentioned Twist Cottage again.

But there is one other thing I need to mention.

My dad hung on to Twist Cottage. He didn't sell it. With all the money he got from the insurance, he didn't need to. But later on I found out that he rented it out from time to time. He demanded an awful lot of money, but the men who rented it always paid.

It was always men. They would go with their cruel, nagging wives. Or their screeching, senile grandmothers. One took his mother. Another went with a peculiarly vindictive aunt.

The women only stayed there a short time.

None of them ever came back.

The Shortest
Horror
Story
Ever Written

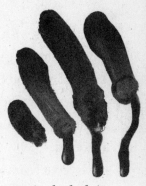

I want to tell you how this story got included in this book.

About a week before the book was published, I broke into the offices of Orchard Books, which are located in a rather grubby street near Liverpool Street station. Maybe you haven't noticed but the book you are holding at this very minute was originally published by Orchard and I wanted to get my hands on it because, you see, I'd had an idea.

Generally speaking, publishers are stupid, lazy people. Orchard Books has about twenty people working for them but not one of them noticed that a window had been forced open in the middle of the night and that someone had added a couple of pages to the collection of horror stories that was sitting by the computer, waiting to be sent to the printers. I had brought these pages with me, you see, because I wanted to add my own message to the book. Nobody noticed and nobody cared and if you are reading this then I'm afraid my plan has worked and you are about to discover the meaning of true horror. Get ready—because here it comes.

Twelve years ago I desperately wanted to be a writer and so I wrote a horror story (based on my own experiences) that was rejected by every publisher in London because, they claimed, it wasn't frightening enough! Of course, none of them had the faintest idea what horror really meant because they had never actually committed a murder, whereas I, my dear reader, had committed several.

My uncle Frederick was my first victim, followed by my next-door neighbor (an unpleasant little man with a mustache and a smelly cat), two total strangers, an actor who once had a bit part in *EastEnders* and a Jehovah's Witness who happened to knock at my door while I was cooking lunch. Unfortunately, my adventures came to an end when a dim-witted policeman stopped my car just as I was disposing of the last body and I was arrested and sent to a lunatic asylum for life. Recently, however, I escaped and it was after that that I had the wonderful idea that you are reading about at this very moment and that can be summarized in three simple stages. Drop into the offices of one of those smarmy publishers in London and slip a couple of pages into somebody else's book (with many apologies to Anthony Horowitz, whoever he may be). Exit quietly and stay in hiding until the book is published. Return only when the book is in the stores and then wait in the background, until some poor fool buys it and follow that person home . . .

Yes, dear reader, at this very moment I could be sitting outside your home or your school or wherever you happen to be and if by any chance you are the one I've chosen, I'm afraid you're about to learn a lesson about horror that I know you'd prefer to miss. Orchard Books is also going to wish that they'd published me all those years ago, especially when they start losing readers in particularly nasty ways, one by one. Understanding will come—but I'm afraid you're going to have to read this whole story again.

Start at the beginning. Only this time look carefully

at the first word of each sentence. Or to be more precise, the first letter of each first word. Now, at last, I hope you can see quite how gloriously, hideously mad I really am—although for you, perhaps, it may already be too late.